Erin stepped inside but then seemed to stop short. She'd no doubt seen the empty bed.

She let the door swing shut as she turned toward the bathroom. He'd left the light on and a small amount crawled across the floor. She moved to the closed bathroom door. "Max?"

He grabbed her from behind, slipping one hand across her mouth. His other hand clamped over her wrist, relieving her of the syringe before locking her back against his chest. The instinctive urge to kill came out of nowhere. *Not her,* he thought. *Winchette.*

Quashing his thoughts of violence, he instead opened intuitively to her, wanting to reinforce the bond between them. He'd done this before with certain women . . . commanded them. But Erin was different. Warm. Caring. *Maybe she commanded him.*

DEADLY
SEDUCTION

CATE NOBLE

ZEBRA BOOKS
Kensington Publishing Corp.
http://www.kensingtonbooks.com

ZEBRA BOOKS are published by

Kensington Publishing Corp.
119 West 40th Street
New York, NY 10018

All Kensington titles, imprints, and distributed lines are avail-
able at special quantity discounts for bulk purchases for sales
promotion, premiums, fund-raising, educational, or institu-
tional use.

Special book excerpts or customized printings can also be
created to fit specific needs. For details, write or phone the
office of the Kensington Special Sales Manager: Attn.: Special
Sales Department. Kensington Publishing Corp., 119 West
40th Street, New York, NY 10018. Phone: 1-800-221-2647.

Zebra and the Z logo Reg. U.S. Pat. & TM Off.

ISBN-13: 978-1-4201-0171-3
ISBN-10: 1-4201-0171-4

First Printing: February 2010

10 9 8 7 6 5 4 3 2 1

Printed in the United States of America

For Nolen M. Holzapfel
Brilliant, Devoted, Wonderful

Sweetheart, you amaze me . . .

Acknowledgments

Kudos to the usual suspects:

Karen Kearney, thanks for pulling rabbits out of hats.
Jenn Stark, thanks, *chica* . . . for everything.
Lori Harris, thanks for being there.
Luanne & Jim Pruett, thanks for a place to hide.
And hats off to assistant editor **Megan Records** and the folks at Kensington Publishing.

As always, I own the errors.

Prologue

"I count four rebels. Confirm, over." Hades melted back into the jungle, once again indistinguishable from the night.

"Check." Taz's whisper came over his earpiece. "One circling the perimeter, one guarding the cave. The two we followed in are chowing down by the fire. Last supper."

That the Thai rebels were confident enough to have a fire meant they were still juiced from hijacking the missile convoy two nights ago. The rebels clearly thought the hard part was over, thought all they had to do now was turn over the merchandise and collect their pay.

"Good," Hades breathed into the mic. "Bastards won't know what hit them."

With less than an hour before sunrise, they barely had time for a wham, bam, in-and-out. And if the Burmese extremists currently funding this little exercise in Armageddon showed up to take possession of their new toys before Hades and Taz finished this op, their collective pooch was screwed. Raiding the encampment with the Burmese also on-site would ramp up the odds from two against four, to two against fifteen. A major suckfest.

Damn. There was that phrase again. Suckfest, suckfest. Who used to say that? Not Taz but . . .

A sudden jabbing behind his left eye truncated the thought. Hades's vision dimmed as the ice pick of pain wrenched deeper into his brain. The swiftness and severity sent him reeling to one side. What the hell?

Nausea burned his throat as the vertigo worsened. A salty, acid-tinged taste puckered his mouth. He stumbled into a tree and grabbed for it, ready to puke. Gritting his teeth, he drew air in through his nose.

Breathe.

Stay on task.

Don't think of anything except the primary objective.

Breathe.

With his brain still half paralyzed with pain, he struggled to grasp the concept. Primary . . . objective. What was it again?

The rebels. The missiles.

Jesus! How could he forget? The Burmese extremists would arrive soon. They didn't have much time. If they failed—

"We *will* complete the operation," he whispered.

And the moment he refocused one hundred percent on the current operation, the pain, the disorientation vanished. His sense of relief was so profound that endorphins flooded his system, helping him to recoup instantly, with a bonus hard-on. Gotta love testosterone, baby!

Twisting his head from side to side, Hades cracked his neck.

"Repeat that last transmission," Taz whispered.

"I said, time to close down this freak show. Ready?"

"Roger that."

"Hold your position three minutes while I neutralize their scout. Then move in."

"Over and out."

Hades crept away, stealth once more his ally. This particular camp, built around one of the many caves that honeycombed the area, had been used so frequently that a trail encircled the site, making it easy for the rebels to navigate with only a sliver of moonlight.

Made them easier to kill, too.

As nasty as the Thai rebels were in their own right, he had to keep in mind they were only couriers—hired to transport the contraband. The real stench came off the Burmese extremists. The fact that the extremists planned to sell the weapons to al Qaeda terrorists made Hades's blood boil. Anything *al Qaeda* was the spawn of pure evil.

And while the thought of capturing one of the Burmese extremists and making him talk was tempting, gathering intel wasn't part of this assignment.

Ensuring that the SOBs didn't score any fireworks to kill and maim was as good as it got this go-round. But God help the bastards next time.

Circling a rock outcropping, Hades hunkered down. The jungle was hyperquiet now, sharpening his senses. The moss beneath his boots felt spongy, the air scented with a funky mix of spore and mold. A slow, steady trickle of anticipatory adrenaline kept his muscles warm, ready.

He slid his black SOG fixed blade knife between his teeth, freeing his hands as he mentally rehearsed, mapping the steps he'd take.

Just ahead a twig snapped, telegraphing the rebel guard's approach.

Hades waited until the guard passed. Then in one fluid motion he straightened and stepped onto the path behind the guard. Ensnaring the man's shoulders with one arm—while slapping his other hand over the man's mouth—Hades snatched him backward.

Immediately the guard tried to drop low. Hades almost smiled. He'd seen this move before with the Thai military—the quick slump to see if the six-foot-three muscle-bound American could keep up with the Thai's superior agility and speed.

But Hades countered just as quickly. His hand dropped, locking across the guard's jaw and twisting his neck to expose his throat. The SOG flashed downward and across, slitting the man's jugular and windpipe.

The guard convulsed and dropped his weapon, horrified at the pulsing sensation of his very life spurting out onto the dirt. He raised his hands to the gushing wound. For naught.

Scooping up the dead man's AK-47, Hades followed the path back toward the camp. Thus far, the job had been easy. Clockworkish. Which left him vaguely unsettled. Why?

Don't question. Just act. Be like Taz.

Taz moved like an invisible grim reaper—strong, silent. Deadly. Be like Taz.

Roger that.

Despite their lack of radio contact, Hades suddenly *knew* that Taz had just slain a rebel who'd stepped away from the fire to piss. At times like this the two men's psychic bond heightened to an unholy link. Which made them a powerful team. If *they* ruled the world—

"Shit." Taz broke the silence. "One of 'em failed to raise your mark by radio. Now he's headed your way."

Too late. Hades and the rebel spotted each other at the same time.

Having led with his gun, the jittery rebel squeezed off two rounds. Hades dove sideways into the thick brush and scrambled away unharmed, knowing he'd never be that fucking lucky again.

Staying low, he paralleled the guard, who now screamed for backup, officially mooting their silent-death MO. If the extremists were close, it was game over.

High overhead, a band of monkeys screeched as they scattered through the treetops, their sleep disturbed. Great. As if the gunshot hadn't been warning enough.

Taz's voice came through his earpiece again. "Nice and quiet. That's you, mate."

Kiss my ass, Hades thought.

Grabbing a baseball-size rock, he tossed the stone a good twenty feet away. When it landed, the guard swiveled toward the sound. Hades pounced, taking the man down with a full body slam before he could fire again.

Just before snapping the guard's neck, he caught a glimmer of the man's final thought—*Don't fight. Surrender.*

Kind of late for that.

"You good, mate?" Taz asked.

"Yeah." A little too good. Like this was a video game he could play blindfolded, points awarded for kills. He was defending champ. And he would remain champ. Ready to take on the next level.

Hades cracked his neck again, this time seeking to relieve the ripple of unease that tick-tocked inside his head. What was wrong here? Fuckups traveled in packs. So far this op had been too easy.

Stay focused.

"All clear," Taz said, confirming he had eliminated the fourth rebel. "I'm going in."

"I'll be right behind you."

Rain started to fall, the heavy drops pinging like beads as they struck the canopy of leaves. Hades ignored it as he crept cautiously into the rebel camp. The fire spewed smoke now, doused by rain and a kicked-over stew pot.

Snuggled in a lush valley between jungle-clad low mountains, the camp lent an ominous meaning to the road less traveled. He glanced around the camp. The place was neater than expected. Orderly.

Moving closer, he paused to check the slain guard lying near the mouth of the cave. Damn it, what was taking Taz so long?

"You find the goodies?" Hades whispered into his mic.

"Not yet. This cave's got more than one room."

"Make it fast." They had less than forty minutes to get back to the extraction point. If unexpected company showed up—

"Found it," Taz reported. "And— Well, well."

"What?"

"Get in here."

Hades ducked into the cave, eager to see what had his partner sounding pleased. Had Taz stumbled onto an even larger cache of weaponry?

"Come straight back twenty feet, then left," Taz said.

The larger cavern was dimly lit by Taz's shaded flashlight. Hades spotted Taz's pack on the ground at the same time he sensed the presence of others.

Females.

Two dark-haired women cowered in the corner, their feminine scent contrasting with the foul smells of bat guano that permeated the cave. The women were prostitutes, known to service the rebel brigand. That they were bound and gagged confirmed they weren't trusted.

One woman let out a muffled cry.

"Shhhh . . ." Taz attempted to calm her as he

moved closer, but the woman physically cringed as if trying to make herself smaller.

Then Hades got a glimpse of the woman's thoughts and did a mental backup. She recognized Taz and was frightened . . . because Taz had raped her before, more than once. Right there on the cave floor. Hades shook his head. That was impossible. She was wrong. They'd never been here.

Still the woman was terrified, sobbing behind her gag. It made Hades recall another woman crying. A woman from his past. A man had been bent over her. Not Taz, surely, but another man. Intent on . . . rape.

God! He couldn't stop it back then, but he'd be damned if he'd let it happen again. If Taz so much as touched the woman, he was going down.

At that thought, pain perforated the inside of Hades's head. *What is past is forbidden.* He staggered backward, equilibrium shattered as what felt like an axe slammed into the base of his skull.

Focus!

"Leave them," Hades snapped.

But Taz had already tugged the woman upright, ignoring her awkward struggle of refusal.

"She said no!" Hades tackled Taz. In spite of their bond, in spite of all they'd gone through, he'd kill Taz if he took the woman against her will.

His head now threatened to split into pieces. The pain became a dual-headed monster. One half breathed fire when he thought about the woman—the *other* woman from his past. And the idea of fighting Taz—his brother in arms, a man he'd sworn to die for—caused saw blades to cut into his nervous system.

"What the hell is your problem?" Taz roared.

The pain quadrupled, causing Hades's grip to weaken. He tried to maneuver the other man back into a spread eagle, no easy task since they were physically well matched. "Leave her alone!"

"You goddamn idiot!" Taz yelled. "I want to release her. They're innocent women, for God's sake. No need for them to die." Taz freed an arm and slugged him full on.

Hades's neck whiplashed, his jaw feeling like it had shattered, yet part of him welcomed the pain. It actually seemed to clear the internal agony.

"Hit me again, motherfucker," Hades taunted. Grabbing Taz by the ears, he slammed the man's head against the stone floor.

"Gladly!" Taz head-butted Hades's chin with a solid *crack* before grabbing his throat.

Fresh agony exploded inside Hades's brain and with that he gained perfect clarity. Jesus—what were they doing here? This wasn't real—

Instantly a new spiral of pain ripped down his spine. *Don't think. Remember the primary objective.*

The rebels.

The missiles.

"The mission is not complete," Hades ground out between anguished breaths. "We have to destroy those missiles before the extremists arrive."

Taz's blank stare cleared, as if he'd hit an internal RESET switch. Nodding, he released Hades.

Rolling sideways, Hades pushed unsteadily to his

feet, then stood over Taz. "And we have a goddamned chopper to meet."

Blood trickled from Taz's nose. He ignored it, holding Hades's gaze before accepting a hand up. "I still owe you one, asshole."

A flicker in the opening to the cave caught Hades's attention. "Behind you!"

He shoved Taz sideways as one of the rebels that had been left for dead charged forward, knife in hand. Though gravely injured, the man managed to bury the blade in Hades's shoulder before Taz attacked the man and quickly finished him off.

"I swear I checked him before!"

"Yeah, well. *Now* we're even." Hades breathed heavily, panting.

"That should have been in my back." Taz pointed to the knife protruding from Hades's shoulder. "You want me to—?"

At Hades's nod, Taz dug a bandanna from his pocket. Grasping the hilt, he yanked the knife straight back before jamming a cloth against the wound.

Hades grunted. The pain sharpened, but faded quickly. Too quickly. It always did. Déjà spooky vu.

They needed to get out of there. Before . . . before . . .

"We're wasting time. Set the charges." Unsheathing his SOG again, Hades moved to the far wall where the women huddled.

Having just witnessed the guard's death, the women's fears distorted their expressions. Rape was no longer their only concern.

He sent one woman a calming thought. Immediately her features softened, baffling her companion, who clearly viewed the two men as dangerous.

Women were easy to influence; in different circumstances, he might even implant a tie between them, making her totally acquiescent. Except she wasn't his type.

The thought struck him as peculiar, because for the life of him, he couldn't recall his *type*. And damn it, he had one. A fantasy lover who made his blood heat with nothing more than a come-hither gaze. *She* wasn't easy. *She* wasn't persuadable. *She* wanted him for *himself*.

The SOG made short work of the women's bindings. Hades waved them toward the entry. Disbelieving, the women edged sideways before climbing to their feet and fleeing toward the mouth of the cave.

Taz jammed a detonator into a brick of C4 and activated its timer. "That's the last one. Ten minutes and counting. Go!"

Grabbing his backpack, Taz hustled toward the cave's entrance. Hades followed. Outside, they began running, charging through the jungle. The eastern horizon was beginning to lighten. Dawn was imminent. So was something else.

Once more, Hades had the feeling that this was familiar. The jungle. The rushing. The suffocating sense of impending doom.

Don't be fooled again. Don't trust anyone.

That voice was different, yet familiar. *Run. Get away. Hide.*

Shit! Heat started fissuring inside his head as if

trying to block the newer voice. But now he knew how to combat it.

Jabbing a finger into his knife wound, Hades tore his flesh open, inviting the searing pain. Or rather, the mental lucidity it brought.

They weren't running *to*.

They were running *from*.

"They're coming. Go faster. Get away." That was Taz, and the terror in his voice was unmistakable.

Hades ripped away the earpiece and radio and let them fall to the ground. Taz did likewise, matching him stride for stride as they veered off the muddy path.

Pain spiked beneath Hades's skull. Withdrawing his SOG, he sliced his palm open, clearing his mind once more.

All of this was familiar because they'd played this game before. And lost. They always . . . fucking . . . lost.

"Do you remember?" he shouted to Taz.

"They always come at the end of a mission." Taz had his knife unsheathed, too, and slashed his forearm through his shirt. "They control us. Our thoughts."

"Not always. We can't let them win this time. Remember our plan."

Hades cut into his own flesh again. This time the throbbing in his head subsided long enough for a startling memory to burst forth.

Remember. Who. You. Are.

"I am . . . Max. Max." Jesus. He wasn't Hades. He was . . . "Max."

Behind him the air woofed with the report of a

gun being fired. Something struck and pinched his upper left back. Goddamn it! Reaching over his shoulder, he grasped the silver dart, yanked it free, and tossed it away.

He shifted his knife and cut deeper into his hand, again and again until the fog lifted. *Remember. Remember.*

He was Max Duncan. C. I. Fucking-A. His partners, Dante and Harry, were dead. The three of them had been on assignment.

Betrayed.

Max had been captured. Held.

And Taz—

Sweet Jesus. Max wouldn't have survived without Taz's help. Taz had taught him to remember; had beaten the shit out of him to force him to remember, to keep the will to live. And Max had returned the favor. Over and over. They'd keep doing it until they were free. Or dead. They'd sworn a solemn vow, sealed in blood. All or nothing.

"Run!" Max shouted. "Remember our plan. Four. Zero—" The sedative had started to kick in, slowing his feet. He knew what came next. He *knew.* "Go. I'll meet you there."

"Won't leave you behind!" Taz looped Max's arm around his shoulder and attempted to drag him. "Never leave . . . a man behind."

"Damn it! I gave you an . . . order!" He tried to shove Taz away. "If you escape, we have a chance."

Another gun fired and Taz flinched as he, too, was darted. "Crikey! Not again."

"Remember plan." Max fell to the muddy ground as if in slow motion. "Remember . . . who you are."

His muscles locked up one by one now, a chain reaction that left his body paralyzed. His face felt cold. Icy needles stung his eyes. At what point had the rain turned to sleet?

Max blinked, desperate to recall the memory of warmth. A fire. Friends gathered around flaming logs. A woman's soft touch. Waking to lovemaking. Soul-stirring kisses. His fantasy lover was back. Soothing his body as she kissed her way down his chest, lower, lower—opening her mouth to take him in.

Memories. Real or imagined, he needed those memories. He needed to pretend someone cared. That it mattered to someone that he lived or died. For where they went next was frigid. Desolate. Barren.

The agony inside his head mushroomed, totally blotting out his vision. No more dawn, no more hope. All was dark.

He tried to talk, couldn't. He heard voices. Not English. Russian? Thai? Martian? Yeah. Familiar Martians. And they were drawing closer. They brought the cold. *Remember. Remember.*

"B-b-but they set the bombs. The mission was accomplished." An uncertain voice. Male.

". . . they fought over the women." This man, the Russian, was older. Heartless. "And neglected to look out for one another."

"B-b-but in the end . . . he pro-pro-protected Taz." The man stuttered, nervous. Always so nervous. He feared the Russian, knew secrets about the Russian.

Secrets the nervous man worried could cost him his life.

"Another failure," the Russian snarled. "Should have . . ."

"B-b-but . . ."

"We will start over!" The Russian shouted angrily now. "I won't rest until it's perfect."

Chapter 1

Bangkok, Thailand
September 13

Rocco Taylor stood in front of the one-way glass and studied the young Thai male seated alone in the CIA interrogation room; the illiterate, sharp-eyed grifter who claimed to be the son of the missing prison orderly, Ping Skihawtra.

Ping had helped Rocco's best friend and fellow CIA operative Dante Johnson escape a jungle prison six months ago. Since Dante still recalled little about his own imprisonment, the Agency was eager—scratch that, *desperate*—to interview Ping in hopes he knew something about the other missing operatives, Harry Gambrel and Max Duncan.

Especially Max. Max had saved Rocco's life once. Rocco would kill to return the favor.

So when he received word a week ago that Ping's son had surfaced, he'd busted his ass to get here—

no small feat considering his star billing on the Thai government's official shit list.

Now . . .

He stared at the memo he'd just received. According to the document, Ping's only child had supposedly died after leaving home *ten years ago*. Talk about a total suckfest.

"Why did it take so long to uncover this little fact?"

"I'll work that issue later," Travis Franks, his boss, said. "*Supposedly* isn't fact. Stick with what we know. Ping had one son, Luc. Age twenty-four. What's this kid's ID say?"

"He claims producing it would endanger his life. Translation: He doesn't have any."

Which in this part of the world wasn't too unusual. Births and deaths frequently went unannounced and unrecorded. A person's heritage was word of mouth.

And in this case, the word of mouth wasn't good. According to Diego Marques, a reliable-slash-controversial contact of Rocco's, this kid—who used street names like Deuce Wild—had dabbled in everything from running numbers to running meth. In fact ol' Deucey boy was on the wrong side of two different loan sharks, which probably explained why he'd shown up today demanding a face-to-face with Travis Franks, plus a ten-thousand-dollar retainer as a show of goodwill.

After seeing this memo, Rocco's *show* would have included tossing the little con artist out.

Except the kid had produced the ultimate get-out-of-jail-free card: a copy of the homemade blood chit Dante had given Ping for his help.

"He's still a link, albeit a crooked one, to Ping. And our best shot at finding Max and Harry." Travis handed the photocopy of the chit back to Rocco. "Find out how he got this."

"That won't take long." Rocco had dealt with enough backwater snitches to know their game. They'd demand outrageous sums, but in the end they caved for chump change. A hundred bucks bought their life history.

"Grimes and Pike will go in with you," Travis said.

Grimes and Pike were analysts that Travis had commandeered. Since the conversation was being recorded, their role was simple: intimidation. Travis would stay here, out of sight, watching and listening.

"At least he speaks English." Moving toward the door, Rocco cracked his knuckles. He'd play bad cop, an easy role considering how pissed and tired he was. "Let's get on with it."

The interrogation room was standard-issue Hollywood. Western film images set certain expectations, after all. Dingy gray walls, a rectangular table, seven mismatched plastic chairs. The obvious one-way glass mirror—*Hi, Travis*—drew the eye since the other walls were bare.

The kid didn't react to their entrance, pretending to nap, his feet up, arms folded across his chest. Joe Cool. Right. Except Joe never napped with neck muscles that tense.

Turning his back to Deuce—*you're neither important*

nor scary, kid—Rocco directed the analysts toward two chairs closest to the door.

When he looked back, the kid's eyes were open, black and shining with intelligence. Recognition flashed then disappeared with a blink. This kid thought he knew Rocco. Except Rocco never forgot a face.

They'd never met.

Interesting.

Rocco pulled out a chair, but didn't sit. Propping one foot up, he pretended to flip through the papers he'd carried in.

"So you're Luke Skywalker." Rocco purposely mispronounced the name. "Mind telling me how you got this?" He waved a copy of the chit.

The kid yawned and stretched. "I told them I'd only speak with Travis Franks."

"I am Travis Franks."

Snorting, the kid unfolded from the chair, moving with that barely leashed grace of a Mack Daddy black belt who'd lived too long on the streets.

While the kid was taller than most Thai males—five eleven or so—Rocco had four inches on him. And eighty pounds. In a street fight, the kid could probably hold his own, but this was about posturing, throwing it out on the table. And Rocco ruled that game. He straightened, forcing the kid to look up.

"You are not Travis Franks," the kid sneered. "And you are wasting my valuable time."

The kid stealing *his* line irritated Rocco. "So you've met Mr. Franks before?" He knew Travis would be listening intently.

The kid met his gaze. "No."

There it was again. Recognition. *He knows me. How?* Photograph? Surveillance video? Rocco gave his mental Rolodex a whirl. One name popped out: an enemy.

Did this kid work for Minh Tran?

Tran was a particularly nasty drug lord whose men had almost killed Rocco once. Rocco wanted Tran out of business, and it was a decidedly mutual feeling.

"Let's start over." Sitting, Rocco forced nonchalance and waited until the kid sat, too. "Here's the deal. I work with Travis Franks, but he's a busy man. Now you tell me how you got this copy and I'll tell you how quickly I can get Travis on the phone."

"I possess the original chit, which I will only produce for Mr. Franks."

"And how did you get the original?"

The kid opened and then shut his mouth, going mute with a single shake of his head.

"No speakie English all of a sudden, huh? Fine. Here's my theory for the report they'll forward back to headquarters." Rocco tilted his head toward Grimes and Pike. "You heard the rightful owner of the chit, Ping Skihawtra, was seeking to make contact with Mr. Franks to collect a reward. You decided to steal the chit and cash it out yourself. Seeing as Mr. Skihawtra and his wife haven't been seen in a number of months, I'm guessing you got rid of them and took on the identity of their dead son."

Bingo. The kid's cheeks flushed angry scarlet.

Rocco knew he'd hit a nerve and pushed ahead. "Unfortunately, the chit is only good for Mr. Skihawtra. So this"—he waved the paper—"is virtually useless. Unless you have something else to offer?" *Something I can use to find my friends.*

Disgust flashed across the kid's face as he climbed back to his feet, holding Rocco's gaze the entire time. "Fuck you. That good enough English for you, Mr. Daniels? Oh, wait. Perhaps today it is 'Fuck you, Mr. Pierce.'"

It was a struggle not to react. The two names, Matt Daniels and Franklin Pierce, were aliases Rocco had traveled under during some of the covert trips he'd made to Thailand searching for Max and Harry. Aliases the Agency didn't even know about.

Clearly, Deuce knew more than he should. And he dared Rocco to correct him in front of the others.

"Hold that thought." Dismissing the two analysts, Rocco waited until they were alone before playing his hunch. "If Minh Tran is behind this, you can give him a message for me: Tell him I've booked his one-way ticket. To hell."

The kid's mouth fished open. "You think . . . get your own message to Tran. I came to offer Mr. Franks a deal regarding my father, but . . ." Muttering the rest beneath his breath, the kid headed toward the door, bristling with indignation.

Rocco was baffled. What the hell was going on here? Genuine dislike had lit up the kid's demeanor at the mention of Minh Tran, as if the kid hated Tran every bit as much as Rocco did.

"Wait." Rocco's bullshit meter suddenly quieted.

Uh-oh. Was the kid telling the truth? "Can you prove you're really Luc Skihawtra?"

"What does it matter? You just said the chit was worthless. Or are you interested in those other things I might know?" The kid paused to allow an imaginary *ka-ching!* to register. "Like your recent travel agenda?"

The kid flicked his wrist. There was a flash of silver, followed by the *slish* of a switchblade ejecting. Christ!

Rocco drew his own weapon and chambered a round in a nanosecond. How had the kid smuggled that past the metal detectors? "Glock, paper, scissors. I win."

The kid's gaze skipped upward from the gun, dismissing it. "If I had intended harm, it would be done. This is—what do you call it—show and tell?"

Luc flipped the knife and caught the tip of the bare blade between this thumb and index finger, displaying the knife.

It's called showing off. And yes, Rocco recognized the black market Italian Beltrame switchblade he'd bought during his last trip to Bangkok. Unless officially authorized, he never entered another country armed. Which meant his first task on foreign soil was securing a blade—a decent one.

He knew exactly where and when he'd dumped that piece. The question was how did Deuce know?

"Look, kid—"

"Kid? I don't need this." Deuce—Luc—dismissed Rocco with a derisive snort. "Tell Mr. Franks that when he is ready to get serious—"

The door opened just then, and to Rocco's

surprise, Travis entered, carrying the bulging case file on the missing agents. Travis pointed a remote control at one of the ceiling panels before turning to Luc.

"I'm Travis Franks. And the rest of this conversation is off the record." He slid a leather ID holder across the table.

Rocco lowered his weapon, but kept a close eye on the kid. The switchblade had disappeared up his left sleeve.

"I'm interested in talking with your father. I also want to hear how you know so much about my friend here." Travis nodded toward Rocco. "And how you came to hear the names Daniels and Pierce. If your info is really good, I'll pay well."

Luc studied the ID then handed it back. "How many zeroes in *well*?"

"Enough to cover your debt to Mongkut and Pham." Travis mentioning the loan sharks seeking Luc was both a trump and a threat. "But the real money rides on questions I have for your uncle."

Nodding, Luc sat down once more, gesturing to chairs as if bidding Travis and Rocco to take their places. As if *he* were running things. This damn kid reminded Rocco of himself. His younger, cockier self. Christ, when had he gotten so freakin' old?

To be perverse, Rocco stood, but Travis sat. Good cop.

"For starters, we need to establish you are indeed Ping Skihawtra's son," Travis said.

Luc appeared to have anticipated the question. "I have no ID, but I can tell you some key information about the American who gave my father this chit. A Mr. Dante. I can also tell you names of two prison guards that this Mr. Dante particularly disliked. They were brothers, Som and Aroon. And they called Mr. Dante by a number: 703."

Rocco already had his cell phone out and was waiting while the international connection went through. Silence hung in the air, thick and familiar. He realized the tension he felt was hope. The hope of finding Max. Harry.

Dante answered on the third ring.

"Quick question—I'll explain later," Rocco said. "Name the prison guards you hated most and what did they call you?"

"Tell me you found those bastards, Som and Aroon. They were twins," Dante said. "But I'm drawing a blank on names. Shithead? Dirtbag? Prisoners had numbers there and—"

"Yours was 703. I'll call you back." Rocco closed his phone and nodded to Travis.

"Let's start with your father," Travis said. "Where is he?"

"Dead."

Rocco and Travis exchanged glances. The news wasn't completely unexpected since no one connected with the prison had been located. Still it was disappointing.

"My father was killed at the prison the morning after the escape," Luc went on. "What your Mr. Dante probably didn't realize is that the warden had recruited my father to help him escape. My uncle said my father had gone back to the prison to collect his pay."

"Wasn't your father required to turn over the chit in exchange for his thirty pieces of silver?" Rocco asked.

Luc ignored Rocco's taunt and directed his response to Travis. "The chit was a secret between my father and Mr. Dante. Apparently, my father thought he was being clever, collecting from the warden as well. And I am not defending him. His greed and stupidity cost my mother her life when she went to identify his body."

"How did you learn about your parents' fate?" Travis asked.

"From my uncle," Luc said. "But he just found me two months ago. My parents were killed back in March. I have since returned to their village, but everything—my parents' home, my uncle's home, even the prison—are gone. Destroyed."

"I want you to look at something." Travis tugged at the file he'd brought in. Part of it split open and spilled onto the floor. Not missing a beat, he quickly snatched it up and grabbed a stack of eight-by-ten photos. Riffling through them, he pulled out several aerial shots and a topo map of Thailand then shoved the rest aside.

Travis laid the photos out on the table. "This is where your father's village is. And the prison was here. Correct?"

Luc moved closer and frowned. "How old are these satellite shots?"

"December of last year," Travis said.

Luc pointed to a spot several inches from where Travis had. "Actually the prison was here." He moved his hand again. "And my parents and uncle lived here. Did I pass your test?"

"For now. Did your uncle work at the prison, too?" Travis asked.

"No. But he and my father had no secrets." Luc's nostrils flared. "My father gave my uncle the chit and all his notes and sent him ahead. He was supposed to meet my parents later in Bangkok. When my father didn't show up, my uncle returned to their village and saw the damage. He's been hiding ever since."

"I want to speak directly with your uncle," Travis said. "In addition to seeing all your father's papers."

Luc nodded. "You do understand those are two separate negotiating points? That means two retainers."

Rocco couldn't believe the kid's gall. He was also tired of being ignored. "It sounds like we can get everything we need from your uncle."

"Perhaps. But try finding my uncle without my help."

"It's premature to talk money," Travis interrupted. "Until we've established you, or your uncle, have something significant. Something I want."

"And how do we do that—quickly?"

"Do your father's papers mention the others who were held at the prison?" Travis asked.

Rocco held his breath, silently willing Luc to say *yes. Two prisoners.* Max. Harry.

Luc paused, squinting. "As far as other prisoners, my father's notes say nothing. However . . ." He waited until both Travis and Rocco looked at him before going on. "I know where the new prison is. But that will cost even more zeroes. Immediate zeroes."

New prison? Rocco bent forward and slapped his open palms on the table in front of Luc. "Where is it?"

Clearly unwilling to give up anything for free, Luc held his ground, going mute again.

"Your rush for fast money destroys your credibility," Rocco snapped. "Afraid Mongkut's men will get you? Believe me, we have the same concern—that they'll slit your throat before our deal is complete."

"My rush is my business. And you are not the only potential buyer." Luc tilted his head toward the jumbled mess of photos that Travis had shoved aside. "I bet I could find plenty of others who would pay for information on him. People who hate Westerners."

Rocco looked at the topmost visible photo. A group shot, the file folder covered all of the men pictured except one: Dante.

Biting back disappointment, Rocco rapped the photo with his knuckle. "Him? He's safe and sound. Game over."

"No." Slanting Rocco a *you idiot* look, Luc tugged the photo completely out into full view. "I mean him."

The man Luc pointed to was Max Duncan.

Rocco shifted his weight onto the balls of his feet. "So help me God, if you're screwing with us—"

Travis held up his hand. The eternal referee. "Trust me, Luc, if that man is alive, it's worth a lot of zeroes." Tugging out his phone, he used the push-to-talk. "Bring it in."

Moments later, the door opened. Grimes came in and set a briefcase on the table, then exited. Travis spun the locks, opening the case before swinging it around for Luc to see.

Rocco knew there was fifty grand, U.S., inside. More than enough to pay off both loan sharks. To this kid, fifty grand probably felt like a million.

In Rocco's mind it was nothing. Hell, he knew Travis would gladly fork over ten times that amount if it got definitive answers on Max and Harry.

Unexpectedly, Luc ignored the money and instead pinned Travis with an earnest expression.

"That will do for starters. But here's what I really need: my uncle is in jail in Australia and he's very sick. You get him out and into a safe house and I'll tell you everything you want to know."

Chapter 2

Northeast Thailand Jungle
September 17

Consciousness tightened cold fingers around Max's larynx, forcing him up. But not fully.

That goddess/bitch—awareness—gave nothing freely. He couldn't talk, he couldn't see, but the void that swaddled him was heinously familiar.

He'd been buried alive.

Left behind.

Again.

Panic boiled beneath his skin. He attempted to move but his arms and legs didn't respond; he was paralyzed.

His mind, however, was anything but and his thoughts leapfrogged, frantic and chaotic. He needed to break free. He needed to find Taz. And then—

Pain slashed the inside of his skull, a razor scraping live tissue from bone. It was a brutal reminder that even the smallest of thoughts about escape were intolerable.

Max panted, sucking air in and out, uncertain why it helped but grateful it did. Slowly the pain diminished, grew tolerable. He wished for light, but all remained dark.

Count: twelve thousand one. Twelve thousand two.

Though the voice had only been inside his head, it startled him. Silence pressed in again. A name teased the tip of his tongue, but the pain spiked and stole it just as quickly.

Just count. Twelve thousand five. Twelve thousand six.

Max listened, realized something—someone?—inside him was ticking off seconds: had ticked off millions of them. He followed the hypnotic count—*twelve thousand eight, twelve thousand nine*—and was rewarded with a name: Hades.

It was more than just the name they called him. Hades was the part that counted. The part that kept his memories, his secrets, secure. But at what price? Was it true he'd go insane without his alter ego? Who had told him that? Taz?

Taz! Holy God, where was his friend? Had he escaped?

Max tried to recall their last assignment. He and Taz had been—

The thought was instantly short-circuited by the sensation of being thrown off a cliff. G-force kicked him in the stomach, turning him inside out as he free-fell.

He hit bottom, landing headfirst on concrete. He

felt his brain splatter, but he didn't die. No, he never died, no matter how badly he wanted to.

Right now he just wanted to puke, a sensation made worse by the awareness of flickering light in the back of his skull where grainy video flashed unevenly, like film that had jumped the track. It felt as if he'd just stumbled, drunk, into a theater mid-movie.

He concentrated, catching words. *Title: War, version 7. Title: Apocalypse, version 3.*

Oh. Hell. No. He wasn't doing any of it—

Another blinding blow hit. This time a fist punched through his chest, squeezing his heart, stealing his breath. The pain was beyond anything he'd endured and it carried a promise that it could get worse. Much worse.

Don't question and it goes away.

Hades was back.

Max began counting again. *Twelve thousand twenty, twelve thousand twenty-one.* The numbers threaded meaninglessly through his mind, an endless progression that helped him go numb.

At thirteen thousand the pain vanished. But still he felt sick. Hot and internally sweaty. The peculiar clamminess was familiar.

Sweet Mary.

He remembered. It was a sign. He was coming to.

This time when the urge to puke rolled over him, Max welcomed it, clawing to the surface of clarity.

He still couldn't see. He was tied down on a table, flat on his back. His head was turned to one side and strapped firmly in place so he wouldn't choke if he vomited.

Recognition hit like an anvil. He was in the lab with Dr. Rufin, being prepped for another mind fuck. A guard was present, too. As much as Max disliked Rufin, he disliked the guards even more.

The bastards thought Max never remembered this. But always, eventually, he did. Step one, the stripping away of old memories, was the worst. If Max tried to hold on to a memory, he was punished. And the pain he endured was nothing compared to the agony of watching those he loved being tortured.

The carefully nurtured false visions they'd implanted of home and hearth—of him as a beloved husband and father—were sown for no other reason than for usage in obtaining his compliance. Max would plead, bargain, beg for their lives to be spared. But in the end, even total capitulation was not enough. He had to endure, suffer. So they could prove their point.

Step two was a black hole, the part Max never remembered. Hell, maybe there were twenty steps in that black hole process but always they extracted a promise. Max swore to do *X* in exchange for *Y*. No questions asked.

The kicker was that no matter how perfectly Max performed, the promises were always broken. He was deep-sixed, put on ice until the next time.

Weeks, sometimes months, were lost while Max was in that horrible state Rufin reverently referred to as "stasis." Like it was pleasant.

And while Rufin wasn't as ruthless as Zadovsky, the difference was inconsequential.

Light seeped in through Max's closed lids as his

senses came back online, albeit unevenly. A foul smell smothered him, as if something dead lay rotting beneath him. His stomach muscles clenched.

Without warning his hearing switched on with eardrum-shattering feedback. He prayed no one saw him flinch. If he gave any outward indication of awareness, they'd put him under again.

Memories of being darted like an animal spun over him. Rufin and the guards kept tranquilizer guns locked and loaded. Max recalled coming to instantly once and springing off the table in a raw burst of energy only to be hit with four rounds of the darts. That much tranquilizer at one time had nearly killed him. Except he was never that lucky.

The noise modulated to a low hiss. Beneath the static he heard voices—real ones—but the drugs in his system made it difficult to distinguish words. What had they given him this time? They purposely used different drugs to avoid predictability and addiction.

"Almost ready . . ." Rufin's voice grew faint again.

Summoning every bit of concentration he could muster, Max latched on to Rufin's thoughts before the man shuffled away. That Max had been inside Rufin's head before made it easier to reestablish a mind link.

Taz had taught Max how to slip into another person's mind, into the pauses between thoughts. Mind wormholes, Taz called them.

It was how the two men communicated without words, how they plotted to survive and formulated a plan of what they would do once one or both of them escaped.

Right now, however, Max found Rufin's thoughts nearly impossible to follow. The man was a total nervous wreck and that spelled trouble. Too sedated to exert any influence over Rufin, Max focused on the man's emotions and was nearly blown away by the intensity.

Rufin was worried the current procedure would kill Taz.

Taz was in danger!

Max immediately redirected his energy, probing the room, mentally seeking Taz. Where was his friend?

That Max couldn't pick up Taz's presence alarmed him.

Rufin began speaking to the guard, dismissing him. "Prepare room number two." His voice dropped, but only for a second. "I'll start the new medication as soon as h-h-he's up from stasis."

Rufin was talking about Max now and it took every speck of Max's willpower to remain unmoving and silent.

As the door to the lab closed, Max mentally scanned the room to make certain the guard had left. Prying one eye just barely open, he followed the tile floor until he spotted Rufin's shoes. The scientist had moved to a station along the opposite wall and had his back to Max.

Opening his eyes a bit more, Max searched the rest of the lab. His gut clenched as he glimpsed the piece of equipment Rufin worked at, the cylinder-shaped chamber used for programming. The coffin-like place was evil.

And Christ! Taz was inside!

Max nearly catapulted up from the table. The desire to save his friend clashed with the blind fury that wanted to snap Rufin's neck. God help anyone who killed another of his friends.

Especially Taz.

Taz was the only person alive Max trusted. And vice versa. Everyone else had sold them out. Or left them behind.

Max had to get free.

He was Taz's only hope.

Dr. Rufin checked the ancient computer. BUFFER FULL. He waited for the cache to clear, for the program to continue.

So much for the state-of-the-art equipment he'd been promised. Of course, the Thai government— if it truly was the Thai government he worked for— hadn't kept their word on anything thus far. Which had initially made it easier for Rufin to justify his failures. To ask for more time.

But time was up.

If the next trial didn't go as promised, the government would shut him down. *Him*, not the lab.

They wouldn't abandon the project; the potential was too great. No, they would simply bring in another scientist. Rufin would be retained to answer questions, most likely from a jail cell. And then . . .

He rubbed the tight muscles in his neck as an

imaginary finger slashed across his throat. In truth, he'd known his days had been numbered since the shadowy Thai agents took over this facility two months ago following Dr. Zadovsky's death.

It had only taken the threat of torture to induce Rufin's full cooperation, especially after being told that everyone associated with Zadovsky's secondary operations in Jakarta had been jailed or killed. The one exception being Zadovsky's secretary, on whom the agents had quizzed Rufin briefly. That Boh-dana may have escaped gave him hope.

Zadovsky had double-crossed the Thai government by working a secret deal with the Indonesians and that had naturally infuriated the Thais. Rufin had patiently answered all their questions, but toward the end of their inquisition, he began to realize the Thai agents were fishing for information.

Like most outsiders, they knew Zadovsky engineered viral bioweapons and antidotes, but they hadn't realized until recently that those projects merely provided funding and diverted attention from Zadovsky's experiments in mind control. Experiments the Thai agents wanted to continue.

And rather than admit that he'd been left behind to babysit for Zadovsky's prize test subjects—Hades and Taz—Rufin had led the Thai agent in charge to believe that he could complete Zadovsky's work.

Once Rufin had sworn allegiance, the Thai agents had produced a jumble of papers and computer data pilfered from Zadovsky's lab and residence in Jakarta.

Given the ill will between the two countries over

long-standing border disputes—the agent inferred a huge coup. Given the disarray of the material, it was anything but.

At first glance, Zadovsky's papers confirmed what Rufin had suspected all along: that Zadovsky had been passing off Rufin's formulas as his own work. Rufin had been furious to realize that Zadovsky had made a fortune selling the designer drugs Sugar-Cane and JumpJuice—both of which had been created by Rufin.

When he'd calmed down enough to dig deeper into Zadovsky's work, Rufin found that basically all of Zadovsky's credited genius was stolen. From Rufin and others.

With one huge exception: the miraculous Serum 89, which Zadovsky had created while working with neurotransmitters and psychotropic drugs. Without doubt, Zadovsky's decades of clandestine experiments in mind control had put him light-years ahead of anyone else.

Serum 89 had been a critical success. Using the serum in conjunction with the neural reprogramming that Rufin had perfected had yielded unprecedented results. They had proved numerous times that they could make a man do almost anything.

And with Serum 89, the survival of test subjects surged. Rufin's work to control the deadly side effects and seizures had been crucial to that success.

Unfortunately, by the time Rufin perfected all the adjunct systems, they'd been down to two test subjects. And the Serum 89 was gone.

Creating more had proved impossible. In fact,

after poring over Zadovsky's journals for the hundredth time, Rufin concluded that the highly revered Russian scientist had somehow lost the recipe and the priceless research for Serum 89.

Ironically, Rufin's knowledge of Zadovsky's work, combined with his own attempts at replicating the serum, had now inadvertently put him light-years ahead, too. If anyone could reproduce Serum 89, Rufin could. Eventually . . . right now no one could get it right on the short timeline the Thais had given. Too much of Zadovsky's data was still missing.

Eager to distract his own thoughts, Rufin checked the computer screen in front of him. Still downloading.

Grabbing a tablet and pen, he scribbled a computation but then crumpled it after realizing it was something he'd tried weeks ago. The nagging feeling that he was close haunted him. That and the certain knowledge that whether he succeeded with these experiments or not, the Thai government would kill him.

Fortunately, Rufin wasn't as gullible as he'd led his Thai handlers to believe. While he'd long dreamed of escaping *with the data*, it had only been recently that he'd figured out a way to actually pull it off. If anyone deserved to profit from it, he did.

Now if his luck would just hold a bit longer . . .

The computer beeped, drawing his attention.

"Finally." He pressed ENTER then moved to the viewing window on the hyperbaric chamber.

Taz, the older of the two remaining test subjects, was inside. How strange that Rufin didn't think of them as human anymore, but with his own life at stake, ethics meant little.

Of course, even stranger was the notion of Taz and Hades working willingly with *him*. Taz, who had twice tried to kill Rufin, was now his unwitting accomplice and savior. Soon Hades would be as well. Once these newest programs were installed, Taz and Hades would give their lives to protect Rufin.

Still, it truly unsettled Rufin to know he'd eventually have to sacrifice Taz.

In many ways, Taz had been more fascinating to study with his uncanny ability to stabilize and adapt. It had appeared that no matter what they threw at him, he'd survived. Flourished. At least for a while.

Lately, Taz's ability to recuperate seemed slower. Inarugably, they'd made some seemingly irreversible errors with him. Zadovsky had likened it to faulty wiring that did too much damage to the circuitry before it was detected. But wasn't that how progress unfolded?

Rufin consoled himself with the thought that he'd still have Hades. They had proceeded more cautiously with Hades and it had paid off. Hades was the real gold mine. A nearly perfect specimen.

Hades was *almost* there, and once Rufin fully controlled Hades, could make him do the morally unthinkable on command—

A hand clamped down on Rufin's shoulder, spun him around. To his horror, he found himself looking into Hades's eyes. Eyes that glittered with that now-you-die expression Rufin had witnessed many times.

Instinctively, Rufin's hand went to his side. Too late he remembered he'd left his tranquilizer gun on his desk and dismissed the guard.

His bladder released as his vision tunneled. It was over.

Max tightened his grip on Rufin's neck. So easy to crush his windpipe. "Don't you dare pass out! Free him. Now."

"I c-c-can't."

"Oh yes, you will!" Max shoved the scientist closer to the chamber. He needed to get Taz out before one of the guards returned. "Shut it down."

"I can't interrupt the process," Rufin pleaded. "P-p-please."

"Fuck your process." Max reached around the scientist and grabbed for one of the latches that sealed the chamber.

Behind them a door crashed open. Swinging Rufin around in a semicircle, Max vised an arm around the scientist's neck and yanked him close to use as a human shield.

The guard that had rushed in, weapon drawn, took one look at Rufin and skidded to a halt.

"Tell him to back off or I'll kill you," Max said.

But before Rufin could open his mouth, a second guard burst in the side door and fired his gun.

Max felt a bruising punch as a dart jammed into his neck. He ripped it away, praying the tranquilizer had not fully injected.

Releasing Rufin, who had fainted, Max dropped

low. He grabbed the computer console away from the chamber and slung it toward the first guard. The equipment crashed to the tile floor, creating enough diversion to allow Max to take cover behind a counter.

The second guard rushed to the opposite side of the counter, demanding that Max surrender. When that didn't work, the guard started shouting threats.

That's it, just keep talking, Max thought. He edged along the cabinets, homing in on the guard's voice before leaping over the countertop and slamming the guard into the floor. The guard's body went limp.

Screaming for his partner to rise up, the first guard fired.

Max ducked behind a desk, avoiding the dart. He heard a door slam and realized the first guard had fled the room. Great! He'd sound an alarm. Max wouldn't have long.

The room tilted now. Yanking the guard's side arm from its holster, Max climbed to his feet, tried not to think about the impossible odds.

Fighting to maintain his equilibrium, he lurched toward the chamber that imprisoned Taz.

Max remembered being trapped in it, being unable to escape.

He also remembered his vow.

"I'm here, Taz. And I won't leave . . . without you."

Chapter 3

Rocco swept his binoculars over the prison. Built into a hillside, the Vietnam War–era structure had only one visible entrance and was exactly as Luc Ski-hawtra had described.

Ignoring the buzz of biting mosquitoes, Rocco focused on the empty prison yard. The tiny fenced enclosure covered less than one hundred fifty square feet.

Divided into three rectangular sections, the yard looked more like dog runs at a kennel. Except these were human-sized. Heavily fortified with razor wire and sporting copious overhead camouflage, the yard itself was visible only at ground level. The single guard tower in the corner was deserted.

Luc had reported watching the person they believed was Max Duncan pace from one end of the cage to the other, zombiesque.

God, had it really been Max? There was a strong possibility that Luc was wrong, that he'd only seen someone who resembled Max. But Luc had sworn the prisoner looked exactly like the photograph, which was unlikely after two years of imprisonment.

Rocco recalled how pathetic Dante had looked after eighteen months of imprisonment and abuse. A walking skin sack, a ghost of his former self. It sure as hell hadn't helped that Dante had also been sick with malaria, gangrene, and a host of other ailments.

Still, if Max had been able to preserve his health, his strength, maybe. Just maybe . . .

And what about Harry? Luc hadn't recognized any of Harry's photographs, which didn't mean he wasn't still alive. Perhaps Harry was sick, too. *If* the men were even here.

It had been over six weeks since Luc had spotted Max. A lot could have happened in that time.

It outraged Rocco to think of his friends being held and tortured. Worse was the burn of knowing that for most of that time no one had even been looking for them.

"Does anything look familiar?" Rocco asked Dante.

Dante was the leader of the six-man extraction team currently hunkered down in the thick jungle surrounding the prison.

They'd been in Thailand less than twelve hours, having hiked in across the Cambodian border. Since they were in the country unofficially, they'd risk only one helicopter ride: the trip out.

"Negative," Dante said. "Which doesn't mean squat."

It was believed Dante had been held at multiple locations, but no solid documentation existed to support the theory. Would they find that proof here?

And how many more of these little bunkers of horror still existed in this godforsaken place, tucked under dirt and trees in ways that made them impossible to detect even with enhanced satellites?

Rocco raised his binoculars again. In the late afternoon shadows the place appeared abandoned, a fact belied by the background hum of a diesel-powered generator. The infrared readings they'd done earlier had detected four human heat sources inside the facility, but the generator kept one area clouded.

The lack of security bothered him. Was it a trap? In spite of all the precautions Travis had taken, had word of their rescue mission been leaked?

"Hold up." Dante indicated he was receiving a radio transmission, most likely from JC or Riley, who were working recon.

"Come back then," Dante said after a few seconds. "And stand by."

"Anything new on infrared?" Rocco asked.

"Same as before."

"So we go in expecting more."

"Exactly." Dante again motioned that he was receiving a message.

This time, though, Rocco heard it as well since JC broke in across all channels.

"We're hearing gunfire inside," JC hissed. "Riley's got lots of movement on IR, all centered in the east corner. Looks like we've got two bodies down."

Two bodies. Max. Harry.

"Move in," Dante ordered. "Now."

Rocco drew his pistol. Times like these made him appreciate the countless drills they'd done in the Army, ones they still did. Action and training supplanted emotion. Repetition cemented skills.

Thompson remained outside as lookout, while the rest of them swept up to the building behind JC and Riley. Two shots from JC's silenced handgun destroyed the lock on the entrance.

Inside the small anteroom, they surprised a guard who was crouched near a door. At first Rocco thought the guard was waiting to ambush them, but the shocked expression on the guard's face confirmed they were unexpected.

As soon as the guard saw them, he slid his weapon to the ground and raised his hands in surrender. JC, the team's linguist, moved forward and secured the guard's hands while quietly demanding answers.

Rocco pointed to the unusual weapon the guard had dropped. "Tranquilizer gun," he mouthed to Dante.

"He claims a prisoner broke free and tried to kill the doctor. Inside there," JC whispered as he nodded toward the closed door. "They use the tranq guns to subdue prisoners."

"Ask him how many people are here, including prisoners," Dante said.

JC spoke to the guard again, in perfect Thai dialect, and then turned back to Dante. "There are only two prisoners kept here. And both are Westerners."

Two Westerners.

Max and Harry.

"He says there's only one other guard here besides him. Plus a doctor. A third guard went to pick up supplies. He thinks the guard inside is dead, maybe the doctor, too. He says the prisoner has the guard's pistol," JC finished.

"Keep grilling him," Dante said. "Find out everything he knows about the main players and any other prisons. Zeke will stay with you. Riley's going with us."

Rocco flattened himself against the wall and edged toward the doorway as Dante and Riley moved to flank the opposite wall.

Dante reached for the doorknob. Twisting it, he shoved the door open but hung back.

"We're Americans!" he shouted. "We have the place surrounded. Lay down your weapons!"

The man inside the room started swearing. It was a voice Rocco thought he'd never hear again.

"American? Give me a name, rank, and serial number or I start shooting."

"Max!" Dante shouted. "Jesus, is that you? It's Dante Johnson. We're here to take you home."

"Bullshit." The words, though slurred, were punctuated by the *zing* of a gunshot. "I've got two hostages. I want the building and perimeter cleared and a vehicle brought to the front door with a full tank of gas."

"He probably thinks you're dead," Rocco whispered to Dante through his mic. "Let me try."

Dante nodded grimly.

"Max!" Rocco shouted now. "It's Rocco Taylor, buddy. No one's BS-ing you, man. It is Dante. He was held in a prison a hundred miles south of here. It's a long story and it really sucks, but we're here now. We came back for you. We're here to get you out."

"Rocco?" Max's voice sounded raspy now, like he was confused. Or weak.

Rocco again remembered how sick Dante had been. Max was probably in even worse shape. "You remember Riley? JC? Look, Dante and I—"

"You're lying!" Max cut him off. "Dante's dead."

"He's not. But if it's any consolation, he doesn't believe you're alive either. Look, let me come in. I'll just stand in the door, okay? You'll see."

"If it's a trap"—Max's voice didn't waver—"I'll kill you."

"It's not a trap. And if you shoot me, I'll have to kick your ass." Easing forward, hands elevated, Rocco slowly shifted into the open doorway.

The room beyond was rectangular, twenty by forty, and looked like a combination infirmary, laboratory, and autopsy suite. Wrecked equipment was strewn about. A man wearing a white lab coat was lying on the floor. The slight rise of his chest confirmed he was alive.

"That's far enough," Max shouted. "I'm coming out."

Rocco did a double take as a man crawled out from behind the flashing console of some machine and struggled to climb to his feet.

"Max? Holy God!"

When Rocco found Dante in a Thai jail, he'd been wasted, emaciated. Max, however, looked completely the opposite. Spectacular. Better than ever.

Wearing only a T-shirt and boxers, Max's well-muscled arms spoke of a regular workout, likely enhanced by steroids. His hair was shorter than Rocco had ever seen it, a high, tight military cut.

"Rocco?" Max's voice sounded slurred, thick.

"It's me, buddy. In the flesh. Easy with the pea shooter." He nodded toward the pistol Max had just lowered.

Drawing closer, Rocco focused on Max's eyes. That's where Max's damage was hidden, behind that tortured gaze. His soulless expression hinted at an even worse suffering. What the hell had been done to him?

"Rocco. It is you." Max blinked back tears. Then just as quickly his features grew steely as he jerked the gun back up. "Wait! There's still another guard around."

"We already got him. Outside. What's the status of these two?" Rocco nodded to the man in the lab coat and another man whom he could only see the feet of.

"Dr. Rufin . . . passed out. The guard's dead. You gotta help me—" Max pitched sideways.

Rocco surged forward to grasp his arm. Max's eyes were fully dilated. What the hell was in those darts?

"Take it easy. You don't have to do a thing," Rocco said. "We're here. To take you home."

Home.

The word didn't register in Max's mind. Where was *home*?

He had a fleeting impression of mountains that

was quickly snatched away by an explosion inside his head.

This time, instead of struggling against the pain, Max embraced it, welcomed it. For whatever reason the discomfort helped him to stay present, to fight the effects of the drug. And since the drugs also wreaked havoc with his ability to reach out for another's thoughts, he stopped trying.

Someone else was speaking now, and Max realized another man stood next to Rocco. Max took in the man's black garb, the compact submachine gun he carried.

He met the man's unblinking stare. A host of images flipped through Max's mind, including the woman they'd once fought over. "Dante."

"Sorry it took so long," Dante said.

So long? Max tried to recall the last time he'd seen Dante or Rocco, a calculation that was impossible since he didn't know what day it was. "How long?" he asked.

"Two years."

Two. Years. *They betrayed you. Left you behind. You can never trust them.*

"Whoa! Easy!" Rocco's voice registered.

Max felt a hand close over his wrist and tug the gun away. That he hadn't even realized he'd raised his arm and pointed the weapon shook him. Now, he knew what a robot must feel like.

Dante, Rocco were good guys. Time didn't change the fact they were brothers in arms.

"Sorry . . . don't know what to think," Max said.

"You're entitled. Are you injured?" Dante asked.

Max tried to shake his head, felt dizzy. "Tranqed. Don't want to go . . . under again." Bad things happened whenever he was sedated.

"Riley!" Dante snapped. "Get your med kit over here."

Max swung his fist, missed. "No. Meds."

"Whatever you say, buddy. I just want Riley to check your vitals."

Buddy. Had he almost decked his friend now? "I thought . . . you died."

"Lot of that going around." Dante cleared his throat. "Right now we need to find Harry. Is he here, too?"

Harry. Max struggled to recall a face that matched that name. Harry Gambrel. Harry and Dante had been with Max. In a fire. *Two years ago.*

No, not fire. An explosion. Screams. *Forget about them. All that matters is Taz. And—*

Once more Max's head began to pound. He rubbed his temples. "Harry's dead. But Taz isn't. Owe him my life . . . got to save him."

Dante looked around. "Who is Taz? And where is he?"

"Give me a minute," Riley said as he moved in and dropped to one knee.

Max realized he was lying on the floor now.

"I want to get your blood pressure," Riley continued. "Any idea what you were given?"

"Get Dr. Rufin up. He'll know." Max shoved away the BP cuff Riley held. "Don't worry 'bout that. Just get me back on my feet and over to that tank. Taz is inside. He's my . . . friend. Brother. One of us."

"Jesus. We'll get him out." Rocco moved in close now. Hooking Max's arm, he hauled him to his feet and supported him.

Riley immediately moved away, toward Rufin. The pungent scent of ammonia filled the air as a capsule was waved under Rufin's nose. The scientist came up sputtering, then nearly passed out once again as he saw the black-clad newcomers.

"Do you speak English?" Dante barked at Rufin.

"Y-y-yes."

"What was he drugged with?" Dante nodded toward Max.

"Sedatives, a mixture with pen-pen-pentobarbital."

"What dose?" Riley asked.

"Adjusted for his weight." Dr. Rufin looked around on the floor. "I need to see the d-d-dart."

"Screw that. Just help me get this open." Max lurched away from Rocco and began to unfasten the latches on the chamber.

"No!" Dr. Rufin tried to surge up but shrank back as three guns were leveled at him. "Th-th-the procedure has been interrupted."

"You know what you can do with your procedures?" Max broke away the last latch and lifted the chamber's clamshell lid. Inside, strapped down to the flat surface, was Taz.

"Hold on, Taz!" Max tugged away the bulky eye goggles while Rocco worked to remove the oversized headphones that were secured with tape.

Max knew the awful images, commands, which were input with the devices. *Do this, or they die.* How many times had Max lain in this machine and watched his friends, family suffer? Had felt intolerable pain rip through his body.

That Taz didn't move, didn't respond, worried Max. He frantically ripped away scores of circular diode patches that were stuck all over Taz's torso, arms, and legs.

"He's alive." Riley had moved in. "I've got a pulse, but it's going through the roof."

Max shifted away to give Riley better access. "Whatever it takes. Save him."

Turning away, Rocco stormed over and snatched Rufin up by the lapels. "I ought to kill you."

"Dibs," Max said.

"Fair enough." Rocco shoved Rufin toward Max. "What the hell have you been doing here?"

But before Rufin could respond, Dante snapped his fingers. "Quiet! Go ahead."

Max realized the men all wore mics and earpieces; that meant at least one other person was outside keeping watch.

Dante swore, then addressed Max and the others. "The Thai military's put out an alert for a rogue chopper in this area. We're outta here."

Max nodded to Taz. "He comes with us."

"Absolutely." Dante began giving orders. "JC, video all this. Zeke, gather anything we can carry out. Then escort the doctor."

Rufin started to protest but Zeke grabbed him and secured his wrists behind his back. Then Zeke thrust a photograph in Rufin's face. "Where is this man? Harry Gambrel."

Rufin barely glanced at the photo, his gaze instead

following Dante, as if recognizing who was in charge. "These are the only t-t-two men here—b-b-besides the guards."

"Look again," Zeke said. "This is an old photo."

"I swear." Rufin eyed the photograph then shook his head. "I've never seen him."

"He's telling the truth." Max pointed to Taz. "We've been the only prisoners at this place."

"Get them out of here," Dante said. "I'll set the charges."

"Don't blow this up," Rufin pleaded as he was escorted away.

"I'm not about to leave it behind for someone else," Dante said. "Let's move!"

Rocco had hoisted the still unconscious Taz up in a fireman's carry. Riley edged closer as if preparing to grab Max in the same manner.

"I can walk," Max said. "Just give me an arm."

Outside, it was growing dark. Disorientation hit Max like a load of bricks. *Leave and you die.* He sucked in huge gulps of night air in an effort to combat the rapidly swelling paranoia. Damn it, they were being rescued. So why the tension? Fear?

Something's out there . . .

He leaned heavily against Riley as it became increasingly difficult to move his feet. He concentrated on fighting the drug. They were going home. They were free.

Shots rang out.

"Sniper at seven o'clock." Riley's hiss reminded Max that the others were communicating with their radios. "Shit! Zeke's down. Rufin's running like a bat out of hell. In the wrong fucking direction!"

"Go. Help Zeke." Max pushed away from Riley.

"Just follow Rocco," Riley said before turning away. "The chopper's straight ahead."

Rocco was running now. Or trying to. Taz was bouncing like a ragdoll over his shoulder. "Come on, Max!" Rocco shouted back to him. "Twenty more yards. You can do it!"

The *whoop-whoop* of a descending chopper scoured the air. Shots pelted the dirt around Max, making him wonder who the good guys were. Who the hell was shooting at them?

He felt his head whiplash as a rocket of heat tunneled into the back of his skull. Extreme agony shattered his senses. Then everything slowed.

Max knew a moment's clarity, followed by total relief from the pain. For one sparkling second, all answers were his. But at what cost? A bullet in the head?

"Ten more yards, buddy!" Rocco's voice grew more distant. "You're almost home."

Max started to fall. Someone grabbed his arms, nearly wrenched them out of their sockets.

"I got you, buddy."

Dante.

Max felt a pounding jostle, followed by a bone-jarring slam.

He was on the floor of a helicopter, sandwiched between Taz and Zeke. Riley's voice grew faint as he shouted orders.

The gunfire had grown louder, more intense.

Empty shell cases clattered to the chopper's floor like holy rain as Dante and Rocco sprayed the ground with automatic fire, giving them cover as the chopper ascended and spun away.

The *rat-a-tat* of bullets morphed from lullaby to dirge as darkness closed over Max.

He'd never make it.

Chapter 4

"Paging Dr. Houston—call on line four."

Unaccustomed to hearing her name on the PA system, Erin checked her cell phone. The display was dead. Again. A not-so-subtle reminder that the replacement battery she'd ordered sat unopened on her kitchen table. Another sign she was losing it.

She hurried toward the nurses' station, resisting the urge to smack her own forehead. *Physician, heal thyself.* She counseled people daily on the pitfalls of prolonged stress. She needed to get a grip . . . and fast before these annoying little slips morphed into big uglies.

Alice, her friend and the nursing supervisor, held up a receiver as soon as she spotted Erin. "No rest for the weary," Alice said.

"Thanks." Erin pressed the phone to her ear. "This is Dr. Houston."

"It's Marguerite. Dr. Winchette would like to see you. Are you free?"

Working for Dr. Stanley Winchette, the head of the hospital's psychiatric research division, required learning his secretary's verbal shorthand. Marguerite's "are you free" meant "get your ass down here now." Still, the woman's acerbic mannerisms paled in comparison to Winchette's.

"Yes." Erin checked her watch. It was twelve-thirty. Since she worked half-days on Wednesdays, she was usually at the gym, kickboxing, by this time. "I'm on my way," she said even though Marguerite had already disconnected.

She'd have to catch a later class. The alternative, to skip, wasn't an option. The intense workout was one of the few things that KO'd her stress. It got her mind off work and helped her clear her head.

Alice, who had given her the token three-foot radius of privacy, moved back in and held out her hands for the stack of patient charts Erin had balanced on the counter.

Alice then pretended to reel sideways from their weight. "Is it me, or do these files get thicker with every new 'paperless' program they institute?"

Erin shrugged, knowing her friend didn't expect a reply. Dr. Winchette's dislike of digital media meant everything in his department got printed, in triplicate, just to buck *their* system. Winchette's vocabulary didn't include "ecofriendly."

"I wish you were going tonight," Alice said.

"Tonight?" Erin drew a blank.

Alice rolled her eyes. "Hello? Cindy's bachelorette party? Chippendale dancers? Men with big, honking muscles? Jeez, girl, you do remember big honking muscles, right? Or do I need to call nine-one-one for your libido?" She dropped her voice. "I'm almost afraid to ask, but when was the last time you let your hair down? Did something wild and crazy like have wild monkey sex?"

"Ewww."

"Not with a monkey, of course. A real man?"

"As opposed to a fake one?" Erin deflected the question with humor, but Alice was tenacious.

"When was your last booty call? I'm talking someone with a pulse, no batteries required." Alice crossed her arms. "And please don't tell me you haven't had any since what's-his-doodle moved out."

"Perry." They'd broken up two years ago for reasons Erin couldn't even recall. "I'm sure I've had some since then."

Hadn't she? Now that she thought about it, her more memorable forays had involved a fantasy lover and a vibrator. But instead of relieving frustration, it seemed to make it worse.

"Some? You need to move HOT SEX higher on your list. Tonight's eye candy will help remind you what you're missing."

"I really can't go. I'm on call for Penny."

What Erin didn't mention was that she'd volunteered to be on call as it gave her a legitimate reason to come back late tonight, when the administrative offices were deserted.

Since Dr. Winchette spent one day a week in Springfield, Massachusetts, overseeing the construction of a new clinical test facility, Wednesday was the only night he didn't keep to his usual ungodly hours, the only night she could search the lab and storeroom where her father used to work.

"Fine. I'll take pictures, you know, to jump-start your imagination." Alice wagged her brows before turning away to answer another ringing line. "See you tomorrow."

Erin made her way down the two flights of stairs leading to the basement level, her thoughts matching the staccato tapping of her functional pumps. It dawned on her that she could probably walk these halls blindfolded. The lack of windows and outside doors prompted many to compare the basement to a maze. No wonder she sometimes felt like the rat in the maze. *Searching, searching.*

As always when she came this way, her thoughts sank. How many times had she walked these very same stairwells with her father before he'd retired "early" nine months ago, listening to his diatribe on exercise? And how many times had she walked them afterward, the weight of his suicide nearly breaking her?

Suicide. She blinked back angry tears wondering how much longer she could keep up the act. No way had her father taken his own life.

No one who knows what I know, who has seen what I've seen, leaves this business alive, her father had seemingly prophesied in a cryptic journal entry. Had he truly expected to die?

Marguerite spotted her and waved her directly toward the double doors to her right. "You can wait there. He'll be right with you."

Steeling herself, Erin stepped inside the very room that used to be her father's office. Funny to think she'd practically grown up here, had slept many nights on the shabby old plaid couch that used to be in the corner. Following her mother's death when Erin was only two years old, her father simply brought her along when he had to work late. Or he'd have the housekeeper drop her off when she left for the day.

Her nose wrinkled at the faint smell of stale cigars. While the ancient facility was currently tobacco-free, for decades everyone had smoked in their offices. No amount of paint could ever cover it.

She took a seat in front of the massive mahogany desk that Dr. Winchette had moved in when he'd taken over the office, converting it to a formal space used only for meetings. He was, after all, in charge of one of the country's oldest mental health research programs. She eyed the montage of diplomas, citations, and certificates on the walls. Even more plaques, awards, and photos cluttered the credenza.

She ignored them, her gaze coming to rest on the solitary picture frame that sat on the desk. It was an old photo of her father and Winchette back in their college days. Alpha-Geek-Geek. Horned rim glasses, white lab coats, and overflowing pocket protectors. Her father used to joke that if she looked up the word "nerd" in *Webster's*, this picture would illustrate it.

The two men had acted the part as well. As a child, Erin had spent countless hours watching and listening to her father and Dr. Winchette argue over an experiment. The two men would stand at the huge blackboard that used to grace the entire back wall and argue with chalk, both of them scribbling equations so rapidly that she'd get whiplash trying to keep up.

At the time she couldn't grasp any of it, but watching their process had always been both amazing and unsettling. The charged air, the parry and riposte. A stranger would have thought they were indeed fighting a duel. But always in the end, they'd formulate a new hypothesis that would leave *them* cackling like children.

"It's how we work," her father had explained when she was older. "I am rock-solid reason, Stanley is unruly brilliance. We spark and collide, ultimately creating bold new worlds."

She stared at the photograph, wondering again if her father's posthumous warning to trust no one included Stanley Winchette, who had once been his nearest and dearest friend.

Though her father never discussed it with her, Winchette had insisted that the nosedive the two men's personal relationship took following her father's resignation amid unsavory rumors had been a temporary glitch born of embarrassment.

Winchette had then gone on to draw a parallel between his professional relationship with Erin. *"God knows you and I have had our awkward moments, but we've moved on."*

The door opened and Dr. Winchette entered briskly. All business, he went directly to the leather chair behind the desk.

"Erin. Good. I know this is short notice." He set his briefcase on the desk's smooth surface and looked at her. "I'm leaving for Springfield this afternoon and I may be tied up for several days. Colby Deets is at the Toronto conference, so—" Winchette broke off as his cell phone began to buzz. "Excuse me. I'm waiting on a call."

Erin sat forward while Winchette checked his phone. That he was going to ask her to cover for him was totally unexpected. Was it also an olive branch?

She hadn't anticipated getting a second chance so soon, not after her alleged screwup of a case several months ago. Winchette had practically accused her of sexual misconduct when a patient of his insisted he'd work only with Erin after she filled in during one of Winchette's absences.

Just because Winchette later retracted his harsh words hadn't meant all was rosy. In fact, Winchette had only recently allowed her back on his team. But only after making sure everyone knew it was mostly out of loyalty to Erin's late father.

That hadn't been their first *awkward moment*, as he liked to call them. More than once Winchette had virtually ridiculed Erin's interest in clinical hypnosis. Or at least he had until she'd won a lucrative research grant for a study of alternative treatments for post-traumatic shock disorder.

And even though a friend of Winchette's, a veteran allergic to most antianxiety medications, had been cured of several crippling phobias with Erin's help—Winchette still referred to her work as "woo-woo."

"That wasn't the call I'm waiting for," Winchette said. "Now where were we?"

"I'd be happy to fill in while you're gone," she said.

Winchette cleared his throat. "That won't be necessary. Colby Deets is already headed back. However, his flight has been delayed until tonight. Since I'm pressed for time, I thought you could ride with me to the airport and take a few notes."

Mortified by her presumptiveness, Erin felt she had little choice but to nod. And since Winchette knew she didn't work Wednesday afternoons, any excuses she made up now would ring false.

Pulling off his glasses, he let out a heavy sigh. "I'm sorry, Erin. I just realized I haven't even asked how you're feeling." He pointed to his phone. "I've been dealing with village idiots all day, which is no excuse."

"You're busy. And I'm fine."

"You don't look fine." Replacing his glasses, he peered at her. "Trouble sleeping again? Perhaps you should go back to Dr. Shelton, do a little follow-up."

Dr. Shelton was a private practice therapist who specialized in grief counseling. Erin had been so shocked by the news of her father's death and the subsequent assertions of suicide that she'd taken Winchette up on his recommendation to see Dr. Shelton.

And it had helped her to work through the initial stages of guilt and doubt. Guilt over not recognizing her father's alleged depression symptoms followed by the uncertainty of wondering if there was truth to the vague whispers that her father had leaked secret information. While initially Winchette had privately defended her father, the cloud of suspicion hadn't ever gone away.

"I appreciate your concern," she said. Liar, liar.

"Your father worked in the psychotherapy field," Winchette had told her at the memorial service. *"Who would know better than him how to hide the symptoms? Especially from his only child and closest friends."*

That hadn't been the first time Winchette had quoted, practically verbatim, some of Dr. Shelton's words. She'd quit seeing Shelton after suspecting he had been feeding Winchette reports the whole time. Toward the end, Shelton had seemed intent on discovering what Erin knew of her father's work. Which at that time had been nothing. Not that she knew much more at this point.

But now that she suspected foul play, she damn sure wasn't going back to see Shelton. The discovery of her father's warning against trusting anyone was too fresh.

"I think it's just my schedule," Erin went on. "I've been pulling night shift twice a week to accommodate Penny's maternity leave. It'll straighten out in another week or two."

Winchette smiled, warming to his fatherly role. "When Penny gets back, why don't you take a few days yourself? Have you been up to the lake house at all?"

"Not for a while." She struggled to keep her voice smooth. The lake house was a tender subject, but not for the reasons Dr. Winchette assumed. In fact, it was her last trip to the lake that had proved the best therapy: that of turning her grief into rage.

After delaying the trip for months, she'd finally gone to scatter her father's ashes, to honor his last wishes. And give herself closure. She'd purposely gone alone, not wanting to share the symbolic last moment she'd have with her father.

She hadn't expected to find his letter, hidden where he knew she'd find it. She also hadn't expected to discover, there in the heartbreakingly beautiful Shenandoah Mountains, that her father had actually expected he would be silenced over his accusations of plagiarized research. Accusations that had subsequently gotten twisted and deflected back at her father. It was just so wrong!

Don't ask questions. Don't press for answers. Just get the data I've collected on the Lethe Project to Professor Ralph Inger. He'll know what to do, whom to contact.

Her father's work had been highly classified, so contacting anyone had worried her. But then she'd learned Professor Inger was dead, too. An automobile accident. And Inger wasn't the only one having fatal accidents. Two other scientists mentioned in her father's notes had also died recently. Moreover, the files on this so-called Lethe Project weren't where her father had indicated.

She was careful to put her father's letter in a safe-deposit box while she searched for substantiation. To go public with so little meant running the risk of further tarnishing her father's reputation.

Truth be told, she was running out of places to

look for his life's work. Which meant she either needed to abandon her search or enlist someone's help. But who could she trust?

Don't think about it now.

"Perhaps when I return we can—" Winchette cut himself off once again as his phone rang. "Blast."

Erin took advantage of the interruption and stood. "Before we leave, I need to run by my office. Can I meet you in the lobby?"

"Five minutes," he said. "I'm cutting it close already."

Erin barely had time to get back to her office after being stopped twice by coworkers in the hallways. When she reached the lobby, it was deserted, but she spotted the shiny black Town Car idling out front beneath the portico. The driver opened the back door, where Winchette was already seated.

As soon as she was settled, they took off. To her relief, Winchette was all business.

Handing her a clipboard, he started talking before she retrieved a pen. "This is my patient roster. The first one is Kenneth Parson. He's one of five veterans participating in a study for a new antianxiety med. His PTSD includes hallucinations. The others in the study—we'll get to them in a moment—exhibit similar symptoms. All have shown marked improvement at the lowest dosages with the exception of Mr. Parson. I conferred with the manufacturer and received approval to increase his dosage."

Erin scribbled as Winchette moved down the list. It wasn't unusual for his entire roster to include drug study patients. As a matter of fact, over the past few months he'd grown increasingly vocal about his desire to focus exclusively on such studies. Almost like he was obsessed with these patients.

In fact, Colby Deets had let it slip that the Springfield facility would be nothing but research and development, a joint collaboration with several major pharmaceutical companies. Bristling with self-importance over his role as Winchette's newest pet, Deets had made it clear that he expected to be reassigned there as well.

"Hold on." Once again, Winchette impatiently tugged his cell phone free and held it out to glance at the caller ID. His scowl deepened. "I have to take this one." He opened the phone. "Winchette."

Erin looked out the window, taking in the crowded freeway as she idly wished for this excursion to end. Maybe a getaway *was* what she needed. Time alone to regroup. Maybe Alice was right. Maybe a good old-fashioned booty call would help reset her circuits. Ground her back in the real world of flesh and blood lovers, not imaginary men who existed only in dreams.

"Did you say there were *two* men? Good Lord! When did this happen?" Dr. Winchette's voice rose. "No need to do that. I can let Dr. Houston know."

His tone was impossible to ignore. She noted the rising flush in his cheeks. He was getting more agitated by the moment. And judging by the accusatory look he'd just thrown her way, she was involved.

Guilt climbed up her spine.

"What is their ETA?" Winchette looked at his watch now. "I'm on my way. And I don't want those men taken to the Naval Hospital. Tell them I'll call back with the name of a private facility with a neurologist on staff where these men should be taken. Also find out who the agent in charge is and whom he reports to. That's the person I want to speak with."

When he disconnected, Erin cleared her throat, waiting for an explanation of why her name had been mentioned. "Is everything okay?" she prompted when he remained quiet.

"No. It's not." Clearly displeased, Winchette pressed the intercom button.

"Yes, sir?" The driver's voice came over the speaker.

"There's been a change of plans. I need to return to the hospital at once."

Erin frowned. "You're canceling your trip?"

Dr. Winchette peeled off his glasses before responding. "I'm needed for an urgent matter in California. Two men have been recovered and are en route to San Diego."

"Recovered" meant the men had been missing; likely captured. Winchette being called in meant the suspicion of psychological abuse. His experience and background in mental coercion techniques, psychological warfare, also meant the case was ugly, messy.

"One of these men apparently worked with Dante Johnson," he went on.

Aha. Erin nodded, careful not to overreact. Dante was Winchette's former patient, the one that had requested Erin take over his case.

Far from a model patient, Dante had resisted assistance, bending only when his job required it. Initially it seemed he'd been around just long enough to cause trouble—for her—before disappearing.

Then he'd contacted her a few months ago, wanting to voluntarily complete their session. They'd since developed a great rapport.

Erin had learned a lot about Dante and the type of person it took to do the job he did. She'd also gotten a glimpse of what he'd gone through. Pure hell.

"Are these men in the same shape as Johnson?" Dante had been brought in near death. Recalling all the scars on his body made her shiver. She also remembered his rantings. The horrible nightmares.

"Worse perhaps," Winchette said. Both are unconscious; one was shot in the head. They haven't even landed in San Diego yet and there seems to be doubt whether either will survive the flight. I promised to make a couple calls, pull some strings."

"What can I do to help?"

Winchette looked directly at her now, his gaze resigned. "You need to accompany me to California. Someone at the CIA has requested your presence as well."

Chapter 5

Calder Center, San Diego, California
September 19

It was after 6 p.m. by the time Erin and Dr. Winchette made it to the Calder Center hospital.

Fighting rush-hour traffic in an unfamiliar city left her with a short temper that matched her sour mood. With the hospital's main lot torn up because of the new parking garage going up, the surrounding streets were jammed. The closest spot she could find was still two blocks away.

Winchette had been on his cell phone nonstop since they'd deplaned. At first she'd been pissed with his secretiveness, thinking it was a ploy to keep her in the dark. It was painfully obvious that he was not thrilled about her coming.

But during the ride, she'd realized that Winchette's caginess was mostly due to his own lack of facts. Winchette viewed "I don't know" as a sign of weakness. Brushing her off, acting too busy to talk, was his signature *modus operandi* in those situations.

The scant details he had shared about this case were intriguing. Two men, both unconscious, had been pulled out of what she half-jokingly referred to as the CIA's Cosmic Lost and Found Box.

These were the *don't ask* patients who were smuggled into hospitals and kept under wraps. They usually disappeared with an equal measure of stealth, leaving a wake of hushed speculation about their identity and circumstances.

That was another thing about Lost-and-Foundees: a higher authority dictated when they came and went. In Spyville, ships didn't just pass in the night. They just totally disappeared, their existence likened to ghosts. *Spooks.*

In this case, one of the men, Max Duncan, was a colleague of Dante Johnson, himself a Lost and Found alumnus. She knew two other operatives had originally disappeared with Dante a couple years ago. But according to Winchette, only one of those missing men had been recovered.

So who was this other man brought in with Max Duncan? That he'd been dubbed "John Doe" could mean anything from a true unknown to an honest-to-God Elvis recovery. Given that the men had been routed here, to a private facility, meant Mr. Doe wasn't a threat or high-profile criminal, like say, bin Laden, but still her curiosity was piqued.

She already knew a little bit about Max Duncan, from Dante talking about him. And she'd seen a photograph once. The guy had been dark fantasy material. *I could give you an orgasm, but then I'd have to kill you.* Of course, most everyone she'd met who worked with Dante had that quality. Alice had nick-named them the Macho Squad.

Leaving her carry-on luggage in the rental car's trunk, Erin snagged her briefcase and purse and hurried toward the hospital after Winchette.

Winchette went straight to the information desk in the lobby and was given two badges. He handed one to Erin.

"Dr. Giles is expecting you," the clerk said. "Take the red elevator to the third floor."

"Giles is the staff neurologist I mentioned. We've worked together before," Winchette said before stepping into a crowded elevator.

Since he was licensed to practice in a number of states besides Virginia and California, Winchette had an established network of colleagues.

That Giles had worked with the intelligence com-munity before made it easier to cut hospital red tape. Giles had had the two patients admitted quickly and anonymously, keeping them isolated from staff and other patients. From what Erin gathered from the phone conversations she overheard, Giles was al-ready deferring completely to Winchette.

As soon as they stepped off the elevator, an older man with thin sandy hair approached and intro-duced himself as Dr. Giles.

"You must be Dr. Houston. Welcome to San Diego," he said. "Stanley, good to see you again."

Winchette nodded. "I was just telling Erin how

invaluable your discretion and assistance are in this matter."

Her smile tightened at the small lie.

Giles's shoulders, however, straightened. "Glad to help. We can talk in here." He led them into a small alcove hear the nurses' station.

Winchette was all business now. "Any change in their condition?"

"No. Sedation levels were increased due to seizure activity during the flight. I've maintained that dosage since I knew you were en route."

"Yes. We'll review that in a moment. Have you had a chance to order MRIs?" Winchette asked.

Giles nodded. "As a matter of fact, the patient with the head wound was just returned to his room. I believe the other patient is still down in radiology, but I'll check on that. I've also secured an unused meeting room at the end of the hall for you and your associates."

"Associates?"

"The two agents that accompanied the patients. Johnson and Taylor?" Giles looked from Winchette to Erin. "Er, they flashed CIA identification after I questioned their presence. Then they grilled me like a sandwich."

"Ah, *them*," Winchette said. "Where are they now?"

"Getting cleaned up. I gathered they had a long flight and were kept on their toes with the patients' seizures and other problems. They said to tell you they would be back shortly."

Winchette's pained expression said that he wasn't looking forward to dealing with either of the

CIA operatives. Dante Johnson and Rocco Taylor had both managed to clash with Winchette during Dante's hospitalization. She'd bet none of them had any fond memories of the other after that.

"Here are the patient files, by the way." Dr. Giles picked up two folders from a table. "I've kept everything segregated. Even their rooms, 320 and 322, are at the far end of the hall."

Winchette took the files and handed them to Erin. "Why don't you go on to Mr. Duncan's room? I'll be along shortly."

While his brusque dismissal was irritating, it didn't surprise her. Winchette was jostling for control, no doubt practicing for a face-off with Dante.

She welcomed the chance for a few minutes alone. When she reached Max's room, she paused outside to read his file. Most of what she saw confirmed what she already knew. Maxwell DeWayne Duncan, Caucasian male, age thirty, had been wounded during an extraction, his head grazed by a bullet that could have easily killed him.

In addition to a skull fracture, he suffered a concussion and a deep scalp laceration, which had likely been crudely stitched in the field. She was a psychologist, not a medical doctor. She'd missed all the blood and guts training, but she knew enough to recognize that while Max's injuries sounded slight, they could render a patient vegetative for life.

You're lucky to be alive, Max.

He'd been kept in a drug-induced coma to ease brain swelling, a standard procedure, which also helped forestall further seizures. Max's prognosis, while incomplete pending further tests and assessments, seemed more promising than the second patient's.

John Doe had been found unconscious and had suffered multiple seizures, with increasing frequency. Doe, too, was heavily sedated but that he suffered no obvious injury was puzzling. And ominous. Much was omitted here. A familiar sensation rippled over her, the one that warned she should be alert and keep her ears open.

She flipped back to the earliest report in Max's file. According to it, he'd arrived at a Singapore hospital less than twenty-four hours ago. The initial CT scan revealed a fracture at the base of the skull and several small hematomas, which were suspect in the seizures.

There was no indication that he'd ever regained consciousness, which could be attributed to the sedatives given to him at the Singapore hospital.

Erin paged through the last of the reports, but nothing she saw indicated the circumstances of how Max had been found or what hellhole he'd been pulled from. The fact that his medical records originated in Southeast Asia was somewhat telling. Hadn't Dante Johnson been held in a prison in that same area?

She needed to speak to Dante. He could fill in the blanks about what conditions Max was held under. She would also find out more about Max personally, to help him better.

Straightening her blazer, she pushed open the door. As soon as she entered Max's room, her earlier irritation with Winchette dissipated. Professional compassion flooded her system.

Setting the files and her briefcase on a corner table, she moved closer, her eyes taking in the unconscious man strapped to the bed. Surrounded by a host of monitors and IV poles, Max's skin was ashen, his head partially bandaged.

As she drew closer, she did a double take. Aside from the paleness and bandage, Max appeared to be in excellent health. She had anticipated that he'd look, well, a hell of a lot worse. Dante Johnson had been so sick and emaciated following months of torture.

And while she had no idea what further injuries lay beneath the sheet, Max's physique, what she could see of it anyway, appeared normal, even robust.

She could guess at the conjecturing taking place. Did the CIA think Max had earned preferential treatment by bartering information? Dante had complained bitterly of being treated with suspicion after being in enemy hands for eighteen months. Max would likely be viewed more harshly.

She scowled. In light of the circumstances surrounding her father's death, that whole conjecture game left a bad taste in her mouth. It was so easy to toss stones.

Assume nothing, her father always said.

She stepped closer to the head of the bed and let her gaze sweep across Max's face. Immediately she felt a softening in her knees. The pictures she'd seen of him before paled by comparison.

Max Duncan was one of those drop-dead gorgeous

types rarely seen outside the pages of glossy magazines. Long lashes fanned down, toward sharp cheekbones. His beard was thick, but not heavy. She'd guess he normally kept his face clean-shaven.

His file indicated no next of kin, but the fact that Max was so attractive made it difficult to imagine there wasn't at least one femme fatale pining away over him.

In fact, hadn't there been a rumor that Max had been involved with the same female operative that Dante Johnson had initially blamed for his capture? That Erin knew Dante and Catalina Dion were together now didn't mean she was privy to all their secrets.

Max's hair, what she could see of it, was practically blue-black. Stick-straight and short, it was also matted with dried blood.

She made a mental note to ask one of the nurses to wash that part of his hair. A small thing perhaps, but she liked to think that if she were the patient, someone might remember the kindness of a little grooming.

"Hello, Max. My name is Dr. Erin Houston." She kept her voice low and even.

Just because a patient appeared unconscious didn't mean he couldn't hear. Countless studies reported patients being aware of everything said during surgery, even though they had been fully anesthetized.

"I'm going to check your pulse," she continued.

But the moment her fingers grasped his wrist, she jerked to a stop, feeling as if an invisible force coursed through her, holding her in place. To touch him was electrifying.

She couldn't take her eyes off him. Her breath caught as desire shot through her. A vision of kissing him flashed in her mind, a memory so real she closed her eyes.

In her mind's eye, she was standing in Max's embrace; he'd been searching for her and had been furious that she'd been . . . lost. His desperation, born of thinking he'd never see her again, never touch her again, was tangible and she ached to soothe him, to reassure him.

Except this wasn't her fantasy anymore. It was *his* and he wanted her naked and open and longing for him. Only him.

Yes . . . yes . . . yes . . .

The intensity of the moment peaked and burst so rapidly Erin stumbled sideways. Throwing her arms out to catch her balance, she turned away from the bed. Mortified.

What the hell had just happened?

For a moment she'd felt . . . possessed. Taken. Owned.

Damn Alice! Clearly her friend's suggestion that Erin didn't have a sex life had brought all this up.

Get a grip.

Drawing a sharp breath, she looked back at the bed.

And stared into Max's fully open eyes. He didn't move, didn't speak, but as he held her gaze, his pupils constricted.

"Max! Can you hear me? Can you blink?"

He blinked. This was not the sightless gaze of the comatose.

Erin scrambled to grasp his hand once again. "Can you feel me squeeze?"

He blinked again.

She placed her fingers beneath his. "Can you squeeze my hand?"

At first there was nothing, and then she felt slight pressure. A definite response!

One of the monitors started beeping loudly. She glanced at the flashing display. His blood pressure kicked up, spiking over two-twenty. His hand grew slack now, and when she looked back, his eyes had closed.

"Stay with me, Max!" She squeezed his hand again, but got no response.

The door opened just then, and Dr. Winchette and a nurse came into the room.

"And then I want—" Winchette broke off his instructions as soon as he heard the beeping alarm. "What's going on?"

"The patient just opened his eyes and responded. Twice," Erin explained. "Then his blood pressure shot up."

"He's going into a seizure." Winchette grabbed the syringe from the nurse and marched straight to the bed. He quickly muted the alarm, then injected the syringe contents directly into the IV port.

"But—" Erin's voice faded as the flashing numbers on the machine began to drop and slow dramatically.

"It's not what you're thinking, Erin. I've seen what

you described enough to know it's a precursor to a tonic-clonic seizure, which this patient has a history of." Winchette turned to the nurse. "I want this new medication carefully monitored. And let me know as soon as the other patient is back in his room."

He turned back to Erin. "The MRI machine was down for a short time earlier, but Dr. Giles is working to expedite our other patient through the queue. Now, we're scheduled to meet with our *associates* in a few minutes. I'd prefer you let me handle the explanation of this incident."

She wanted to protest, but when she opened her mouth to speak, her mind abruptly went back to Max as if something pulled her toward him.

What was wrong with her today? Had the combination of stress, lack of sleep, and jet lag gotten to her?

She cast another look at Max, and again felt an irresistable tug. "I need to gather my things," she said to Winchette. "I'll be there shortly."

Max followed the voices, but found it increasingly difficult to keep up. The woman was talking now, her voice almost as soothing as her touch. *Come back.*

He heard the door shut but sensed he wasn't alone. The angel had stayed. Thank God!

Erin. Her name is Erin.

Though he couldn't see her, he knew she'd moved back toward his bed. He prayed she'd touch him again. An image of her shimmered in his mind. Dark red hair, glossy like a burnished halo. And big eyes. The kind you fell into.

Angel eyes.

Establishing a link with her had been easy. And . . . pleasurable. He'd wanted more, had wanted to deepen and explore their bond. She wanted more, too. No, needed more.

He reached out to her now, felt her confusion and embarrassment, but couldn't maintain a connection. Whatever that man, Dr. Winchette, had given him was fast acting, peeling away his tenuous grasp on reality.

Unfortunately, Max hadn't had the strength to establish a lasting link with Winchette. He'd tried to see the man's thoughts, but had come away with scattered impressions and bad vibes.

Only one thing was sure. Winchette reeked of subterfuge; he intended harm. And he was on his way to find Taz.

Run, Taz. Hide!

"I'm here, Max."

Max was aware of Erin's hand grasping his, but her touch, her words, were ripped away as the drug rolled fully over him, leaving him with that familiar sensation of being uncertain whom to trust. Once again he'd been cast adrift in stormy seas.

For now hope was lost.

But the next time he came to . . . he vowed that he would kill anyone who came near him.

Chapter 6

Four men were huddled in the hallway a short distance from Max's room.

Erin recognized the tall blonde, Rocco Taylor, but her gaze widened as she realized the man standing next to him was Dante Johnson.

Because they'd done subsequent sessions by telephone, she hadn't seen Dante in months. He looked nothing like the frail tortured man she recalled. He'd gained weight, muscle mass. But it was his eyes that told the real story. The haunting emptiness was gone, replaced by something profoundly peaceful.

She extended her hand. "You look fantastic, Dante."

He smiled. "Good to see you again, Dr. Houston. You remember my partner, Rocco Taylor?"

"Mr. Taylor." Erin kept it formal.

Rocco didn't. "Doc. You look fantastic, too. Still gorgeous as ever."

Erin wanted to cringe at his obvious flirting, which

she didn't take seriously, nor did it offend her. She just wished he hadn't done it in front of Winchette.

The third man stepped closer, his hand extended. "I'm Travis Franks. We met once briefly in Virginia."

While not much older than Dante, Travis Franks had that calmly authoritative air that bespoke high rank. *He's seen much misery yet he's not bitter*, she thought as she shook his hand.

"Of course she remembers all of you," Winchette interjected snidely. "It hasn't been that long."

It was impossible to ignore the shimmering tension. Belatedly she realized Winchette's rudeness was meant to establish dominance. He liked to posture by giving orders, which was difficult to do on someone else's turf.

Of course, Travis Franks was equally off turf. But he had two people with him, which to Winchette's way of thinking meant Franks was ahead, probably with bonus points since his people were also male.

Like it or not, the sexist good-old-boy mentality had yet to die out.

"Let's move to the conference room," Winchette said. "This way."

Once inside the small meeting room, Winchette asserted himself at the head of the table. Erin took the seat immediately to his left. Travis sat opposite her.

Winchette started talking before Dante and Rocco were seated. "Let me state up front that if you want a prognosis on these two men, it's entirely too early. I am still waiting on test results and I haven't even had a chance to examine John Doe yet. Based on what

I've seen thus far, however, I'm not optimistic. As Dr. Houston and I just witnessed, Mr. Duncan's seizures are increasing in frequency and severity, which will require deeper levels of sedation to control."

"I don't get that," Travis said. "I had hoped the seizures would subside once the swelling in his brain decreased."

"Hope has no scientific bearing, Mr. Franks," Winchette said. "Facts are facts. And from what I understand, those facts appear even more dire for your John Doe. Speaking of Mr. Doe, have you been able to obtain any history?"

"Not yet. His fingerprints are being run as we speak," Travis said. "And as I mentioned earlier, I don't want to advertise his existence, so the process may take a bit longer."

"If he's not one of your men, what is his status? Friend or foe?" Erin asked.

"For now, John Doe should be treated as an ally," Travis said. "At least until we debrief them—which we can't do until they regain consciousness."

Erin had worked with enough security agencies to recognize the double-talk. "At least until we debrief," meant that even though Max Duncan was one of their own, he'd be scrutinized closely before being "welcomed" back to the fold. And John Doe would be treated like a leper.

"What do you make of their physical shape?" Winchette asked. "They look pretty—what's the word—buff?"

"Compared to how I looked?" Dante asked. "Yeah. But before you call him buff, look at him without a

shirt. Max is sporting some hellacious scars. So is
Doe. They've been burned, cut, whipped, and who
knows what else."

Erin felt her stomach clench at the confirmation
of torture.

Winchette changed tactics. "Well, friend or foe, I
want these men transferred to Virginia immediately. Given that mind manipulation is also suspected, they need to be in a specialized facility." Dr.
Winchette looked at Travis again. "Now, I'd like to
hear details about the circumstances these men
were found in."

Travis reached for his briefcase. "I have photographs taken during the recovery operation. I'm
hoping you can shed light on some of this laboratory equipment." He slid a stack of photos toward
Winchette.

Erin shifted sideways so she could see them, too.
The first ones showed a crude laboratory. Then
there were close-ups of the counters and cabinets.
She saw nothing unusual or particularly dangerous.
Microscopes. Titration equipment. Beakers.

She pointed to the label on one of the bottles. "Is
that Chinese?"

"Yes," Travis said.

"You're having translations done?" Winchette
asked.

"Of course. We have some actual samples, which
will be tested as well." Travis peered over the top of
the photographs Winchette held, clearly eager for
him to move on. "Shuffle ahead and tell me if you've
seen anything like that."

Dr. Winchette flipped through the photos and abruptly stopped. "What the devil?" He bent closer. "It looks like an old sensory deprivation unit."

As Erin stared at the photograph of the cylindrical chamber, a sense of horror prickled up her spine and her mind began to spin. *She remembered this.*

Jeez, how old had she been? Five or six? It had been one of those nights when her father had been called out to the hospital on an emergency. As a single parent, he'd simply taken her along.

She'd been in his office alone, watching her favorite mermaid cartoon, when she'd had to go to the bathroom. She'd gone in search of her father, opened the wrong door. She remembered seeing this machine—or one like it.

She didn't know which had scared her more, the way the machine seemed to glow—or the muffled voice of someone inside screaming. She had promptly wet her pants and run away. When her father found her hiding beneath his desk, she told him what she'd seen and heard.

He'd hugged her and laughed. Then told her it was just a bad Halloween joke someone had rigged up. A joke meant for adults, not small imaginative children. He'd gently chided her for wandering around. He'd also sworn to tell no one about her little *accident* if she agreed to tell no one about seeing the joke.

But it had been months before he'd taken her to his lab again. And even longer before he left her alone while there.

That image had haunted her sleep back then. And

to see it now. Dear God! She had a brief image of Max trapped inside the machine. In intense pain—screaming.

She blinked away the image. Why was her past haunting her now? Was this one of the things in her father's files that she needed to locate?

"Are you okay, Dr. Houston?" Travis asked.

Erin realized she'd gasped and apologized. She cleared her throat, suddenly self-conscious. "I'm fine. It's just that this looks rather . . . surreal."

Winchette glanced sideways at her, but didn't comment further, leaving her to wonder if he had recognized the machine.

He began flipping through the rest of the photos more quickly. There were shots of another man, the John Doe she supposed, strapped to a table, his eyes and ears covered with optic and audio input devices. Diode patches were visible on his skin.

That she somehow *knew* those diodes delivered muscle stimulus, some punishing, some positive, seemed to emphasize the awful certainty that Max had been subjected to this treatment as well. Her heart ached for him—for anyone who had been subjected to that.

"I'd say this confirms that someone was attempting a type of brainwashing," Winchette said.

Travis clasped his hands on the table in front of him, leaning over them slightly as his gaze leveled with Winchette's. "But what type? Are you familiar with that machine?"

"Only in the vaguest sense. I've seen photographs of similar sensory deprivation units, but that one has clearly been modified. Unfortunately these pictures tell me little. I need to know the specific audio and visual stimuli that were used." Dr. Winchette tamped the photos into a stack and settled back in his chair. "Did your men learn anything from the people running the facility? What did you say the name of the scientist who escaped was?"

"Dr. Rufin." Travis reclaimed the photos and looked pointedly at Erin. "I know this will not be discussed beyond these walls, but as far as the rest of the world is concerned, Dr. Rufin is still in our custody."

Disinformation, Erin thought.

Travis went on. "And we learned nothing; though I do expect to have Rufin back in our custody soon. In the meantime, I have a damaged laptop and two external hard drives that I hope will yield some clues."

Winchette perked up. "I'd like to see that as well. I have staff with specialized training who can decrypt and analyze that type of data."

Travis shook his head. "Thanks, but I'd prefer you and Dr. Houston concentrate on helping these men regain consciousness." He spoke directly to Erin now. "One of our operatives is still missing. I hope that Max or John Doe can provide clues to his whereabouts. I do not want to waste any time waiting for their memories to sort or surface—or whatever. I was hesitant to do so in the past, but this time I suggest we start off using hypnosis at the first sign of a memory gap. Your extraordinary work in the field of hypnotherapy speaks for itself."

"I'll be glad to work with these men," Erin said.

Especially Max. She shook her head at that thought. She'd be happy to work with both men.

"It's premature to have that conversation," Winchette said. "Particularly since neither man has regained consciousness."

Erin squirmed. She had hoped Dr. Winchette would mention her encounter with Max. That he hadn't effectively muzzled her.

"Any clue how soon they'll come to?" Dante asked this question.

"None. I should point out that, typically, the longer a patient remains unconscious—the less likely that they'll regain it," Winchette warned. "So it's critical I get my hands on everything seized in that raid. To understand what was done. And while I'll do everything in my power to help these men, I have much better resources in Virginia. So about moving them . . ."

As Dr. Winchette outlined his proposal for transporting the men, Erin's gaze drifted back to the stack of photos.

The horde of self-doubts that had crept into her mind had helped her regain a sense of healthy skepticism. And right now that skepticism reminded her that the incident she had recalled happened over twenty-five years ago. Maybe she wasn't remembering any of it right; she'd been so small. So impressionable.

And while she'd never mentioned it again, her father and Winchette *had* worked together back then. Winchette should have recognized the machine immediately.

Unless . . .

Was he purposely not mentioning it out of a sense of loyalty to Erin's father?

Or had it had been one of their classified projects, which meant Dr. Winchette couldn't mention it. A sour taste flooded her mouth at the idea that her father and Winchette may have participated in mind-tampering studies. No! She couldn't bear the thought of her father doing anything unethical.

She glanced up and found Dante watching her. Shifting in her seat, she tried to refocus on what Winchette was saying. Something about—

A loud buzzer cut off his words.

"Fire alarm," Dante said as he and Rocco moved simultaneously toward the door.

But before they reached it, a mechanized voice came over the public address system. "Code red. Alert level two. All visitors proceed to the nearest exit. This is not a drill."

Taz had the technician pinned by the throat. "That was a stupid thing to do."

The alarm the tech had triggered clanged loudly, adding a new dimension to the headache that had started the moment Taz awakened completely disoriented inside the noisy, tubelike space.

His first thought, that he'd come awake during a programming session, had proved false when this man, a total stranger, had rushed in and freed him. *Freed him.* Where were the guards? Where was Dr. Rufin?

Taz had taken the man down and given him ten seconds to answer four questions: Where am I? How did I get here? What day is it?

And where is Hades?

The man babbled about two unconscious men who had been brought to the hospital under military escort. A hospital in San Diego, California.

Two men. The other had to be Hades.

"Where did they take Hades? Is Dr. Rufin with him?"

The man's eyes bulged as he struggled to speak. "Don't . . . know . . . Dr. Rufin." The alarm seemed to grow louder.

Taz grunted and threw the man across the room. The man hit a wall and slumped to the floor, unconscious. But Taz had seen his last desperate thought: police swarming in and taking Taz down.

No way.

Dashing out the emergency exit, Taz found himself in an alley between two buildings. His eyes felt sensitive to light, as if laser sabers were being thrust into his head. Dizziness tangled his steps. Leaning against a large metal trash bin, he vomited.

Get a grip, mate. He sucked in air, willing the nausea to pass.

Run, hide and *mission incomplete,* repeated in his head. Since he had no idea what mission they'd been on, he went with the first suggestion. Escape and evade.

He looked down at his bare feet, suddenly confused by the concept of freedom. He and Hades had planned for this, right? But what was their plan?

The string of garbled images and words running through his mind made no sense. *Stasis*. He had to wait for stasis to clear. Then it would make sense. For now all he needed to do was avoid capture.

He'd escaped several times before, but had always been captured. The punishments were ungodly—and they never suffered alone. He couldn't go through that again.

Running to the end of the alley, he waited as a tractor trailer maneuvered into position at the loading dock. The bleating of the backup warning bounced around inside his head like a pinball machine on tilt. Taz waited for the driver to go inside before moving around the truck, using it for cover.

The rest of the alley was deserted. The sun was low in the sky, heralding evening. He headed for the row of hedges lining a fenced-in tennis court. HOSPITAL EMPLOYEES ONLY, the sign read. Following the hedges, he let himself in the unlocked gate. A plain concrete block building stood beyond the clay court.

The men's locker room was empty. He searched the stalls and found a discarded wire hanger, which he used to force open the door marked MAINTENANCE.

Inside that small closet was a second door. That one opened into a large garage area filled with lawn equipment.

"King Solomon's mine," he whispered.

He helped himself to a dark blue jumpsuit and pulled on a pair of rubber boots. Looking around, he found a battered hard hat and a pair of sunglasses.

When he buried the hospital gown in the trash

can, he pulled out the folded newspaper on top and eyed the banner: *San Diego Union-Tribune*, September 19th. How long had it been since he actually knew where he was, much less the date? It seemed like a fucking eternity!

He eyed the paper again. He had a vague notion of having been to California before, but trying to recall specifics was useless.

Mission incomplete, echoed in his mind.

Find Hades.

Find Rufin.

Take what is yours.

The confusing jumble of words, commands, made no sense. Thinking didn't help—in fact, the act of reasoning, questioning, seemed to compound the pain in his head. He felt dizzy, spacey. And until that passed, he needed a safe place to hide.

And then—he'd unlock the mystery of what he needed to do.

Chapter 7

Outside the hospital, Stanley Winchette stepped away from the others to answer his cell phone. Because most of the crowd stayed as close to the building as police allowed, that gave him an opportunity to slip toward the relative privacy of the parking lot.

"Winchette here."

"What have you learned?" Abe Caldwell demanded before breaking into a hacking cough. "Sorry, I'm fighting a damn cold again."

Try emphysema, Stanley thought, not for the first time. Funny that once, in the early stages of their partnership, Abe had implied trepidation about Stanley's age. As if at fifty-nine Stanley had had one foot in the grave.

How ironic that five years later, Stanley felt better than ever, while Abe was mired in denial. Of course, back then, Abe had also believed his grandfather's pharmaceutical conglomerate was close to patenting a miraculous antiaging drug that would keep Abe eternally forty-nine, eternally chasing women and money.

Abe's hobbies were expensive. He liked anything macho and daring: big game hunting in Africa, treks to Nepal, yacht races through the pirate-infested waters of Southeast Asia, for example. The last time Stanley had seen Abe, the man had sported a goatee and had let his hair grow long enough to catch in a ponytail. As if that made up for the receding hairline.

"So what have you learned," Abe repeated.

"It appears these men were indeed used for Zadovsky's secret experiments. And judging by their physical condition—" Stanley still couldn't get over Max Duncan's superb physique. Supposedly John Doe was equally magnificent. "They are one-hundred-eighty degrees from what we saw with Dante Johnson."

"Which confirms what we'd suspected: that Zadovsky hid more than any of us imagined," Abe said. "Any idea what the potential exposure is?"

By that, Abe meant the chance that he and Stanley would be connected to Zadovsky's nefarious experiments. After Zadovsky's death, Stanley had been so certain that he and Abe would be exposed that he'd even selected his own method of suicide: an overdose. Zadovsky blowing his own head off had been a little much.

Unfortunately, the CIA had not been able to move into Jakarta fast enough to snatch Zadovsky's files, which were quickly claimed by the Indonesian government. As rumors swelled on the international front that decades ago Zadovsky had been courted and funded by several Allied nations, the strategy shifted to ass covering. Most countries wanted to put distance between themselves and Zadovsky.

Somehow, in the ensuing mass confusion, Abe, through his uncanny sources, managed to gain access to the Indonesian files only to learn that the records seized were in such bad shape nothing could be surmised. Ironically, it turned out that the research Abe had previously turned over to Stanley, the bits and pieces of data, the shocking video that had been smuggled out of Zadovsky's lab, seemed to be more than the Indonesian government even had.

After clinking wineglasses, Abe and Stanley had once again decided to pull out the stops on the side-lined projects and plunge full speed ahead on their own. How could they not?

Mind control was science's Holy Grail, the ultimate quest for power. On an altruistic level, that field of study would likely yield cures to brain diseases like Alzheimer's. Which had been the reason Abe's grandfather had gotten involved in secretly funding Zadovsky's research to begin with.

Abe and Stanley had everything to gain by continuing this research. In a weird way, the two men complemented each other. Stanley was brains; Abe was brawn. And money. Abe's silver spoon paved many paths.

"I am working to contain matters here," Stanley said. "Apparently the CIA blew up the lab in Thailand, taking only what they could carry out. Which, besides the two prisoners, wasn't much. I expect to get full access to everything they got. The real trick is keeping both men stable yet unconscious until I can get them back to Virginia. The last thing we need is for them to start filling in the blanks."

"Excellent," Abe said. "Let me know if there's anything in particular you require."

"I've got this end covered. You need to concentrate on locating this Dr. Rufin. The CIA's putting up a good front, but it won't be long before word leaks that they've got nothing. What have you turned up on him?"

"Nothing useful," Abe said. "Zadovsky portrayed him as an idiot."

A smart way to throw off the competition, Stanley thought. Especially since it now seemed Zadovsky's former research assistant, Dr. Rufin, had been continuing work at a secret lab in Thailand. Stanley couldn't help but wonder if Rufin was the brains behind the arrogant Zadovsky.

"All that trouble Zadovsky went through to tag prisoners," Stanley muttered. "Too bad he didn't tag his employees."

He had been stunned months ago to learn that Dante Johnson had apparently been tracked by Viktor Zadovsky after being *allowed* to escape. The real pisser had been discovering that Abe Caldwell had known all about the tracking devices since he'd supplied Zadovsky with the technology. "For testing," Abe had argued.

Right. How many other secrets was Abe keeping? Stanley looked around, noting people were beginning to head back toward the hospital entrance.

"One more thing," Stanley said. "With Max Duncan surfacing, the Agency is expanding its search for Harry Gambrel. Any word on his whereabouts?"

"He's dead."

"That's what you told me about Max Duncan after Johnson returned."

"I have personal knowledge of Gambrel's demise."

Once again Stanley wondered about Abe's connections and sources of information. "Keep me posted."

"You do likewise." Abe paused to have another coughing fit. "Also see if you can learn how the CIA got word about this lab to begin with."

So your connections aren't as perfect as you claim, Stanley thought.

"I must go now. I'll give you an update after I've examined both subjects."

Disconnecting, Stanley hurried toward Erin.

"Apparently it was a false alarm," she said. "They are allowing people back inside."

"I don't have time for this bullshit," he grumbled. "Where did Travis Franks disappear to?"

Erin pointed to a spot near a side entrance where Travis was huddled with hospital security personnel. "He's over there."

Just then, Travis broke away and motioned them closer.

"Bad news," Travis began. "Our John Doe regained consciousness and panicked while in the MRI machine. The technician apparently thought he was having a seizure and rushed in to help. By that time Doe was extremely agitated and confused. He ended up throwing the tech across the room before fleeing through an emergency exit."

I should have expected this after Duncan started to come to, Stanley thought. "I want to speak with that technician," he said.

"He's in the ER. Being treated for a broken arm and possible concussion. I sent Rocco to check it out."

"When did this happen? Are they searching for John Doe?"

"It happened maybe twenty minutes ago, same time the alarm sounded. Hospital security personnel are searching along with police. For all I know, they may have found him already."

"Then let's get back inside." Stanley barged ahead toward the door. "I need to speak with whoever's in charge and warn them this patient will likely be disoriented and unstable. He will need to be sedated for his own protection as well as to protect others. The next person he attacks may not be so lucky." God only knew what John Doe might do . . . or say.

Inside the lobby, Dante Johnson joined them. "What now?"

"Dr. Winchette and I need to speak with the security chief," Travis said. "Dante, you and Dr. Houston go check on Max. Make sure we don't have a repeat performance."

"If he's receiving the sedatives I prescribed, that shouldn't be a problem." Stanley turned to Erin. "Call me if you hear anything."

* * *

The uneasiness Erin had experienced over being forced to leave the hospital—to leave Max—subsided once she learned they could return. She had worked in hospitals long enough to know that the majority of fire alarms were false, or triggered over minor incidents. Still, each had to be taken seriously.

She also wanted to see those photographs again, to study them. Her confusion about her childhood memories and the troubling image of Max trapped inside had increased. Obviously, she had conjured up the image, projecting Max into the scene.

Except . . .

It wasn't so much a picture she was seeing; it was more the feeling of his desolation of being trapped inside a cylinder like that. There was physical pain, too, as if Max had struggled to hold on to himself. To resist meant punishment.

Someone in the crowd bumped her. She flinched, startled to realize she'd been so deeply engrossed in thought she hadn't paid attention to her steps.

Damn it! What was wrong with her? Where were these images of Max coming from? Why were they striking such a strong emotional and visceral response? How could she explain the strange yet erotic episode she'd had in Max's room?

Enough already.

Was she dodging the real issue here? Indulging in flights of fancy to avoid examining the truth?

Maybe.

Yes.

The sinking feeling in her stomach confirmed it.

The notion that her father could have been involved in this type of research was repugnant. She tried to recall specifics about her father's allegation of stolen research. Research he'd regretted conducting. Until now, she'd never questioned the reason for that regret.

"I see Dr. Evil's still as cheerful as I recall," Dante quipped from behind her.

Erin stiffened. "That's neither funny nor appropriate."

"Sorry. You're right. That was uncalled for. Can we chalk it up to nervous humor?"

Embarrassed that she'd snapped at him, Erin forced a smile. "You nervous? Should I be worried?"

"Actually, sleep deprived is more accurate. And despite my remark, I really do respect Dr. Winchette's expertise. Yours, too. If I hadn't tried those self-hypnosis CDs you gave me, I never would have found Cat. And I will wholeheartedly suggest Max work with you to get back on his feet ASAP. Same with John Doe."

Erin met his gaze. "Level with me. Is this John Doe really an unknown? I remember that two men went missing the same time you did. And now two men have been recovered . . ."

"It sounds crazy, I know, but only one of my partners, Max, was recovered. We're still searching for Harry. As far as John Doe?" Dante shrugged. "We don't know who he is. Max said he was an ally, a brother. That was all I needed to hear, though honestly I wouldn't have left anyone there. Then the mission went south so fast." He quit talking as others drew close.

They had reached the elevators now but a crowd had gathered. "Let's take the stairs," she suggested.

They weren't the only ones in the stairwell, so they didn't speak again until they'd reached the third floor. Inside Max's room, a nurse was changing bandages and IVs, so Erin and Dante decided to stay in the hallway where they could continue their conversation without the nurse listening in.

Dante led Erin toward the quiet end of the hall. "Your turn to level with me, Doc. Do you concur with what Winchette said about their chances for recovery?"

"He didn't give any actual chances," Erin began. "He emphasized that his findings were preliminary, based on incomplete data."

"Then off the record, what do you think?"

The memory of gazing into Max's open eyes, the feel of his hand in hers, quickly came to mind. But on its heels came another memory of the pain he must have endured inside that machine followed by the impression of distrust. The desire to protect Max suddenly swamped her.

She hesitated. "On or off the record, my answer is the same: incomplete data. We'll know more when all the test results are in."

"A lot of people didn't think I'd recover. And I did."

"You weren't brought in with a head injury," she reminded him.

He narrowed his eyes, his focus suddenly intense. "I sense you're hiding something."

Heat bloomed in Erin's cheeks. "Why do you say that?"

"I'm psychic, remember?"

Chapter 8

Erin did remember. Dante had had several incidents of clairvoyance while hospitalized. Winchette had wanted to study the phenomenon but Dante had refused. He later claimed that seizures had ruined his so-called psychic abilities. She made a mental note to remind Dr. Winchette about that.

"I was joking about mind reading," Dante said. "Still, when you saw those photos, I swear you recognized something. I saw a reaction that seemed to rattle you. Was it one of the drug vials? A piece of equipment?"

Erin struggled to keep her features blank. "You saw a purely visceral reaction. You had just described Max's scars and then to see that chamber. It looked barbaric. I'm slightly claustrophobic, so the thought of being closed inside a machine like that gave me the creeps."

"Yeah. Me, too."

"Is that because you had seen it before?" she asked. "When you were held overseas?"

"Not that I can recall. But there are still gaps I can't account for. Dreams that make no sense. Part of me hopes Max will remember more. For both of us. Taz, too . . . whoever he is."

"Taz?"

"That's what Max called him." Dante rubbed the back of his neck.

Erin caught a glimpse of how tense he was. How difficult had it been for Dante to risk his own life to find Max, only to see him get shot?

"You know I'd be glad to work with you again," she said. "To work on closing those gaps." Erin sensed his discomfort in talking about himself, so she changed the subject. "Do you think you'll find your other partner? Harry? And this Dr. Rufin?"

"Yes."

They grew quiet as the nurse who'd been in Max's room approached.

"I'm finished," the nurse said.

"Any change with him?" Dante asked.

"He seems to be resting more comfortably with the new medication," the nurse said. "And his scalp wound is closing nicely. He must heal fast. You can go back in now."

Inside Max's room, Erin went directly to his bedside. Except for a neater, smaller bandage on his head, Max appeared unchanged. The relief at seeing him was tangible and eased a tension that she hadn't realized was building in her chest.

She spoke softly. "Max, it's Dr. Houston. I'm here

with a friend of yours, Dante Johnson. I'd like to check your pulse again."

His wrist felt cool beneath her fingers. His pulse wasn't as strong as before, a reflection of the sedation, no doubt. But with a heartbeat there was hope.

She watched his face. *I'm here, Max. Please wake up.*

He didn't.

Come on, she silently urged. *Give me a sign.*

His features remained slack.

"Is anything wrong, Doc?" Dante had moved closer. "His pulse okay?"

"It's fine. I just lost count and had to start over." Oddly she didn't want to release Max's arm. As if by touching him, she could make him feel better. She felt the electricity again, subtle, but there, and wondered if Max felt it, too.

Aware that Dante watched her closely, she tucked Max's arm beneath the sheets, straightening the blanket before stepping away.

"His records list no family," Erin said.

"He has no blood relatives that I'm aware of. But there are people, friends, who care deeply."

She hoped he'd elaborate. Did Max have a girlfriend? Fiancée? Ex-wife? "Am I correct in assuming you and Rocco are two of those friends?"

"Yeah. And my fiancée, Catalina Dion, is on her way here, too. She and Max were—"

Erin leaned forward. *She and Max were . . .* lovers? Married?

"Extremely close," Dante finished. "I know I once thought there was more." He looked at Max, then back at Erin. "But I didn't have all the facts then. What I thought I knew was far from fact."

It was clear that Dante had strong feelings for both Catalina and Max. It was also apparent that there was much more to their story.

"And I almost forgot this." Dante moved to the minuscule closet and opened the door. Lying inside was a black duffel bag.

Erin stared at it, disappointed with the change of subject. "That's for Max?"

"Yes. It's full of stuff Rocco and I picked up earlier. Will you make sure it gets to his room in Virginia?"

"Part of me is tempted to decline. I remember you getting dressed and wanting to discharge yourself prematurely."

"Exactly. And if Max wants to do the same, he'll need something other than that damn gown. I remember how it felt to have nothing," Dante said. "There are clothes, shoes, dop kit. Some cash. Not enough, but—"

"It's enough," she assured him. It was obvious that he felt guilty for not finding Max sooner, for Max being injured—*for stealing Max's girl?* "I'll make certain it stays with him."

"Hold on." Dante shifted as his phone vibrated. She waited expectantly as he checked the display.

"Text message. No news. But Travis needs me downstairs."

He handed Erin a business card. "Here's my cell phone number. I could get called out again without much notice. And maybe I shouldn't ask this, but I'd like to know firsthand how Max does, okay? Getting info through official channels can be trying. Seriously, I'll owe you one. Call me anytime, day or night."

Erin looked at the card. Being owed a favor from a well-connected CIA operative could come in handy someday. She fished one of her own cards out of her blazer pocket. "Here is mine. Would you keep me posted on the search for . . . Taz?" That sounded better than *John Doe*.

"We'll find him, Erin." Dante paused at the door. "Just take care of Max."

Two hours later, Erin was back in the third-floor conference room, waiting for Dr. Winchette to get off his cell phone before someone else interrupted once again.

She stifled a yawn. It was after 10 p.m., which to her East Coast body clock meant one o'clock.

In contrast, Winchette showed no signs of fatigue and was livid that John Doe had not been located.

"Keep me posted," he snapped before disconnecting and turning to Erin. "If we had been in Virginia, this wouldn't have happened." He scribbled a signature across the orders he'd just drawn up. "I want Max Duncan out of here before another incident occurs."

"Those photographs Travis Franks had." She went straight to the point. "Have you ever seen a machine like that used for mind manipulation?"

He hesitated, and in that moment she knew he wasn't formulating a denial. But rather, an excuse. A diversion to throw her off.

"There was a time when everyone experimented with sensory deprivation." Winchette frowned. "Timothy Leary did something similar with LSD. The annals of science are filled with such cases. All were abysmal failures. No one, save Hollywood, pursued it beyond the sixties."

Had her father? "Obviously someone missed that memo," she said. "How can we figure out what was done to these men—in order to reverse it?"

"Actually, we don't know that anything was done to them. Neither man has regained consciousness long enough to debrief. Personally, I think the photos were a ploy to throw us off."

"Off what?"

Winchette shrugged. "Maybe Travis Franks is trying to cover his men's ineptitude. He knows more than he's letting on. Personally, I wouldn't be surprised to learn that Mr. Duncan was injured by friendly fire."

Erin couldn't hide her shock. "Are you saying his own people shot him?"

Now Winchette let out an exasperated sigh. "I'm saying we don't have all the facts. And certain things I've been told don't add up. Which as you know—"

His phone rang just then. He tugged it free and glanced at the display. "Excuse me, Erin. I need to take this call. Perhaps you could go find coffee? Black."

As she turned to stalk out of the room, Winchette spoke to her again.

"Your father gave me advice once, Erin, about dealing with security matters. He said, 'Some things are better left unquestioned.' I've never forgotten that. Your father was a very smart man."

He turned away, dismissing her as he answered his phone.

Just outside the door, Erin stopped and leaned back against the wall. Did Dr. Winchette think she'd blindly accept her father's idiom and march away to do his bidding? *Coffee. Black.* His request infuriated her. She had no problem acceding to his desire for privacy. But to be sent off for coffee? Please! Talk about a ploy. She'd return and Winchette would change the subject or rush off.

Not this time. She'd wait him out.

Through the closed door, she heard Winchette's voice rise. What now, she wondered, shifting closer.

"I need that device immediately!" Winchette demanded. "If there is a way to track that man . . ."

She knew he had to be discussing John Doe, though the words made little sense.

"I'm getting him out first thing in the morning," Winchette's voice dropped and grew muffled. "Can't keep . . . the level I need here."

Now he was discussing Max Duncan. But with whom?

"Travis Franks agrees. And when the patient goes brain-dead . . ."

Brain-dead? What in the world—

"Excuse me, are you Dr. Houston?"

She jerked, cheeks flaming guilt-red as the hospital's security chief addressed her. "Yes, I'm Erin Houston."

"I'm looking for Dr. Winchette, ma'am. He's not answering his cell phone." ·

"He's on another call."

"This is urgent. We've got a lead on that missing patient."

At that, Erin rapped on the door before thrusting it open. Winchette looked stunned at her interruption.

"The chief of security needs to see you," she said. "He has information regarding John Doe."

"I'll call you back." Winchette practically leaped to his feet and hurried to the door. "Well, what is it? Have they located him?"

"We have a report of a jumper on a bridge south of here, threatening suicide," the security chief said. "He matches the patient's description."

"Good God! How far is this? Get the police on the phone and tell them to back off until I get there." Winchette scrambled to grab his briefcase, stopping just long enough to scoop up the papers he'd completed. "Erin, I need you to get a copy of these transfer orders to Dr. Giles. I've got a private medical helicopter coming in at sunrise. I suggest you get some sleep. If I get tied up, you may need to accompany Mr. Duncan back to Virginia."

Before she could reply, Winchette's phone rang again. He rushed away, motioning the security chief to follow.

Erin stared at the papers without seeing them. *When the patient goes brain-dead.* Granted, the words were garbled and she'd heard them out of context. But what had Winchette meant by that?

Her thoughts were drawn back to her first encounter with Max. His eyes. He had squeezed her fingers. Just before receiving a sedative . . . of course! It was only natural that Max was more likely to respond as the medication waned.

If she could get to him before his next injection, could she wake him?

Back in Max's room she checked his charts. He was due for another dose in about an hour. She could hang around until then. She also noted that the new medication Winchette had prescribed was indeed enough to keep a man comatose. Was that being done on purpose? With the CIA's blessing? *Travis Franks agrees . . .*

She started to set the chart aside, then noticed that new pages had been added. She flipped through the sheets, reading as she went. Max's blood panels were all normal; same with urine tests. That was good.

The MRI report, however, listed several aberrations. *Evidence of numerous, older, fractures. All healed,* the report stated. From torture and abuse, no doubt, she thought.

She kept reading. *Hematomas and skull fracture noted in the September 17th MRI report were not visible. The types of injury noted previously wouldn't heal in less than forty-eight hours.*

The radiologist's comments went on to suggest that the previous scans were older than indicated or wrong.

Erin set the file aside. What the hell was going on here?

Chapter 9

Max opened his left eye. Blinding light spiked in like a jet of boiling water. He blinked, subjecting his right eye to the same scalding pain.

Clarity always demanded a price. And because this was mild compared to the toll normally demanded, he tensed. Ready for more. For worse.

It didn't happen. If anything, he felt a tiny bit better. He turned his head to the side, away from the light directly above his bed.

Reality slammed in. This wasn't the lab and he wasn't coming out of stasis. There had been a raid. He remembered being tossed to the floor of a helicopter.

Max! We're here to take you home. But the word "home" had no meaning. No pictures, no memories came to mind. Had he really been gone two years?

He tried to move but couldn't. What a bunch of bullshit!

He might have been rescued, but he still wasn't free.

He arched against the restraints, felt them tighten across his chest and thighs and arms. Twisting his torso, he managed to yank one arm loose. Then he sat up and tore through the remaining nylon straps.

There were other tubes. Needles. Even a catheter. Christ, what were they planning to do now?

You know. An image glimmered in his mind. Someone still wanted to control them. To experiment with them. The brief glimpse he'd snagged of Dr. Winchette's cold, calculating thoughts confirmed that he and Taz were still in danger.

Taz . . . Jesus. Where was he? Max had to find and help his friend.

Frantic to get out of the bed, he stripped everything away. Pain ripped through him, temporarily grounding him. But the moment the soles of his feet hit the cold floor, the room spun and bucked like a deranged bull.

He held tight to a bed rail and managed to stay upright. Ignoring the ringing in his ears, he corralled his senses through force of will and assessed his surroundings. The blinds were drawn, but the faint lines of ambient light seeping in at the edge were shadowed, artificial. It was night.

Faint memories percolated in the mud that was his brain. The woman—Erin—had been here. He'd made a connection with her, but was it strong enough to allow him full control? She'd argued with the nurse over his medication and they'd taken off in search of new orders. He didn't have long.

His ass suddenly cold, Max lurched away toward

what he assumed was the bathroom. He wrenched open the door. Turning on the water, he scooped handfuls into his mouth, and then splashed his face, feeling it soak into his parched skin. He couldn't get enough of it.

He shut off the water and stared at his reflection. Dark circles hung beneath his eyes. His cheeks were drawn, his lips cracked. The face in the mirror was familiar, but why did it feel like it had been a long time since he'd seen himself? Exactly how long had it been?

Tearing the bandage off his head, he felt his scalp and found a line of stitches. The spot was tender, but when he tried to recall how he'd been injured, the ache in his head roared back to life.

Doesn't matter. Just leave.

Straightening, he slipped back into the room. Inside the tiny closet he found a black duffel bag and dug through it. The clothes looked brand new, unfamiliar—yet he sensed they were for him. And if they fit . . .

Out in the hall, he heard female voices. Erin was coming back, with another nurse he'd bet.

"I know Dr. Winchette mentioned changing the dosages. Look, if he doesn't call back within ten minutes, you can call Dr. Giles," Erin was saying. "It won't hurt to hold off on the injection that tiny bit."

"But this patient has been experiencing seizures."

"I'll stay with him, and if one starts, I will administer this." Max sensed that Erin now held the syringe the nurse had carried in earlier.

"I still don't feel comfortable," the nurse began.

"Then I'll take full responsibility. Better safe than sorry, right?"

Max moved next to the wall behind the door, waiting to see who won the battle. *Come on, Erin!*

"If he hasn't called in ten minutes, I'll be back," the nurse said, fear of reprimand heavy in her words.

The door pushed open slowly. Erin stepped inside but then seemed to stop short. She'd no doubt seen the empty bed.

She let the door swing shut as she turned toward the bathroom. He'd left the light on and a small amount crawled across the floor. She moved to the closed bathroom door. "Max?"

He grabbed her from behind, slipping one hand across her mouth. His other hand clamped over her wrist, relieving her of the syringe before locking her back against his chest. The instinctive urge to kill came out of nowhere. *Not her*, he thought. *Winchette.*

Quashing his thoughts of violence, he instead opened intuitively to her, wanting to reinforce the bond between them. He'd done this before with women . . . commanded them. But Erin was different. Warm. Caring. *Maybe she commanded him.*

Desire came out of nowhere as sensations of Erin overwhelmed his system. The sudden flood of input was chaotic. Jumbled. It felt like someone had pried open the top of his head and poured bits and pieces in. The drugs in his system didn't help, making it more difficult to reason.

Since his thoughts no longer made sense, he focused on reading hers. Her relief at knowing he'd regained consciousness was palpable. She'd been worried. About him. He could use that. Controlling her would be easy.

And while she had no intention of drugging him, she believed he was in danger. But from whom? And why?

Those were the wrong questions. The pain in his head spiked. Now it seemed someone used a knife to hack at the inside of his skull, scraping away the thoughts he'd been given seconds earlier like a hunter cleaning flesh from a hide.

Max knew the only way to stop it was to shut down everything inside his head. He concentrated on the externals again. The woman he held. Erin.

"I'll let you go," he whispered. "Don't scream."

At her nod he lifted his hand.

"May I turn around?" She moved before he could respond.

Her eyes searched his. Dark. Mossy. Like smoked emeralds. They were overly large, overly lovely, and missed nothing as she rapidly scanned him from head to toe.

He felt her hand close around his wrist as her fingertips pressed with firmness. His pulse slammed against their light pressure. Her gaze shifted to his face, her eyes reflecting concern.

"I'm Dr. Houston, Max. You're in a San Diego hospital. You've been unconscious for a while and heavily sedated, so let's take it easy. Nod if you understand." She spoke softly and slowly like one would with a child. Or an idiot.

He must have nodded, because she glanced away, toward the bed. "Why don't I help you back to—"

"No." He needed to get away. But where to go?

Once more he tried to bring order to his thoughts. Words and images avalanched inside his head, and the longer he was on his feet, the worse it got.

"Please." She had stepped closer. "The injury you suffered wasn't minor."

He jerked, remembering gunfire. "I was shot, right?"

She nodded. "The bullet grazed your skull, fractured it, but didn't penetrate. You had a couple hematomas, blood clots. And you've had some seizures."

Seizures. He remembered being strapped to a table and given electric shock therapy, but— "I don't remember being hit."

"It's not unusual. Amnesia following a traumatic head wound is common. And it's usually short term. Let's get you settled and I'll explain it more fully."

"Don't bother with that. Tell me where the shooting took place."

"I'm not sure. Southeast Asia, I believe. I can call—"

"No!"

With a slight flinch, she eased backward. "Anything you say, Max. But I am concerned."

"Save it. Now where is Taz?"

"Do you mean the man who was brought in with you?"

"Yes. Take me to him."

"I'm sorry. I can't." Tension flashed across her features as he compelled her to answer honestly. "He . . . he regained consciousness and left the hospital a few hours ago. We're searching for him now."

Being that Taz had already gotten away meant he was in better shape than Max. But Max was supposed to be with Taz; they had something important to do. *Mission incomplete.*

Nausea climbed through him. He shifted backward using the wall to support himself. The hunter with the skinning knife was back now, digging inside his head. He pinched the bridge of his nose, desperate to recall the mission, but things started to fall out of focus again.

He pushed away from the wall. "I've got . . . to leave."

"You haven't recovered enough to be out of here."

"I need to get dressed." He pointed to the black duffel bag on the floor. "Is that mine?"

"Yes. One of your friends, Dante Johnson, brought it. He, um, knows exactly what you're going through, Max."

Your friends left you for dead. They deserved to suffer. Pain slashed up Max's spine one vertebra at a time. *Escape. Evade. Find Taz.*

"Put the bag on the bed and open it," he said tersely. "Hand me clothes."

"Max, you are in no shape to go anywhere. You still need medical attention."

"Clothes," he snapped. "Now."

With a small sigh, Erin tugged out jeans and a shirt. Her thoughts were easy to pick up. She was stalling, hoping someone came in. But not Dr. Winchette. She mistrusted him, too.

Max ripped his gown off, ignoring Erin's gasp of indignation. "You're a doctor, for Christ's sake. I can't be the first man you've seen naked."

"Those scars." She pointed to his torso. "You've been . . . hurt."

"Hurt" didn't come close. "I survived."

He focused on getting dressed. The clothes were stiff, but they fit. Snapping the jeans, he slid the confiscated syringe into his pocket before jerking a black T-shirt over his head.

"Shoes?" he prompted when she just stood there.

Erin dug and tugged out a pair of leather deck shoes and dropped them on the floor in front of him. He slid his feet in, grateful to forgo laces. Again a perfect fit.

"Max, let me call someone."

"No calls."

He turned the bag upside down now and dumped the remaining contents onto the bed. More clothes. Shave kit. A cell phone and wallet caught his eye. He scanned the crisp hundred-dollar bills tucked inside, trying to recall the last time he'd had any use for money. He shoved the wallet into a rear pocket, then pulled the battery out of the cell phone to disable the built-in GPS before dropping it and the phone into another pocket.

All of a sudden Max was hungry. Ravenous. When was the last time that he'd eaten something that wasn't delivered through a tube? It felt like days.

He crammed everything back into the duffel bag and slung the strap over one shoulder.

"I have to advise against self-discharge," Erin said.

"I didn't ask to come here, so I'm not asking to leave." He crossed to the windows. Opening the blinds, he peered down.

"Max, you can't climb out! Look, let me go with you. I've got a car. I'll take you wherever you want to go."

He probed her thoughts. Her concern was sincere even though she believed she'd be able to persuade him into returning. Since he actually wanted her along, it was expeditious to let her think that. A willing hostage was infinitely more compliant.

"You can come on one condition," he said. "I'm calling all the shots. And we're not telling anyone good-bye."

"But—"

"Take it or leave it."

"I'll take it," Erin said.

It was better than him vaulting out a window and disappearing like John Doe had.

And short of sedating him against his will—hard to accomplish since he now had the syringe—there was little she could do to physically prevent him from leaving. Better to go with him. Help him work through the disorientation.

The thought that she didn't want to be without him came out of nowhere. She ignored it.

After what Max had been through—*the million-dollar question*—confinement of any type was probably highly stressful. Once she got him in the car and they talked, she'd make him see reason.

"What's in there?" Max nodded to the tiny back-pack purse Erin had retrieved from the bedside chair.

"The usual. Wallet. Keys. Machine gun."

"Let me see."

"I was joking." But she still held out her bag, wanting him to feel at ease.

He peeked inside and handed it back. "Come on."

Moving to the door, he checked out the hallway. Then he looked back at her. "Which way to the closest exit?"

Erin could have lied, but figured it would only turn out badly if she did. And she really wanted Max to trust her; more, she wanted to take care of him. Felt drawn to him.

Now that the shock of seeing him not only awake but on his feet had passed, other questions arose. Something was not right here and her instincts screamed that Max must be protected.

When Max had seemed to respond to her before, Winchette had blown it off. *I've seen this before.* Winchette had since kept Max heavily sedated. *Travis Franks agrees. And when the patient goes brain-dead . . .*

"Which way," Max prompted.

"To the left," she said. "Toward the end of the hall."

As they moved toward the exit, sounds from the nurses' station, the low murmurs of voices, the occasional soft break of laughter followed after them. With the seven-to-three shift ending soon, the RNs would be busy.

Inside the stairwell, Max disabled the security cameras as they went. When they hit the heavy outside door, he shoved it open without hesitation, not even looking to see if Erin was following. It was raining lightly, but he didn't seem to notice as he paused to inhale sharply. She relaxed, realized she had worried that once she got him this far, he'd just take off and leave her.

"Where is your car?" he asked.

She motioned toward the street. "I'm parked a few blocks from here."

When they reached the sidewalk, the upcoming shift change became obvious. Of the dozen or so people they passed, half of them were dressed in scrubs. Most didn't seem to pay them any attention. The few that did were young nurses and they outright gawked at Mr. Handsome. Erin would bet that if asked in the next five minutes, they would swear that Max had been walking alone. Why did that bother her?

"This one." Erin pressed the key fob, unlocking the doors of her rental car.

"Trunk," Max said.

While he slid his bag in next to hers, she moved to the driver's side. A red SUV barreled around the corner. That fast, Max was there, pressing her back flat against the car as if to shield her.

She gasped, startled by his lightning reflexes. The SUV swerved on the wet pavement, then straightened before shooting ahead to a parking spot.

Max didn't move, and for a crazy moment she didn't want him to. His abdomen pressed into hers. He was solid. Hard. And the feel of his body against hers wasn't unpleasant. She wanted him to stay there. She wanted to fantasize about being in his embrace. She wanted to be crushed by the weight of his rock-hard body . . .

"Look at me." He turned her face up, giving her no choice but to stop her lascivious thoughts and meet his gaze.

The man was tall, six three or four. She tilted her chin. *Big mistake.* Inside, Max's dark eyes had looked black, but now they seemed to glint with a fire that promised a deadly seduction.

Her vision blurred. The rain, she thought. She felt his fingertips graze against her temple.

"I won't let you get hurt," he whispered.

She pressed a hand against his chest. "I'm okay."

"You sure?" His voice was low. An invitation to burn in his arms.

Suddenly self-conscious, she straightened. "I'm sure."

As fast as he'd moved in, he now stepped away. A car horn honked and she realized someone waited for her space. Shoving her handbag onto the floor in front of her seat, she climbed in and started the car, grateful to have something to do.

And as soon as she pulled out into traffic, she realized she had another problem. Where to go? She decided to stay in the general vicinity of the hospital. Even though Max didn't seem like a threat at the moment, that could change. He could wig out on her yet, like his friend had.

"While we drive, why don't you tell me what you do know about Taz," Max suggested. "Don't cut any corners this time, or I'm bailing."

She realized that he was growing more lucid. That was good. "What I said earlier was true. Like you, Taz was brought in unconscious but he came to while having an MRI. He was disoriented and overpowered the technician, breaking the man's arm before fleeing. Must have had a claustrophobia attack that made him panic."

"And where do they believe he is now?"

"We're not sure. We had received a report of a man matching his description out on a bridge."

"Did they confirm it's Taz?"

"No."

"Take me there."

"I can't." Erin felt a mild sense of dread. Was this why Max had agreed to take her along? Because he thought she could lead him to Taz? Now that he knew she couldn't, that she was of no use to him, would he try to get rid of her?

"Can't or won't?" Max pressed.

She tried to stall, not wanting to admit she'd

have to call Winchette to get the location. "I'm not familiar with the city. I just flew in a few hours ago."

Because it was less obvious than checking her wristwatch, she glanced at the dashboard clock while calculating her next move. Usually at shift change the nurses going off duty briefed their replacements, which bought her a little time before anyone noticed Max wasn't where he was supposed to be.

But eventually someone would go into Max's room and discover he was gone.

Just then her cell phone started going off in her pocket. She flinched slightly at the sound, her stomach sinking. It could only be Dr. Winchette. Did he know? How in the hell was she going to handle this? Pretend that she wasn't aware of Max's disappearance? Or try to somehow alert Winchette to the situation?

Without thinking, she tugged her phone out. Max's hand closed around hers before she could answer it.

"You want to be very careful, Doc."

It rang once more then went to voice mail.

"It was probably Dr. Winchette. If I don't answer, he'll just keep calling."

The phone beeped now. Max glanced at the display then withdrew his hand. "You have a message. Put it on speakerphone."

Erin complied. Dr. Winchette's voice came across the speaker. "The bridge sighting was a false alarm. A complete waste of time. I'm on my way back to the hospital now. Mr. Duncan will be moved tonight and

I'd like you to accompany him. I'll be staying behind until they locate this John Doe. Call me as soon as you get this message."

"That answers my question about Taz," Max said, rubbing his temples.

"Are you okay? Look, we could go back to the hospital—"

"Pull over. I feel sick."

Erin whipped the car into a deserted parking lot. As soon as she stopped, Max opened his door and climbed out. Throwing the car into PARK, she exited and raced to help him.

"It's better if you stay seated, Max." She moved in close and hooked his arm around her shoulder to guide him back toward the car. "If you pass out—"

He lurched forward. She swung forward, facing him and catching him in a bear hug. He was too heavy for her to carry, but she could at least break his fall to avoid him injuring himself. Locking her arms around his waist, she leaned into his chest, bracing herself.

Too late she realized the trap as his arms tightened around her. Holding her pinned against him, he lifted her off her feet with one arm.

"Look at me, Erin."

She resisted and he once again caught her chin and forced her to look up. Her breath caught as his eyes held her. They were mesmeric, the irises dark, glittering with hints of silver. And something hypnotic. A sensation of warmth swirled through her, dulling her senses momentarily. Her skin tingled as if tiny electrical sparks were traveling through him . . . to her. She never knew how much she could feel . . . want . . .

She jerked as the bizarre sensation strengthened. "What are you doing? Let me go!"

"We're not going back to the hospital, Erin."

There was a stinging jab in her left buttock as he injected her with the syringe.

"No, Max!"

"Don't fight it," he whispered.

"Like hell I won't!"

But already his voice sounded distant. "I'm sorry, Erin. But I need you. Need your help."

Chapter 10

Mission incomplete.

Taz ignored the words as he studied the hospital from his perch atop the half-complete parking garage. He ran the blade of the stolen knife across the tips of his fingers. The pain was short lived since the cuts began to heal almost immediately. But it silenced the chatter long enough for him to think. To remember.

It finally settled in that he was really free and in control. But he wouldn't rest until Hades was free, too.

Impatience ate at him. *Just a few more minutes, till shift change,* he thought. *And I've already waited this long.*

He had ended up spending the evening at a homeless shelter. Volunteering to scour pots had scored him extra food. God, he'd been hungry. Kitchen duty also kept him out of the main dining room when the police did a walk-through.

"They're always here, always looking for one of us poor bums to blame," Frenchy told him later.

Frenchy had befriended him after Taz inadvertently came to his rescue, stumbling down an alley near the hospital and scaring off some trouble-making teens. Taz's bouts of vomiting hadn't fazed Frenchy, who chalked it up to Dumpster diving.

"Come on," Frenchy had said. "I know where we can get a real meal if you don't mind 'em thumping Bibles while you eat."

At the shelter, Taz also received an outfit of clothes, a shower, and a bus pass by simply signing up to search for work. The bus pass came in handy later, when he and Frenchy returned to the makeshift homeless camp near the hospital.

Taz ended up trading the pass to another guy who knew someone who worked in the hospital.

"They got a couple John Does stashed on the third floor," the guy had reported back. "Rooms 320 and 322."

Mission incomplete.

I'm coming, Hades!

Taz checked the hospital again. Finally! Small groups of people were leaving as others entered. Time to kick his plan into high gear.

He slipped on the white lab coat he'd stolen earlier from a car. Moving tentatively, he made his way out of the construction site.

Once inside the hospital he commandeered a lab cart and headed toward the service elevators. On the third floor, no one gave him a second glance, save the cleaning lady. He winked at her and headed purposefully down the hall.

Room 322 was empty. But Taz knew immediately that Hades had been in Room 320. The discarded hospital gown on the floor, the shredded bed sheets and restraints indicated a struggle.

Had Hades been forced to go elsewhere?

Uneasy memories shimmered. Always they'd been forced to—

Outside the door, he heard footsteps. One person, headed this way.

"Perfect."

Getting answers might be easier than he'd thought. He ducked into the bathroom, his knife ready.

Stanley Winchette paused outside Max Duncan's room and tried Erin's phone again. Still no answer. In his rush to chase down John Doe, Stanley hadn't thought to ask about hotel reservations earlier, which meant she was probably asleep, oblivious to the problems she'd caused.

What the hell had she been thinking, questioning his orders?

When he'd stopped at the nurses' station a few minutes ago, he learned that Erin had disputed Max's medication. The nurse had ultimately called Dr. Giles after Stanley failed to return Dr. Houston's call.

What call? His phone showed one missed call and that was a message from Giles stating he had belayed all action until he could reach Stanley. On top of everything else, Erin's colossal screwup had triggered a game of telephone tag between the two men.

Damn Travis Franks and Dante Johnson for insisting she come along. Now Erin could be the fly in the ointment. Just like her father had been.

Of course, since babysitting two unconscious men was more than Stanley could realistically manage on his own, he would have been forced to bring someone. And while not the total pushover he had hoped she'd be, Erin was definitely more malleable than Colby Deets.

Deets would have raced him here and then dogged Stanley's every step, questioned his every move. Recently, Deets's intense attention to everything Stanley did—especially with Caldwell Pharmaceuticals—had almost become a liability.

In reality, Erin's *faux pas* was simply the last straw in a day that had gone from bad to worse. The few small upticks, like the burst of excitement he'd felt at thinking they'd located John Doe, now seemed more like tripping points.

The bridge jumper had not been Doe after all and that was a mixed blessing. It meant they still had a chance of finding him. Provided that John Doe did, in fact, have a tracking beacon implanted on his person and that Abe Caldwell could get a tracking device here quickly enough.

Pocketing his cell phone, Stanley pushed open the door to Max's room. It was crucial that Max's medications be maintained to avoid any more surprise awakenings. For now, Stanley would sedate him and adjust the next dose after speaking with Giles.

Inside the room he stopped short. The bed was empty, the straps and sheets in disarray. Dear God, not again!

A slight noise in the bathroom had Stanley pressing his hand to his sternum in relief. Max was still here!

Opening his briefcase, he quickly removed one of the syringes he had prepared for John Doe. Uncapping it, he hid the syringe in one hand. After years of working with unstable, delusional patients, he had developed a technique for administering a shot quickly. The trick was making certain they never saw the needle.

Clearing his throat, Stanley rapped on the door. "Max? Are you okay?"

The door swung open. But it wasn't Max Duncan he confronted.

"You!" Stanley tried to recall the name Travis Franks had mentioned. "Taz?"

The man didn't respond, his eyes vacant.

Stanley kept his voice low and even. "We've been searching for you. Your friends will be relieved to know you're unharmed. I'm Dr. Winchette, a friend of Max's. Where is Max, by the way?"

Taz rocked sideways. "Where is Hades?"

Stanley played along. "You mean the man who was with you, correct? I've been taking care of him."

"Take me to him. Now!"

"Yes, of course. But can we talk out here?" Stanley backed up slightly, holding the door open. Given

Taz's size, hitting him from behind was much safer. "Was, um, Hades still here when you first arrived?"

"No." Taz stepped forward, but instead of moving past Stanley, Taz pinned him flat against the bathroom door.

A strong forearm beneath his neck prevented Stanley from screaming while an iron grip at his wrist immobilized the hand with the syringe.

Stanley didn't move, afraid that the slightest pressure would jam the needle into his own skin. Damn it, where was a nurse when he needed one?

"Easy," Stanley whispered. "I want to help you."

"Tell me where they took Hades. Is he already with Dr. Rufin? Must meet . . . Rufin."

"You know Dr. Rufin?" Stanley's mind began racing. Could this man help them locate the mysterious Rufin and recover Zadovsky's files? "Please. We need to talk. You're in danger, but I can help. You must trust me."

Taz snapped Stanley's wrist. Pain spasmed up his arm as the syringe hit the floor.

"Zadovsky is the enemy," Taz snarled, pressing closer.

What the hell? Stanley suddenly had the uneasy impression the other man was literally reading his mind. Except . . . that was impossible.

Taz shook his head. "No. It's not."

Chapter 11

"That was Dante." Rocco snapped his cell phone closed. He and Travis had just taken a table at the deserted all-night diner next to their hotel.

"You told him the latest on John Doe?"

Rocco nodded. After confirming that the suicide jumper fished from the water was not the missing John Doe, Travis had suggested pulling the plug on what was left of the night.

The plan was to catch a little shut-eye and regroup at sunrise. None of them had had more than a four-hour stretch of sleep since the mission began. Hell, for Rocco, a *good night's sleep* equaled five hours. Preferably after hot sex.

"They should be here in a few minutes," Rocco went on. "Cat's going to drop Dante and Marco off here and then go on to the hospital."

It was hoped that Catalina Dion's presence would help jolt Max out of his coma. She'd been friends with Max for a lot longer than Rocco. Close friends.

After being told that Dante and Max had supposedly died on an overseas assignment, Cat must have been elated to learn that Max, too, was alive. The two men resurfacing was biblical in proportion. The equivalent of Lazarus rising.

It made Rocco wonder how Gena Gambrel would react if they found Harry alive. Would all the mistakes and mishaps from their past be forgotten?

Would Gena welcome her ex-husband home with a chance at a do-over?

Probably not. The water under that particular bridge was tainted. Which didn't stop Rocco from wondering if Gena could ever forgive him.

God, maybe his last girlfriend was right . . . men *were* assholes.

Travis's phone started to ring just as their waitress came over and introduced herself as Kimmie. She pointed playfully at Travis's phone. "It's after two a.m. Technically, you can ignore that."

"They'll just keep calling. I'll have the special. Eggs over easy. Be right back," Travis said before moving away to take the call.

Kimmie leaned in close to Rocco. "And what can I get you, sugar?"

He eyed the swells of her breasts as she openly flirted. She was wearing one of those bustier things that made men go stupid in less than sixty seconds. The process was relative to cup size. The fact that Kimmie had dusted her generous curves with body glitter didn't help.

Neither did the memory of his last phone conversation with his girlfriend, Maddy. Or ex-girlfriend, as Maddy had harshly reminded him. *I'm tired of being forgotten at the drop of a hat.*

Damn it. He didn't mean to forget. Maddy deserved better. It was just . . . men were assholes.

He shifted his gaze away from Kimmie. Through the plate glass window behind her, Rocco caught sight of Travis pacing outside the restaurant. Whatever the call, it wasn't good. As he watched, a cab pulled up to the curb, discharging Cat and Dante.

Dante had his sleeping son cradled in his arms. Travis quit his call and motioned for them to follow him into the restaurant.

Travis's fierce scowl telegraphed bad news.

Rocco sighed. Looking at Kimmie, he released the dream of waking up from a good night's sleep with glitter all over his face.

"Better make it two coffees. Black."

"To go," Travis amended.

Rocco stood and hugged Cat, before turning back to Travis. "Don't tell me. There was another John Doe spotting. Why don't you let me handle this one? You go grab some sleep."

"None of us will be sleeping after this." Travis held up his phone. "That was hospital security. Dr. Winchette is dead. His body was found in the bathroom of Max's room. Looks like his neck was snapped."

"Jesus!" Rocco ran a hand through his hair. "What happened? Is Max okay?"

"Max has disappeared. A nurse was making rounds and found his bed empty. She checked the bathroom and found Winchette's body. They think

Max must have awakened disoriented like John Doe did. And he wouldn't have known Winchette from the man in the moon."

Cat drew a sharp breath. "We have to find him."

"Yeah, well, there's more," Travis said. "It appears Dr. Houston is missing now, too. She was last seen going into Max's room. One of the security films from a stairwell caught an image of her with Max just before he disabled the camera. They're checking other cameras around the grounds."

"When do they think it happened?" Dante asked.

"Less than an hour ago. Around shift change, when everyone was busy," Travis said. "The police have been called in but it will take them a while to piece together what happened. That gives us a chance to find them first."

"Erin mentioned having a rental car," Rocco said. "If they're in it, we can trace it with LoJack."

"I'll get her credit card and cell phone records," Travis said. "ATM, too. If he's coherent, Max would know to use cash."

"Shit." Dante looked at Rocco then Travis. "I left a bag with clothes, a cell phone, and some cash."

"How much?"

"A thousand."

"Ouch. You have the cell phone number, though, right?" Travis asked.

"Of course."

"Okay, let Cat start calling that number." Travis turned to Cat. "I think he'll feel safer talking to you."

"I'm on it," she said.

"Dante, I want you to pull his last known ad-

dresses. Find what's familiar. Friends. Family," Travis
continued. "Cat, you've known Max longer. Didn't
he have an uncle who lived on one of the reservations out here?"

"Arizona," she said. "Max lived with him off and on
during grade school. He died, though, when Max was
in the Army."

They grew quiet as Kimmie drew close again.
Rocco handed her enough cash to cover the coffee
and a generous tip.

"Listen up. This isn't going to be easy to hear,"
Travis went on as soon as they were alone again.
"Max is one of us, but he's been held two years,
under extremely questionable circumstances. With
Winchette dead, I've got to assume Dr. Houston's
life is at risk as well."

Cat shook her head. "I know this sounds crazy,
but Max won't harm her. I guarantee it."

"Guarantee?" Travis repeated. "Look, at the risk
of sounding insensitive, if there is something in particular you know about Max that would help us
locate him, I need to know it."

Rocco knew Travis was referring to the rumored
involvement between Cat and Max.

But if Cat felt awkward having an old love affair
mentioned in front of her fiancé, Dante, she didn't
show it.

"It is a private matter," she acknowledged. "And
it's not what you're thinking." She moved closer to
Dante as she spoke and pressed a kiss to her sleeping son's forehead. "What I'm referring to will shed

no light on where Max is. Still, I'll give you a full explanation *after* I tell Dante about it."

"Fair enough," Travis said. "Dante, you and Cat stay here; start tracing Max and Dr. Houston's records. Rocco and I will head back to the hospital and work that end."

Outside, the sky was masked by heavy clouds that promised rain. A lone siren pierced the night. Rocco drove back to the hospital as Travis fielded phone calls.

The tiredness Rocco had felt earlier was replaced by a heavy tension. A woman was missing and a man was dead. Both were last seen in Max's room. And while they lacked witnesses to Winchette's murder, the circumstances didn't bode well for Max.

"Goddamnit! When did that happen?" Travis said into his phone. "Find out and call me back!"

Rocco glanced sideways. "Word on Max?" he asked when Travis disconnected.

Travis released a long sigh. "No. But Dr. Rufin may have surfaced in Bangkok. One of his e-mail accounts was accessed."

Rocco could guess what was bugging Travis. "How many people besides us know?"

"Supposedly none. But we both know how fast that can change." Travis hammered his knee with his fist. "Damn it. I want Rufin! My gut says he's the missing link. Whoever gets to him first will have Max, Taz, and maybe Harry's future in their hands. I just hope to God it's us."

"Can we throw out a false trail, then send some-one in to grab him?"

"Perhaps. The question is who can I bank on?" Travis grew quiet but only for a moment. "How fast could you reach one of your contacts over there? It would need to be someone you'd trust with your life."

Rocco weighed the request before nodding. "I think I know just the guy."

Chapter 12

The route Max took to the San Diego Airport was eerily familiar. *Exit 5 onto Sassafras. First right to remote parking.* Even the swirling patches of fog prodded his memory. Like he'd just driven here last week.

Except he had no freakin' clue what he'd really done last week. Or last month. Or last year. This ability to read and influence others obviously didn't apply to himself.

His concept of linear time was skewed. He kept getting little flashes of recall, but they made no sense, felt out of sequence. Some even felt fabricated.

Wasn't that perfect?

He'd been gone two years. But it felt like more. Like his entire past was gone. Was that the amnesia Erin had mentioned? Or the lingering effects of the sedatives? Hopefully *both* were short term. Because he wanted and needed answers—fast.

Where he'd been wasn't nearly as pressing as the question of what had been done to him. And even that question paled in the face of the near panic he felt over forgetting what he was supposed to do next.

The feeling of something undone, something incomplete, ate at him. What was it?

Without warning, the dull ache that had lumbered in the back of his head since awakening spiked. His vision tunneled. He tightened his grip on the steering wheel, squeezing the hard plastic.

Concentrating on the tactile helped. He noticed he was panting—which also helped. A voice inside his head automatically began counting. *One thousand one, one thousand two.*

Okay, voices in the head weren't good. But neither was the alternative: passing out while driving. He needed a better distraction. Thoughts of Erin crept in. Naked Erin. His mind began to wander in ways it hadn't in a long time. Yeah, that was a hell of a lot nicer than counting.

And almost immediately his field of vision expanded, pushing back the headache.

Okay, he'd just learned something valuable. As long as he kept his thoughts on a present-moment task— say counting, or more preferably, a hot fantasy—he could control the pain. Brief thoughts, little hit-and-run wonderings, small conjectures, were tolerable.

Effort was relative. The longer and harder he tried to remember, the worse it hurt. And trying to recall anything about his imprisonment made his skull feel like it was being pried off his neck.

For now, the simpler he kept things, the better. Erin could help him sift through the messy details later.

He glanced over at her. She looked to be asleep.

He had reclined the passenger seat and buckled her in to add to the illusion.

He didn't feel guilty for drugging her. She would have doped him up without hesitation if he'd displayed any instability.

And later on, when she woke up pissed—no psychic power needed to predict that one—he felt confident in his ability to soothe her. Not that *that* would be unpleasant. Erin had the kind of good looks that hit a man in the midsection. When was the last time he'd felt anything other than a fist there?

Slowing the car, Max pulled into the remote parking lot. Yeah, he'd definitely been here before.

He lowered his window as a lot attendant materialized out of the fog. The lanky kid wore headphones and rocked his head to the beat of music so loud Max could hear it.

"We're pretty full," the kid practically shouted. "There are a few open spots at the back, by the fence. If that doesn't work, the cashier will let you out, no charge."

"Thanks." The rear spots were considered the least desirable to anyone overly concerned with potential theft. Which made them perfect tonight.

"If you hurry, I can flag down the shuttle driver and send him back around," the kid went on. "Otherwise it'll be another fifteen, twenty minutes before the next one."

"Actually we'd prefer to wait." Max nodded toward Erin. "It'll give my wife a chance to wake up."

Taking the ticket, Max drove toward the last row,

checking out cars and pole-mounted security cameras as he went.

While there were better ways to obtain a vehicle, theft was expeditious. A car parked in a remote lot meant the owner was more likely to be gone a longer period, buying time before the vehicle was reported stolen.

And cheap parking also attracted older, easier-to-break-into cars that were less likely to have theft recovery devices like this rental car certainly had. He'd spotted a dozen cars he could easily hotwire, a skill the simmering headache warned him not to question.

Ultimately he felt drawn to an older Ford pickup. The truck had four-wheel drive and a slide-in camper in the bed. On some level the rig looked familiar, making him wonder if he had owned one in the past.

Shifting the car into REVERSE, he backed into the spot beside the truck, which was also backed in. Climbing out, he moved to the rear of the truck. The bulky cab-over camper blocked one of the security cameras and he hoped the thickening fog would camouflage the rest.

The camper's rear door had a cheap lock. Twisting the knob while lifting the door and pushing against the frame popped it open without damage.

Max flicked a switch near the door on, then off. A dim yellow light briefly illumined the shabby but clean interior. In addition to the sleeping space over the cab, the camper had a table fitted above bench seats that converted into a second sleeping space. It also had a tiny galley with stove, fridge, sink.

The cabinet closest to the door held a dented metal tool box. He grabbed a screwdriver and flashlight, and then found an unexpected bonus: a black magnetic box with a spare ignition key.

Moving quickly, Max started the engine, then transferred their bags from the rental car's trunk. Gathering the still unconscious Erin in his arms, he carefully moved her to the front seat of the truck and again posed her as if asleep.

Across the lot, headlights illumined the fog as another vehicle approached. Max climbed in behind the wheel. Tucked behind the visor was the parking ticket. He put on the camo baseball cap that had been left sitting on the front seat. As disguises went, it sucked. But it helped hide his head wound.

He pulled out and followed another car to the exit. The cashier was talking on his cell phone while making change and didn't give Max more than a cursory glance. Twenty-five dollars later, he was headed back to the interstate.

His primary goal was freedom. No way was he going back to the hospital. What little he'd gleaned from Dr. Winchette's thoughts had been sobering. Winchette wanted to keep Max and Taz imprisoned and incapacitated with the use of heavy sedatives. Just like Rufin had.

Why was another issue to address with Erin. Same with the fact that she seemed to distrust Winchette. Or at least that was the impression Max gleaned from her thoughts.

He drove fifty miles south then east before taking an exit and pulling into an all-night gas station with a convenience store.

The truck was below a quarter-tank and he could no longer ignore the fact he was hungry—starving. He was also growing tired. When was the last time he'd slept? Really *slept* versus being drugged?

"Don't ask questions," he muttered, rubbing his temple. Erin was still out cold. Even though he'd given her only part of the drug, he wasn't worried about her waking anytime soon. But he didn't want anyone bothering her while he went inside to prepay for gas so he eased her down on the bench seat and then locked her in.

The store, obviously popular with truckers, was busy. Max filled the counter with premade sandwiches, donuts, cookies, candy, milk, coffee, and orange juice. He grabbed peanuts from the counter display just before the clerk totaled his purchase.

She flirted, teasing him about his grocery selections. "Going camping with an army?"

"Yeah. Old friends."

"The lake's pretty this time of year," she said. "Less crowded now that school's back in."

"The lake?"

"Baldwin Park?" She paused while bagging his purchases. "I figured you were camping there."

"Right." Max remembered seeing the directional sign with camping icons as he exited the interstate. "How much farther is it?"

"Two, three miles. Just turn left when you pull out of here. Which campground are you looking for?"

"Good question," he ad-libbed. "I need to check the note my buddy sent. Guess I figured there'd only be one."

The girl smiled and shoved his bags forward. "Actually, there are two. You'll come to Haverhills first; it'll be on the right. But it's rather, um, old-fashioned; I bet your friends are at the county park. Just keep going to the dead end. Off season, the spots are first come, first serve. If your friends didn't get you a spot, there's an honor system box by the office. If you use cash, be sure it's exact. The sign says someone comes by daily to make change, but I know that doesn't always happen during the week."

"Thanks for your help."

Gathering his bags, Max returned to the truck. Erin hadn't moved. He tucked the bags on the floorboard before pumping fuel.

The gas fumes made his headache worse and made him nauseous. By the time he'd finished, he wondered if he could drive. Fatigue was bearing down fast. He needed to focus: Food—sleep—Erin.

She was still stretched out across the front seat. Max lifted her shoulders and slid in behind the wheel before letting her head rest on his thigh.

Peeling the lid off the coffee, he gulped half of it down and then devoured two of the sandwiches. The food helped more than the coffee, but not enough. He needed to find a secure place to pull over.

Following the clerk's directions, he headed for the county campground. Worse case, he'd park in the woods and grab a few hours' sleep.

As it turned out, the campground had two spots

open. He studied the park map, then grabbed one envelope and crammed money into it.

It was after 4 a.m. now and the tiny solar lights marking the rutted gravel road were practically invisible in the dark and fog.

Lot number seven was small. Farthest from the lake, it was the least scenic, but most private. Grabbing the flashlight, Max climbed out of the cab. A short distance away a dog barked. A muffled voice yelled, "Shut up!"

Inside the camper he lowered the dining table and rearranged the cushions, converting it to a bed. Once again he had the sense that this was familiar, that he'd camped like this before. Often. Grabbing the blankets and pillows from the claustrophobic space above the cab, he finished making the bed.

Back outside, he gathered Erin up and locked the truck's cab. She fit comfortably in his arms, no big feat considering she was unconscious. He laid her on the makeshift bed, and tugged off her shoes.

Yeah, he was definitely attracted to her. The black pants, black top, and blazer she wore didn't look comfortable to sleep in, but he wasn't about to undress her. Tonight wasn't about comfort. It was about sleep. Just enough to take the edge off.

He snagged some of the rope he'd spotted in one of the cabinets and tied her hands loosely. The idea was more to slow her down than to confine her. There was a small part of him that questioned whether he would ever wake up. And if that were the case, well, he didn't want her to feel trapped.

Kicking off his shoes, he crawled onto the bed

beside her. The space was so small he ended up lifting her so he could lie diagonally. Then, since there was no space left, he settled her on top of his chest. His arms encircled her, holding her in place. The truck felt like it was spinning now.

The headache mushroomed and he felt dizzy again. He closed his eyes as lights strobed inside his skull.

Movies.

Pictures.

The images made no sense.

Then he had a brief glimmer of Taz. Where was he? Once again Max had a sense he was supposed to do something. The sense of incompletion made him feel even sicker.

Don't forget . . . our plan.

Taz had shouted those words at him during their last mission . . .

Chapter 13

Northeast Thailand Jungle
October 10
Eleven Months Ago

"I count four rebels. Confirm, over." Hades melted back into the jungle, once again indistinguishable from the night.

"Check." Taz's whisper came over his earpiece. "One circling the perimeter, one guarding the cave. The two we followed in are chowing down by the fire."

"Good. Time to close down this freak show. Ready?"

"Roger that."

"Hold your position until I neutralize their scout. Then we'll move in."

Hades crept through the moonlit foliage. The caves that honeycombed this area were popular with the Thai rebels, who ferried stolen weapons across the borders.

This wasn't the first time they'd raided this particular encampment, but if Hades had his way, it was damn sure going to be the last. Twenty-nine schoolchildren had been killed by missiles linked to this supply line and he was taking it personally.

Circling a rock outcropping, Hades hunkered down. He slid the black blade of his SOG between his teeth, freeing his hands. Off to one side a shadow moved, telegraphing the guard's approach. He waited until the rebel guard passed, then in one fluid motion, he straightened and stepped onto the path behind the guard. Ensnaring the man's shoulders with one arm, Hades snatched him backward.

"Shit." Taz broke in across his earpiece again. "One of 'em failed to raise your mark by radio. Now he's headed your way."

Too late. Behind him a twig snapped.

Hades spun around, taking the rebel he had just captured with him, hoping this newcomer would hesitate at the sight of his comrade as a human shield. Just long enough for Taz to get in place.

Having led with his gun, the new rebel squeezed off several rounds. The muzzle blast lit up the night. Hades felt his captive's body jerk as if bullets were slamming into him.

His captive was screaming now, but not in death throes. Hades caught a few words. *Wrong bullets. Use knife.*

Instead the other rebel threw down his weapon and ran screaming toward the camp.

"He's headed back your way," he warned Taz.

But there was no reply.

The man he held tried to drop low and kick free. Hades countered, slitting the man's throat and shoving him away in one motion.

Pulling out twin nine-millimeter Glocks, one in each fist, Hades raced back toward the camp. In the eerie firelight, he saw Taz on the ground wrestling with one of the rebels. Another rebel moved in from behind, his knife drawn and aimed at Taz's back.

Hades charged forward, both Glocks blazing. The rebel with the knife stopped and straightened as Hades continued firing. But the rebel didn't fall. Taking dead aim, Hades squeezed off shot after shot at the now-fleeing rebel's back.

Wrong bullets. As in *blanks*?

Taz staggered to his feet, having killed the rebel with his bare hands.

"What the fuck?" Taz pulled his own weapon and fired repeatedly at the rebel's corpse. It was all noise.

"Leave it," Hades shouted. *They're coming.* "Run. Get away."

A loud squelching noise filled the air as they took off running.

"Do you remember what comes next?" Taz shouted.

You will do what we say.

We control you.

You have no choice but to comply.

A low-flying helicopter circled directly overhead. Its blinding searchlight snared them in a beam.

"Split up. They can't follow us both," Hades shouted. "Remember our plan!"

Taz nodded. "Two weeks. If you're not there, I'll come looking for you."

"Same here. Now go!"

Hades dashed out of the light but could only evade it for a few seconds. When it picked him up again, it stayed on like a death ray.

He heard a different type of gun fire; the mechanized burst from a pneumatic air gun. Multiple tranquilizer darts hit his back, neck, and buttocks. Shit!

For him it was over. Running would only make it worse. But still he pressed on, would keep going until he dropped.

If he could buy Taz a few minutes . . . to make good his escape.

They were . . . each other's . . . only . . . hope . . .

Chapter 14

Southern California
September 22

   Mission incomplete.
   Max was dreaming. He and Taz had been on a mission. In the jungle. But who had they been fighting? And why? A man lay dead at his feet, his neck broken. Smoke swirled in his mind, blanking out what happened next.
   But not the memory of what he'd done. And who had made him do it: Dr. Rufin.
   The memories from being inside Rufin's head were jumbled. But Max had the gist of things.
   Or did he? In some way he felt like he was just a pawn in some sick game. Is that what it had been?
   Wrong question.
   Without warning, red-hot pokers lashed across Max's eyes, plunging him into total darkness. He wanted to scream, but the searing agony rendered

him mute as well as blind. He felt claustrophobic as if he were being buried alive. Smothered. He needed air. He needed—

Erin!

She was here. Simply recalling her presence helped to ground him. Breaking free of the dream, he found her still on top of him. Still asleep.

His arms encircled her. Holding her was like grasping a magic elixir that defused his pain. Where he burned, she was a soothing balm. And the tighter he held her, the greater the relief.

Mine.

The voice inside his head was back, but this time he had a name: Hades. It was what Dr. Rufin called him. There were more memories, lurking close to the surface, but it hurt to think.

She's mine, Max thought back, seeking to end the silent challenge.

He sensed light seeping in from behind his eyelids. The episode was passing. That he'd come through it with a few memories intact felt like a huge victory.

He blinked, taking in his surroundings. Soft light frosted the camper window. He guessed by the relative silence that it was still very early in the morning.

That he knew exactly where he was struck him as profound. He had fled the hospital, drugged Erin, and then stolen a truck. That was reality. It had a genuine sense of continuity. A sense of continuity that the scene with the dead man lacked.

Aware that he held Erin in what had to be a crushing embrace, he loosened his grip, but didn't release her, still drawing benefit from holding her.

He debated whether to try and rouse her, or to just let her awaken on her own. The drugs should be wearing off soon and he wanted to get back on the road. To find Taz.

That was one of the things he'd remembered. He and Taz had an elaborate plan of where to meet and what to do if they became separated. At least it felt like an elaborate plan. The problem was he recalled few specifics. Like *where*, for instance.

They'd been overseas—Thailand—yes! But he felt certain the rendezvous spot wasn't there. It was here, in the States, at a place he and Taz had both been to.

He noticed he was panting again, to ward off the headache. Time to stop thinking.

He focused instead on the woman sprawled across his chest. She wasn't very tall, maybe five-six, which in Max's book made her tiny. But what she lacked in height, she made up for in curves. The formless jacket she wore hid much.

The fact that she hadn't moved bothered him. He pressed two fingers against her neck and found her pulse weak, but steady. He also found her skin pleasingly soft.

He studied the way her hair fell across her cheek. This close he could see that it was a deep, rich color. Mahogany highlighted with lighter cinnamon red. Unable to resist, he pushed it back. His fingers speared through her hair. It was as silky as it looked. *In for an inch . . .*

The urge to kiss her came out of nowhere. So did his erection. *In for a mile* . . .

"Erin, wake up."

When she didn't respond, he grasped her shoulders, shook her gently.

"Mmmmmm." She snuggled against him, drawing one leg up between his. The pose was intimate and vulnerable. A picture of her naked came to mind.

He shook her again. "Erin. Give me your hands." That her wrists were bound hadn't even registered.

"Just . . . one . . . more minute," she murmured.

"Snooze button's broke, sweetheart. Get up."

Instead, she shifted closer and raised her head. A soft sigh escaped her lips as, eyes closed, her mouth brushed his. She was still half asleep, still half under the influence of the sedative.

And with that tentative half kiss, she had Max's full attention. Was she dreaming of someone special, he wondered. *Did it matter?*

No. All that mattered was that the kiss not end. He lifted his head, making it easier for her to continue her gentle exploration. Erin's mouth hovered close to his, her lips touching so lightly he couldn't be sure if contact was still being made. She stole his breath, leaving him desperate, confused. Aching. For more.

He didn't move as her hands awkwardly cupped his chin, urging him closer, forcing him to participate. Her tongue, tiny and moist, darted forward, tasting him. Tempting him.

She deepened the kiss, drawing his tongue into her mouth. His body responded, his testicles tightening with need. She was pressed fully against him, her breasts crushed against his chest. He wanted them in his hands. His mouth. He wanted to grasp her hips and grind fully against her, fit his crotch into the cradle of her hips.

Except she held him enthralled, held him perfectly immobile with just a kiss. Did doing "whatever it took" to remain free include coercing her sexually? Hell. No. His hands fisted into the blankets.

He couldn't take much more.

Her eyes opened just then and she broke off the kiss with a small cry.

"Let me go!" Erin struggled atop him.

"I'm not touching you."

"Oh!" She tried to push up. The move shifted her lower body, making them both aware of his erection.

Max groaned as she wiggled against him, desperate to get away. He grabbed her hips, to still her, but that made matters worse.

"Max! Please!" The frightened tone in her voice and the panic in her eyes jolted him.

He sat up, letting her tumble to one side as he edged away in the opposite direction. But in the close confines, they still touched.

"You were dreaming." The excuse sounded lame, so he switched to reassuring. "Nobody's going to hurt you, Erin. Especially me."

She tried to raise up and immediately pitched backward.

Max reached to steady her, but there was no calming the fury that swept across her features as she realized that her hands were bound.

"Untie me. Right now." She thrust her wrists up.

"This isn't what you think." He tugged the rope free and tossed it away. "I needed to sleep and I didn't want you to run off, sound an alarm."

More of the events from the night before came back to her. "You drugged me, didn't you?"

"I did. And don't tell me you wouldn't have used that syringe on me, so in my book that makes us even. And I will let you go as soon as I get a few answers."

"Well, I want a few answers myself," she snapped, melodramatically rubbing the chafed skin of her wrists while looking around. "Where are we? Where's my car?"

"We're at a campground about fifty miles outside of San Diego. You car is at the airport, but I brought your bag with us." His eyes roved about the camper. "I borrowed this."

"You stole it? Max, please, let me contact Dr. Winchette. By now, there will be people searching for us. I'll explain that it's my fault. If you let me handle this, we can probably get the charges dropped."

"You're hardly to blame."

"I never should have left the hospital with you."

"I would have forced you to come." *I did force you to come.* "Look, you can call Winchette shortly. In fact, I want to know if Taz has been located."

His response appeased her, even as she assumed it meant Max would return to the hospital. Which he had no intention of.

"Where's my phone? My purse?" she asked.

"Up front. We'll get them after we use the bathroom."

"You'll let me go alone?"

He sighed. "You're not my prisoner, Erin. I understand how bizarre this must seem, but you have no clue what I've been through. Hell, I'm not even sure what I've been through. I had hoped you could help fill in a few blanks."

"How much do you remember, about being rescued?"

"Not much. Bits and pieces that don't make sense. Other things feel like they're within my grasp. As if with a little more time, it'll all come back." He rubbed his temples as the headache restarted. A warning not to question his thoughts. "Mostly it hurts to think. Is that part of the amnesia you told me about?"

"The pain? No. Describe it. Where exactly does it hurt?" She reached for him. He drew back.

It took Max a moment to realize she was only seeking his wrist. To check his pulse. Damn. What had he thought she was going to do?

"I'm fine now" became a true statement the moment her fingertips pressed against his skin. That was twice just since waking that his pain had abated beneath her touch. Coincidence?

"Proper treatment is crucial to a full recovery, Max. We need to return to the hospital."

"Can we shelve this discussion and go find the bathroom?" He scooted toward the edge. "I've gotta piss, but I promise we'll talk after I've had a shower."

* * *

Erin resisted the urge to argue. For one thing, she really did need to use the bathroom, too.

She also needed a minute to shake the last of the cobwebs from her head. Besides leaving her tongue thick and her mouth dry, that particular combination of drugs made her brain feel lethargic. Confused. Is that what Max had felt upon awakening in the hospital?

She was furious that he'd drugged her, tied her up—and involved her in an auto theft. But oddly she didn't feel endangered by him. In fact, she felt the opposite. Protected. Safe.

That he seemed more lucid than last night was a good sign. His headache concerned her, though. It could be nothing . . . or something. But diagnosing it in the back of a truck wasn't an option. He needed to be back in a clinical setting, where tests could be run.

She watched him back off the makeshift bed and kneel on the floor, one hand extended to assist her.

The pose struck her as chivalrous, until she realized he was too tall to stand inside the camper. Heck, his shoulders were too broad for the tiny walking space between the camper's galley and cabinets.

Ignoring his hand, she scooted to the edge of the mattress, but Max didn't move. Instead he pinned her with a gaze that was way too intense, way too desirous. A gaze that had her thinking of him as a handsome man versus a patient.

She looked away, wrestling with her errant thoughts. "I, um, really need to use the bathroom."

"Can I trust you, Erin?"

"If you're worried I'll scream for help or run, I won't. I've heard voices outside, so I know there are people around. And I did come with you willingly, Max. At first at least." She met his gaze. "I should be asking if I can trust you not to leave while I'm in the bathroom."

"Touché." Turning, Max practically crawled out the camper door.

She followed. Once again he held out his hand and this time she let him help her out of the camper. But the moment her feet hit the ground, her knees wobbled.

Max caught her. "Easy."

Dizziness assailed her. Mortified at the thought of being sick, she turned away. But he blocked her, forced her to stay put.

Gritting her teeth, she tried to reestablish her equilibrium. Her cheeks flushed as she realized she'd drifted closer to him. Her hands were braced against his chest, her hips brushing against his thighs in an almost erotic stance. He murmured under his breath, the words inaudible, yet oddly calming.

"Let me see your eyes." He reached out and tilted her head back, his gaze probing. His fingers stroked along the underside of her jaw.

She straightened. What was she doing standing here, letting this man, her thoughts— God, what was wrong with her? She looked around, glad to find their campsite sheltered by trees. No one could see them. "I'm fine. Sorry."

Almost as if he could read her mind, a half smile

formed, then disappeared. "It's a bitch, throwing off the effect of those drugs. Sit. I'll get our bags."

Max had thoughtfully brought along her carry-on bag, which boosted her spirits a little. She followed him along a small path through the trees to a concrete block bath house.

The sun had yet to burn away the ground fog. It swirled at their feet like spun sugar. The voices she'd heard earlier had faded, leaving the campgrounds quiet.

"Looks like we've got the place to ourselves." Max handed her a towel. "Found them in the camper. They look clean."

She grabbed for the handle of her bag, but Max caught her hand and pressed something into her palm.

"The car key," he said before turning away. "So I can't drive off."

"Thanks."

The ladies' room was deserted. She checked her pockets then remembered Max had never given her back her cell phone. After using the toilet, she washed her hands and face, then brushed her teeth.

The showers had individual dressing rooms with a bench seat. She opened her bag and tugged out clean clothes, opting for khaki pants and a lightweight green sweater. The shower revived her.

She dried her hair as best she could using the wall-mounted hand blower, and then applied makeup. She resisted the thought that she was going through all these pains to look good for Max.

"I'm doing it for me," she whispered. Well, mostly.

Disgusted with herself, she repacked her bag and switched her thoughts to wondering how she was going to explain this fiasco to Dr. Winchette and Travis Franks.

Yes, Max had drugged her and taken her along but that didn't excuse the part she'd played in his leaving the hospital in the first place. And while she knew Winchette would be furious that she'd questioned Max's medication, she needed to be prepared to turn those questions right back on him.

Why had Winchette purposely kept Max so heavily sedated? Was it because, fully awake, Max could finally answer questions?

"Some things are better left unquestioned," Winchette had said time and time again.

She disagreed. Questions were pathways to the truth. How long would Max have remained captive if no one had pursued the question of his disappearance?

Travis Franks's photographs of that chamber came back to mind. Did Max recall any of that? Did he know what had been done to him?

While she had no clinical experience, the case histories she'd studied in grad school indicated that most *alleged* brainwashing patients had no conscious memory of the actual process, though many later recalled it with hypnosis.

Medical hypnosis was her area of expertise and the reason she was hired for the position in the first place. Was the real reason Travis Franks had wanted her involved not so much to help Max, but rather to determine what information had been compromised?

She looked at her reflection one last time. She needed a plan. Once Dr. Winchette found Max gone, he'd sound an alarm. People would be searching for them. The problem was she wasn't sure she wanted anyone to find them just yet.

Not until she knew more about where Max had been held and what had been done to him. *Admit it, Erin—you really want to know about that machine.* What had it been used for? Where had it come from? And had her father been involved in any of it? She could never believe that her father would willingly be involved in anything evil.

Max promised they would talk, and while getting him back to the hospital was her primary concern, she had to face another reality. She could very well lose her job over this, so if she had any questions for Max, she needed to ask them now.

Losing her job would also put an end to searching for her father's records at the hospital. Maybe it was time she was honest with Dr. Winchette and asked him point blank about her father's death.

Outside the restroom, the fog was still heavy. She sat on a bench, listening, but all was quiet. Too quiet.

She approached the men's room door and listened, but no sound came through. "Max?"

No one answered. Her stomach sank at the realization that he was gone. He'd given her the key . . . to a stolen truck. How stupid was that?

Furious over having been tricked, she whirled around and plowed right into him.

Max reached out, steadied her.

The disproportionate relief she felt at seeing him morphed into stunned awe as her eyes swept over him. His hair was still damp and a little longer on top than she'd realized. His head laceration was barely noticeable now that his hair wasn't stuck to the suture line. He was healing amazingly fast.

He wore clean clothes, black jeans and another black tee that hugged his muscles. Big honking muscles that would leave Alice drooling.

If Erin had thought him handsome before, he was even more so now. He'd shaved, his cheeks smooth, making her want to touch them again.

Again?

Right. She had dreamed about kissing him. And more.

He smiled, revealing a deep dimple. Then he dropped his hands, breaking the spell.

Erin quickly took a step backward, disappointed that the moment ended.

"Afraid I'd deserted you?" he teased.

"It crossed my mind."

"Come on." He led the way back to the truck. The smell of bacon frying drifted over from some neighboring site, reminding Erin she'd skipped dinner last evening.

Max opened the passenger door. "Look, there were several restaurants, back toward the interstate. How about we head there, get coffee and food. We can talk while we eat."

"You should let me drive."

"No. Just get in."

Having little choice, she climbed onto the passenger seat.

Ten minutes later, he pulled into the drive-through lane of a fast-food restaurant. "Don't worry. I'm going to pull over, but we can talk more privately if we eat in the car. What do you want?"

"Coffee, black. And an egg biscuit."

Max ordered himself four steak and egg biscuits. "With extra cheese."

After getting their food, he swung around to the rear of the parking lot and backed into a space. Digging through the paper sack, he handed her a wrapped biscuit. "I think this is yours."

"Thanks." She set it on the seat and reached for her coffee. The scalding brew tasted divine.

Max polished off one of his biscuits in two bites before she even got hers unwrapped, and then opened his coffee.

"I feel like I haven't eaten in—months. But I'm guessing it's only been a few days."

"I'd still take it easy, try to slow down and chew it well." She immediately regretted her words, fearing she sounded like a mother hen.

Max ignored her advice and wolfed down another biscuit. "You're from Langley? I am—was CIA, right? You, too?"

Erin sipped her coffee, debating how much to tell him. If she wanted honesty from him, she needed to lead by example. "You are, yes. They're eager to debrief you, by the way. I work for the NSA at a research hospital in Alexandria. I've got a doctorate in clinical psychology, but unlike a psychiatrist, I'm not a medical doctor."

"National Security Agency. Big gun. Winchette, too?"

"Yes, but he is a psychiatrist. Head of my department."

"Interesting that they'd call in a squadron of shrinks." Max pointed to his head. "Obviously someone thinks I've suffered more than a scalp laceration. What's the story with you and Winchette? One minute the guy seems to push all your wrong buttons. The next he's like a revered older uncle."

She nibbled on her biscuit. This was why she never played poker. There was no *bluff* in her DNA.

"My father and Dr. Winchette were research partners and friends once. We're not related, but I've known him, well, forever. My parents had no siblings or extended family, so in many ways Dr. Winchette was the closest thing to an uncle I ever experienced. At least when I was little."

As if sensing the topic was a sore one for her, Max changed his line of questions. "What do you know about how I got to Southeast Asia in the first place?"

"Very little, I'm afraid," she said. "You and two other operatives, Dante Johnson and Harry something—"

"Gambrel," Max supplied.

"The three of you disappeared on an assignment two years ago and were believed dead until Dante escaped six months ago."

"I remember Dante and Rocco rescuing me. But Harry . . . was he with them?"

"No. He's still missing. I'm confused about Taz. If he was not part of your original team, who is he?"

"Taz is a friend. We worked together, if not for the CIA, then elsewhere." Max rubbed his head. "This not remembering is getting old. How long before this amnesia passes?"

"It varies. It's not an exact science. You could wake up with full recall tomorrow. Then again, some or all may never return."

"That totally sucks. Sounds more like a crap shoot."

"There are therapies, utilizing things like regression and even biofeedback, that might help. The fact that I'm also a clinical hypnotherapist is one reason I was called in on this case."

"Well, no offense, but the last thing I want is someone trying to put me under again."

"It's not like that. You don't go unconscious, as with sedatives. Believe me, I understand your concerns. Dante Johnson resisted it as well."

"Did Dante have amnesia?"

"You really need to speak with him about that. We're treading close to the line on patient privacy."

"Professional propriety isn't high on my list these days." Max set his food aside. Leaning forward, he pulled her cell phone out from beneath the car seat. "I want to know if they found Taz. Call Winchette and get an update, but use the speakerphone. Tell him you're safe and will explain everything as soon as you're back at the hospital."

She noticed that he'd loosened her phone battery, but snapped it back in place before handing it to her. When she dialed Winchette's phone, it went straight to voice mail.

Max reached over and hit the END button. "No messages."

"Let me try calling Dante Johnson, then. He'll know if your friend was located." She looked around for her purse. "He gave me a card last night."

"Keep it on speaker and keep it short," Max said. "And don't tell him where you are."

Dante answered on the second ring.

"It's Erin Houston," she began. "I was trying to reach Dr. Winchette, but he doesn't answer."

"Dr. Houston!" Dante said. "Are you okay? Is Max with you?"

She looked at Max. "Yes, and we're both fine. Max wants to know if you found his friend, Taz. The John Doe patient."

Dante hesitated. "Max, I know you're listening. And no, we haven't found him yet. But there's more. Dr. Winchette is dead."

"Dead?" Erin felt like someone had struck her. "How? What happened?"

"I hoped you could tell me," Dante said. "He was found in Max's room shortly after you disappeared. Look, tell me where you are and I'll—"

Max grabbed the phone, ending the call before separating the battery again.

"Give me that!" she said. "I need to find out what's going on."

He started the truck, but didn't put it in gear. "You can call Dante back in a minute. He'll arrange for someone to pick you up."

"You can't leave, Max! Dr. Winchette is dead. They probably think that you came to like your friend did and went ballistic."

"That's exactly what they think. Which is why I need you to call and tell them that Winchette was nowhere around when we left."

She noticed that Max winced as he spoke, his words seemingly gritted out between clenched teeth. That he was in pain was obvious.

"I can't let you go off alone," she said.

"You can't stop me. I've got to find Taz."

"You need to go back to the hospital, Max."

"And be a guinea pig? Never. Get out, Erin. Please."

The "please" undid her. "Whether you want to admit it or not, you need help, Max. Let me stay with you. We'll figure out something together. I want to help you."

Instead of replying, his arm shot out across her chest, toward the door. She wanted to scream in frustration that he intended to physically eject her from the truck.

"I hope I won't regret this." He grabbed the seat belt and pulled it harshly across her chest before jamming it in the buckle.

Then he stomped the gas and sped away.

Chapter 15

Boston, Massachusetts
September 22

The last thing Abe Caldwell felt like was having brunch at the nearly deserted club. But this meeting with Salvador Pena had been too important to postpone.

He smiled and nodded, encouraging Salvador to continue droning on about his recent vacation with his great-grandsons. Meeting here was better than meeting at Sal's estate, where Abe would have had to suffer through a photo presentation as well. Fortunately, with Sal, a little fake enthusiasm went a long way. And right now Abe needed every advantage.

Salvador Pena was wealthy and powerful, but still old-school humble enough to insist he owed it all to Abe's grandfather. Sixty years ago, Salvador had agreed to back Abe's grandfather's fledgling drug company. That initial investment in Caldwell Pharmaceuticals eventually made both men billionaires.

Salvador's subsequent reinvestments helped fuel the company's exponential growth and allowed him to expand into other markets like the electronics and software firm Sal's grandson now ran. Abe's grandfather and Salvador had been one of those rare, unbeatable teams of money and genius, their Midas touch and ruthless mindset making every business venture a success.

It all changed ten years ago, however, following the crash of a corporate jet in the Swiss Alps. The sole survivor, Abe's grandfather miraculously walked away unharmed, but permanently altered all the same. Suddenly saddled with a conscience, his grandfather refused to do business "the old way."

Profits at Caldwell Pharmaceuticals plummeted and the board threatened mutiny. Fate intervened in the form of a stroke. When his grandfather was declared incapacitated, Abe became his guardian. With Salvador's backing, Abe convinced the board to let him take up the company reins.

Three years later, Caldwell Pharmaceuticals was back on top. Everyone lauded Abe's brilliance. Some even suggested that perhaps he was smarter than his grandfather. Abe went to great lengths to preserve that image, making certain no one knew the truth—that while going through his grandfather's most private papers, Abe discovered the Golden Goose.

Decades earlier, under a variety of airtight guises and dummy corporations, his grandfather managed to acquire mountains of research projects abandoned in the forties, fifties, and sixties.

By today's standards, the projects ranged from sheer folly to downright unethical. They'd been sold off or jettisoned with the understanding that they'd never resurface and cause the originating parties embarrassment. Some had even been outright stolen.

Abe's grandfather's true genius was his uncanny ability to sort the wheat from the chaff, marrying old hypothesis to cutting-edge technology, which in many cases produced magical results.

His grandfather had also been masterful at obscuring the origins of a project, carefully utilizing only the work of deceased scientists—with one key exception: his collaborative work with Viktor Zadovsky.

After his grandfather's stroke, Zadovsky had been as eager as Abe to continue their secret partnership. No big surprise given the shambled state of the Russian government at the time.

For a while their new partnership seemed to work. The initial successes Zadovsky demonstrated with mind control had been startling. Men who blindly followed commands. Human robots. Human slaves. Human killing machines. Unfortunately, the shelf life of the test subjects was horrendous. *"A minor but solvable problem,"* Zadovsky had insisted.

Abe had been especially interested in the enhanced physical capacities later test subjects displayed. That Zadovsky may have inadvertently created a fountain of youth formula didn't seem to faze the Russian scientist. It had deeply intrigued

Abe, however, who went on to indulge Zadovsky's every whim and overlooked every excuse. The promise of success had been huge.

But that promise vanished with Zadovsky's death—along with millions Abe had invested. Thankfully, not all appeared lost. Always one to hedge his bets, Abe had his Jakarta spies smuggle out whatever bits and pieces of Zadovsky's work they could obtain. Those bits were far from complete, but Abe had faith in Stanley Winchette's ability to reverse engineer whatever they lacked by studying the two test subjects who'd been recovered by the CIA.

One of those test subjects had disappeared, but that was a temporary glitch. Abe already had one of his own men en route to San Diego with a tracking device.

Another *hedge* was the fact that Abe had supplied Zadovsky with the tracking technology to begin with. An experimental nanotechnology that Salvadore's electronics company worked on.

Now as soon as Abe's contact in Southeast Asia found this Dr. Rufin, all the pieces would be in place.

"You've indulged me long enough," Salvador said at last. "Let's get down to business. I've looked over your latest proposal, and if it's as promising as you've indicated, I'm in. In fact, I'd like exclusivity on the deal. Let me provide all funding in exchange for a higher percentage of the profits."

Abe felt a genuine smile break across his face. Discarding his fork, he met Salvador's gaze. "I started to say that's very generous. But I realized it's just you being masterful. Again."

Grinning at the compliment, Salvador slathered butter on a croissant. "Your grandfather and I used to do business that way and look where it took us."

"If he were here now, he'd approve."

Frowning, Salvador grew serious. "Tell me straight. How is he doing? Last time I saw him, he didn't seem to recognize me until right near the end. Even then I wasn't sure."

"Yes. Well, I've had the same experience, Sal. It's . . . unsettling. That's why I'm so eager to get started with this new project. The benefits projected for Alzheimer's patients could help stroke victims as well."

The cell phone clipped to Abe's belt suddenly vibrated with the distinct long-short-short buzz that identified his assistant, Tommy Groene. Tommy wouldn't interrupt this meeting unless it was urgent.

Abe shifted his gaze to their nearby waiter, who immediately approached the table and offered fresh coffee.

"Actually, I'd like a cappuccino," Salvador began.

Abe took advantage of the break. "Make that two. If you'll excuse me, Sal." He stood and headed toward the men's room.

After confirming he was alone, he called Tommy back.

"Sorry, sir," Tommy began. "But I just received word that Dr. Winchette was found dead at the San Diego hospital."

Tommy knew to get straight to the point, with little preamble, but still the bluntness of this news was shocking.

"What?" Abe said. "How?"

"My source at the San Diego Police Department said it appears his neck was broken in a scuffle. They were treating the case as a homicide until the Feds stepped in and took over, citing national security."

"A homicide? Who do they think killed him?"

"The patient he was treating, Max Duncan. Apparently Duncan has disappeared now as well."

"Damn!" Obviously, Duncan hadn't been sedated enough no matter what Winchette had said.

"There's more," Tommy went on. "Winchette's assistant, Dr. Houston, is missing. Presumed kidnapped."

"Oh, that's just fucking great." A damsel in distress would whip the CIA into overdrive. And this particular damsel could have the Agency asking questions about Winchette that Abe didn't want asked. If any of this got traced back to Caldwell Pharmaceuticals—

"Sir?"

"I'm here," Abe snapped. "Have my driver waiting out front. I'll meet you at the office in thirty minutes."

Disconnecting, Abe hurried back to his table. Jesus, he needed a cigarette.

Salvador took one look at him and scowled. "Everything okay? It's not bad news about your grandfather, is it?"

Abe shook his head. "I just got a call. My wife's niece has been in an auto accident down in Hartford. It's serious."

"I'm so sorry." Salvador pushed unsteadily to his feet. "Look, you need to go. This other will wait."

"I'll call as soon as we return."

Salvador crossed himself. "I've got two nieces who are like daughters. Keep me posted."

As soon as Abe got in his car, he lit up and drew deeply on a cigarette. The hit of nicotine was calming and helped him to think. This wasn't the first time he'd been in a tight spot. Hell, compared to some others, this was minor.

His first concern was damage control. He needed to distance himself from Winchette. His second, and equally important, concern was recovering all the data Winchette had.

A grim-faced Tommy waited at Abe's office.

"What do you have?" Abe asked.

"Not much. The CIA is working hard to keep this one contained. They figure they'll have a better shot at a temporary insanity plea if they find Max Duncan before Dr. Houston is harmed."

"Do they have any leads?"

"No. Which is making them dig a little deeper for clues. Inquiries are being made about Dr. Houston's late father and his connection to Stanley Winchette."

"I was afraid of that." Abe steepled his fingers.

Damn it, he'd warned Winchette against keeping Erin Houston too close, but Winchette had insisted he could control the situation. So, how well had Winchette covered his tracks? "It's time to cut our losses. Is Allen in San Diego yet?"

Allen handled Abe's personal security and had been sent to help Stanley Winchette locate John Doe.

"Yes. He's waiting for instructions."

Standing, Abe paced to the small bar in the corner of his office. "Max Duncan should have a tracking beacon as well. Tell Allen to start nosing around, see if he gets any hits on the missing men."

"Should I fly out? With Winchette dead, Allen will need assistance capturing them."

"I don't want them captured. I want them eliminated. And it needs to look like an accident. Allen's good at that stuff. I want you to concentrate on purging Winchette's records. Start at his home. He wouldn't have kept anything at the hospital."

"Yes, sir."

"Send everything you find to our Zurich office. It might prove useful when we locate Dr. Rufin."

"Any news on Rufin's whereabouts?" Tommy asked.

"Not yet. But I'll rattle my contact's cage right now."

Chapter 16

Jakarta, Indonesia
September 22

"One last thing." As was his custom after pocketing his payoff, this snitch—who freaking believed in value-added service—offered a free tidbit. "People are asking about Harry Gambrel again. Lots of cash, U.S., being flashed."

The man seated across from the snitch was careful not to react. Was this a trap?

It didn't feel like one.

First and foremost the snitch was a mercenary. If he had any inkling that he was in the presence of the man formerly known as Harry Gambrel, they wouldn't be having this conversation. The snitch would be off someplace, happily counting *lots of cash, U.S.*

Harry shrugged. "Seeing as we've both heard

that name tossed around before, I'm curious who they're really looking for." *Wait for it.*

Squinting, the snitch scratched his forehead. "An associate of Gambrel's perhaps?" His eyes widened. "Yeah, the old bait and switch. Like the time they claimed to be looking for Dax Harlton. His ex–old lady popped her nose out of a hole, hoping to make some fast cash, and whammo! They nailed her. You know the real kicker? Dax was dead."

Stupid fuck. Harry stood and prepared to leave. "You might be on to something."

Both men reached for the tab simultaneously. Another custom: the snitch liked to act as if he intended to pick it up. Harry watched the snitch's gaze drift from his own bare wrist to Harry's gold Rolex Submariner.

"I've got it covered," Harry sneered. "No worries."

After taking more extreme measures than usual to assure he wasn't being followed, Harry grabbed a cab and headed downtown, confident that his disguise remained effective. Multiple plastic surgeries, new dental veneers, hair dye, and colored contacts assured he looked nothing like the two-year-old photographs the CIA was likely circulating. Hell, he looked damn good now.

The news that the Agency had again ramped up their search for him was old. Ever since Dante Johnson had *miraculously* escaped Viktor Zadovsky's custody, the interest in Johnson's fellow missing operatives had heated up. Max Duncan's reemergence, however, had sent it off the charts.

Jesus, if Zadovsky was still alive, Harry would rip

him to shreds with his bare hands. Granted, the fact
the two men had been partners in crime—partners
in ripping off *others*—should have been a clue that
Zadovsky might not be trustworthy. Unfortunately,
Zadovsky had played to Harry's one weakness: He'd
thrown money in the air and Harry had chased the
whirling bills like a cheap whore.

As Harry had recently discovered, the lying,
cheating bastard had been screwing him from the
get-go. Zadovsky had diverted virtually all of their
joint funds while showing Harry falsified bank
records.

"You can't take it with you" didn't apply to other
people's money.

And if being personally swindled wasn't bad
enough, Zadovsky's suicide had left Harry holding
the bag on several other deals.

Luckily, most of the clients who'd made advance
payments for one of Zadovsky's nasty biohazard
recipes quickly wrote off the loss at word of his
death to avoid guilt by association.

The one huge exception was Minh Tran, who
had fronted Harry a large deposit and expected another shipment of SugarCane, a potent opium by-
product that had taken the recreational drug world
by storm. Produced in small quantities, demand far
exceeded supply. 'Cane was known for its trade-
mark superior high that lasted for hours. No crash
and burn. Its utopian, performance-enhancing
qualities made it a pleasant-seeming addiction.

Then there had been the promise of JumpJuice,
a new chemically altered amphetamine that Zadovsky

touted as the next perfect drug. A single drop under the tongue lasted for hours.

Minh Tran had already paid handsomely for the exclusive right to distribute SugarCane and was drooling over similar rights for JumpJuice. The 'Cane had proved wildly profitable for all of them these last two years.

Then Zadovsky committed suicide. Bastard.

In the flash of a coward's bullet, Harry was bankrupt. Adding insult to injury, it had taken nearly two weeks for word of Zadovsky's death to reach Harry, who'd been in hiding at Abe Caldwell's insistence after Dante Johnson resurfaced.

By the time Harry got back to Indonesia, Zadovsky's lab and personal residence in Jakarta had been wiped clean. He suspected the Indonesian government had most of the lab records even though publicly the government repudiated Zadovsky, claimed he was in the country on a forged passport. *Plausible deniability.* The Indonesians didn't want anyone to know about their secret deals with Zadovsky either.

"Pull over. You can let me out here."

The cab stopped near a busy open-air market and Harry climbed out. He pretended to wander, then took a convoluted route back to his hotel.

Alone in his room, he ordered a meal from room service while his laptop powered up. The RAM-hungry security programs that ghosted his cyber-trail seemed to take forever to settle in.

Among other things, he was expecting an update from Abe Caldwell on the status of Max Duncan and the mystery man extracted with him.

Talk about another stunning betrayal by Zadovsky!

It was now painfully apparent that Zadovsky had been conducting dual experiments—one set in Jakarta for Abe Caldwell's benefit and another set in the secret Thai laboratory run by Dr. Rufin.

It didn't take a nuclear physicist to figure out where the real research was being conducted. Did the CIA have any idea what had been lost when they blew up Rufin's lab?

As it was, the research data the CIA supposedly had—if indeed they'd gotten Rufin's laptop—was the equivalent of a gold mine. A gold mine Harry should have inherited as Zadovsky's silent partner.

Damn it! That was twice in one year he'd been cheated out of an inheritance. Harry's old man was probably sitting in hell, laughing his ass off.

Ephraim Gambrel had never forgiven his only son for leaving the family farm after high school. Harry hated farming and predicted his old man would go belly up along with all the other Midwest farmers. But the stubborn old coot had held on, and just before succumbing to cancer last year, Ephraim sold the farm for millions when a rare mineral deposit was discovered.

The real salt in the wound, however, was learning that Ephraim had left his entire estate to Harry's ex-wife, Gena. Of course, Ephraim probably would have done that even if he'd known Harry was alive.

It was one more score to even with the cheating bitch. Provided he lived that long. If Minh Tran caught up with him, Harry would die before ever getting a shot at settling with Gena.

Room service arrived just as his laptop beeped, signaling an all clear. His appetite now diminished, Harry opened the soda he'd ordered and moved to his computer.

Methodically checking e-mail accounts, he read and deleted threat after threat. Everyone wanted a piece of his alter ego, Mr. Peabody, the name he'd used to conduct business on Zadovsky's behalf. That Harry had a new persona, *Doug Harold*, didn't stop him from monitoring the old Peabody accounts.

Switching browsers, he logged on to a different e-mail account. Abe Caldwell had sent another e-mail that didn't amount to much more than a rant about how important it was that they locate Dr. Rufin before *the competition* did. Like Harry wasn't exhausting every means already.

Since only a select few even knew about Rufin's liaison with Zadovsky, the only competition Harry considered real was the CIA. They had the most at stake and were better equipped than anyone else. Or at least they used to be.

A major disadvantage of faking his own death was that he no longer had direct access within the Agency. Abe Caldwell had some inside connections of his own, but it wasn't the same. And it made Harry nervous.

The longer a mole remained inside, the greater the risk of discovery. The Agency's best protection against leaks was the fact they expected them. A constant undercurrent of paranoia kept everyone on their toes. The Agency also played a pretty mean shell game. More than once their disinformation techniques had fooled their own operatives.

As far as Harry was concerned, everything the CIA said was questionable. They might have Rufin in custody . . . or they might not. Same with seized hard drives and missing *John Does*.

Frustrated, Harry started to log off his laptop. Then he recalled one little-used account. He hadn't heard from Bohdana, Zadovsky's former secretary, in a while. She always went radio silent after a fight and she'd been royally pissed the last time they'd talked.

Harry had smuggled her out of Jakarta, where she'd been in hiding following Zadovsky's death. Not quite ready to be rid of her, Harry had set her up in a Bangkok slum. Her loyalty came cheap enough: the promise of marriage. He trusted her as much as he could trust anyone, which meant he was always cautious.

As Zadovsky's secretary, Bohdana had played the dumb bimbo perfectly. If Zadovsky had been se-ducible, she would have slept with him had Harry told her to.

He found one e-mail from her, dated a few hours ago. Clicking the IN box, he read the subject line: FROM YOUR LOVING NIECE.

Suddenly alert, he leaned forward. That Bohdana had written meant all was forgiven. Like he cared. *That she'd written in code meant something else.*

He copied her e-mail to a separate program so the original appeared unread. Then he opened the copy.

Dear Aunty,

I am sorry to have neglected writing these past months, but my new position keeps me very busy. I wanted to let you know that my cat returned. I had been so certain I would never see her again after she wandered off. She is pregnant so I will bring you a kitten when I come to visit.

He deciphered the code he'd taught her, then reread the message. Dr. Rufin had sent her an e-mail asking for her help in getting out of Thailand!

Harry stood and paced to the window. Tempering his excitement was the perpetual question: Was this legit or was it a trap?

Who the hell knew anymore?

One thing was certain: He was long overdue for a bit of a break. And while he never relied on luck, he did acknowledge its existence. The old adage that even a blind squirrel occasionally found a nut manifested more often than blind squirrels believed.

Tugging out his cell phone, he punched in a number, and hit SEND.

Chapter 17

Southern California
September 22

Max drove due east, his thoughts changing like the landscape outside the car's windows. They'd gone from the shore near the Pacific Ocean, through the desert, and were now headed into the mesas and mountains of southwest Arizona. Mesas and mountains that were familiar. Had he lived here?

The magic eight ball that seemed to be his mind turned up the following reply: *No answer. Ask again later.*

Damn it! It was bad enough that the last two years had been stolen from him, but not to know where he'd lived before that? There was no tug of home and hearth. No sense that he had left a heritage or that he belonged any one place. Maybe he'd been a rolling stone. Maybe that's where this pull he felt to *keep going* came from.

While his ultimate destination continued to evade him, the direction felt right. Heading east also got them farther from San Diego.

Erin had remained quiet since learning about Winchette's death. They had obviously been close. Or had they? He remembered she said her father worked with Winchette, that they'd been friends. *Once.* As if maybe they hadn't been later on.

Max didn't share her grief or whatever she felt, but he allowed her space.

He used the driving time to think—or not think— which became an experiment of sorts.

Trying to recall virtually anything from his past gave him a headache. And rather than risk the pain escalating to the point of blinding him, he would purposely switch his thoughts to something different— the billboards, other cars, numbers, Erin—until the pain receded.

Interestingly, after dropping the effort to remember details, he was frequently rewarded with a clue about the same matter. *Boom!* A bit of data would surface in his mind.

Unfortunately, the phenomenon wasn't consistent. When he tried to do it more intentionally, he failed.

That same lack of consistency applied to other areas, like trying to read Erin's mind. One moment her thoughts were transparent, easy to slip between. She'd been thinking about her father and Dr. Winchette working together. The moment after that, he'd hit a brick wall.

The same brick wall he kept hitting every time he attempted to reach Taz. Was Taz having this problem, too? Or did the problem lie within Max? Had this head injury/amnesia bullshit that was disrupting his memory also screwed up the link to Taz?

Or was something wrong on Taz's end? Was Taz injured? Unconscious? Dead?

A memory of Rufin warning against interrupting Taz's procedure came to mind. What had Rufin meant by that? Jesus, had Max inadvertently short-circuited his friend's brain?

Max's headache spiraled. Immediately, he shifted his attention back to the road.

They were traveling a dusty two-lane highway. Avoiding the more heavily patrolled interstate meant slowing down as they passed through tiny towns. Which gave Max a chance to watch for another vehicle.

Assuming the worst case meant he had to presume the CIA had already discovered where he'd left Erin's rental car. A quick rewind on the security tapes from the remote parking lot meant they'd also know exactly what Max had driven off in. The camper-pickup was now a liability. And they'd likely be watching other airport parking lots, too.

Good thing there were plenty of other choices.

He circled the block and pulled around behind an old filling station. The CLOSED sign in the front window wasn't what caught his eye. The portable sign near the road had. CONSTRUCTION AUCTION SAT. NIGHT, it read. Arrows pointed to the adjacent fenced-in lot filled with dump trucks, backhoes, cement mixers, and an assortment of passenger vehicles that looked destined for a junkyard.

Erin sat up. "Why are we stopping here? Did you remember where you're supposed to meet Taz?"

"No. We need a different vehicle."

"So you're just going to steal another one?" The contempt in her voice was undeniable. She probably thought he was a weasel.

"Yes. I'm stealing another car." At least he was an honest weasel.

He attempted to reach for her thoughts, but it backfired with a spike of pain. He winced.

She unbuckled her seat belt and scooted close. "Max, we need to get you to a hospital."

"That's not going to happen. Voluntarily at least. Look, you asked to come along. If you'd like to part ways now, you can stay here." He didn't want her to leave, not until they'd found Taz. Maybe not even then.

"I do want to help you." She sounded sincere. "I just don't want to cause anyone else harm or end up in jail."

"You won't. Gather our things. I'll be right back." Climbing out of the truck, he grabbed a few tools from the back of the camper.

The building didn't have an alarm, and in less than a minute, Max jimmied the lock and slipped inside. Greasy gears and spare parts were scattered all over the floor. The desk was covered with tools and oil cans, but beside it was a small file cabinet marked KEYS/TITLE.

Max pried the handle lock off and tugged the drawer open. Several sets of keys were tagged

TAURUS. He grabbed all of them, then lifted a pair of bolt cutters from the desk.

Erin sat on the truck's bumper, their bags at her feet.

"Hang tight," he said.

The bolt cutters worked magic on the locked fence chain. He pulled the truck inside the lot and closed the gate. The first two cars he tried had dead batteries. The third fired right up.

They didn't speak again until Max was headed back to the interstate driving a dusty blue Taurus.

"Is that what they teach on The Farm?" she asked.

She was, of course, referring to the CIA's covert training facility, nicknamed The Farm.

"Do you mean breaking and entering, or how to use bolt cutters?"

"Either."

"I don't remember."

"Amnesia or selective memory?"

"A little of both."

"So what next?" she asked.

"When we were being held, Taz and I agreed that if we escaped and were separated, we'd go to a special meeting place."

"You remembered!" Her voice was animated as if she was pleased he was opening up to her. "That's great. Where?"

"I don't know. I'm getting everything in half measure. That's one of the halves still missing." Max glanced at the rearview to assure no one followed. "You mentioned hypnosis earlier. Could it help me retrieve the missing parts of my memory?"

"Possibly. Have you ever been hypnotized before?"

"No. What do you need to do it?"

She sat up straight. "Mainly, we need a quiet place. Somewhere you feel comfortable enough to relax. The process itself is fairly simple. I'll guide you, verbally, through a series of mind and body relaxation techniques with the intent of getting you into a trancelike state. Then I'll make suggestions that you recall previous exchanges with Taz."

"And what if I'm not gullible enough to hypnotize?"

She gave him a look. "You need to be open to the idea, or it won't work. It's also not unusual for it to take more than one session. Ideally, it should be done in a clinical setting and—"

"That's not going to happen."

"Nonetheless, as a doctor, I'm obligated to point that out."

"I'd say our situation is beyond the scope of legal disclaimers, but you bring up a good point." He glanced sideways at her. "You may be a doctor, but I'm not your patient, Erin. I never hired you. And if anyone assigned you by proxy, I hereby revoke it. Now here's what I suggest: Let's get a few more miles down the road, and then we'll find a motel. It's the middle of the afternoon, so most places off the interstate ought to be quiet. Worst case, we can clean up and grab a little sleep. We only got about four hours last night."

"Is there any way I can call and get more news about Dr. Winchette? Maybe at a pay phone?"

He detected the slight catch in her voice. "We'll come up with something. Tell me more about Dr.

Winchette. You said he was an associate of your late father's. Did you lose your father recently?"

She nodded, but didn't elaborate. He caught a fleeting image of hostility. Had Erin and her father not gotten along well?

Max suddenly had a spontaneous memory of his own parents. "My father was an alcoholic. He died when I was twelve."

"And your mother?"

He tried to recall her. "She . . . left when I was born and died a short time afterward. I've only seen photographs of her."

"What about siblings? Extended family?"

A memory glimmered close, then disappeared, leaving him frustrated. "No brothers or sisters. My uncle, Stony, raised me. Stony was . . . a good man." Max slowed, changing lanes. His head had started to ache again. Big surprise. "It's strange, feeling like I have to dig for my own past."

"Don't push it," Erin said. "Just let it come naturally."

"That's part of the problem. Nothing feels natural. Right now I feel like I have to weigh each memory to be sure it's legit."

"Do you feel some memories are not legitimate?"

He recalled the dream he's woken to that morning. The dead man lying at his feet. The image returned now, but instead of a broken neck, it seemed that the man's throat was slit.

"I'm not certain." What he was certain of was that his headache had suddenly flared dramatically. *Don't think and it goes away.*

He directed his focus to the passing scenery. "How does that one sound?" He pointed out the window to a faded billboard. "Sunset Inn. Clean, quiet rooms. Next exit."

"Sounds great."

Max stopped and filled the car's fuel tank first. Erin wasn't hungry, but he picked up snacks and bottled water before heading for the motel.

There were two cars at the Sunset Inn. Max paid cash for the room and filled in the registration card as Mr. and Mrs. John Smith. The older gentleman behind the counter didn't bat an eye.

They were assigned a corner room on the far end. Max brought their bags inside the musty-smelling room before fiddling with the ancient air conditioner.

"Will that be too noisy?" he asked after Erin came out of the bathroom.

"You tell me. Actually, it might help filter out road noise. White sound."

"So how are we doing this?" He sat on the bed and watched as she pulled the heavy drapes shut. Since she'd left the bathroom light on, the room wasn't completely dark.

She had dragged the straight-back chair in the corner closer to the bed.

"Basically, you close your eyes and follow my voice. I'll begin with some relaxation exercises, getting you to tense then release certain muscles. Don't try to anticipate what I'm going to say next. Just relax into the moment. It usually helps if I utilize imagery that's relaxing and secure to you. Most people use something like floating on a cloud, or swinging in a hammock."

"A cloud couldn't support my weight."

That made her smile, which in turn made him feel good. "Okay, scratch clouds," she said. "Give me a tangible description of tranquility."

"The ocean. A quiet beach. Not an island, though. Lots of sun."

"Waves? Seagulls?"

"Yes on the waves. But ditch the gulls." Max tugged off his shoes. "Can you do this without a swinging pocket watch?"

"That only happens in old movies."

"You promise I'm not going to start barking like a dog when someone says the number three?"

"That only happens in Vegas." She tilted her head to one side as if sensing his misgivings. "Worried?"

"Nah. Do I need to take off my clothes?"

"Max!"

"Kidding. Yeah, I am a little apprehensive." *Little?* "Just take it easy with me, okay? This being my first time and all."

"You'll do fine."

"Let me use the bathroom then." When he came out, he noticed that Erin had grabbed the small note pad from beside the phone.

"For notes," she said.

Max stretched out diagonally on the bed. "What kind of questions are you going to ask?"

"You want to know where you and Taz agreed to meet, right? I'll focus on that, ask you to remember talking with him and what you discussed. I suggest we keep it simple this first time. We can do another session later."

Max nodded. The throbbing pain was centered behind his eyes now, but he wasn't about to mention it, for fear Erin would refuse to go further. And now that he'd made up his mind, he wanted to get on with it.

"Let's do it."

Pushing aside her misgivings was easier than Erin would have believed. Max agreeing to try hypnosis was major. If she stuck to her guns, insisting that it only be done in a conventional clinical setting, Max would refuse.

She hoped that if they had even a partially successful session, Max would agree to return to San Diego. She briefly considered formulating a mild suggestion that they surrender, but ultimately rejected the idea as too manipulative.

One of the basic tenets of hypnosis was transparency, honesty. They were after the truth—Max's unadulterated memories. Neutrality on her part was crucial; that he trust her was equally crucial.

She had few expectations about the outcome, but she hid her pessimism from Max to avoid influencing his own attitude toward the process. His belief that he could go under and magically retrieve his lost memories would hopefully make it easier for him to relax.

Like a lot of people, Max misunderstood and resisted the notion of hypnosis. To some it smacked of silly stage acts; to others it flirted with mind control.

And if anyone had the right to fear mind control, he did.

Once he settled down, she took her time guiding him through a series of rote relaxation exercises. She was careful to keep the guided imagery of the ocean and beach quiet but not isolated.

It took almost twenty minutes before she noticed his facial muscles relaxing. The line of apprehension that had marred his brow seemed to ease right before her eyes.

"You're safe and in full control, Max," she repeated, before beginning another relaxation sequence to take him deeper.

When she'd finished that, his breathing was shallow and his mouth gaped open slightly.

"I want you to think of your friend, Taz. The two of you were close," Erin began. "You trusted one another. You depended on each other. You had a bond."

Max nodded almost imperceptibly.

"And that bond grew stronger with each day you were together. You discussed plans about helping each other. You can recall the sound of his voice as he spoke. You agreed to meet someplace if you were separated. Nod if you recall talking about that meeting place."

Again Max nodded. Erin glanced at the clock. Nearly thirty minutes had passed. That was enough for now.

"You will recall everything you've remembered upon awakening, Max. Now it's time to return." She began a reverse counting sequence to bring him back to normal alertness while assuring him that the process could be readily repeated in the future.

"And, one. Open your eyes, feeling refreshed and alert and able to recall everything easily."

Max blinked and drew in a deep breath, but he didn't move.

"Pretty relaxed?" she prompted.

He closed his eyes and nodded.

"What do you remember, Max?" she asked. It wasn't unusual for a patient to want to drift off to sleep. But discussing the session first was important. Talking also reengaged their attention.

"The beach." Max turned toward her and looked directly into her eyes. Then he patted the edge of the mattress. "Sit here. And I'll tell you."

Erin moved without thought. Max looked so tranquil, so at ease. *Don't break the spell.*

His gaze held hers as she eased onto the bed. In the dim light his eyes took on that silver glint again.

"Tell me what you remember," she said again.

Max rolled onto his side, drawing closer as he faced toward her. His thighs pressed against her buttocks, but when she went to scoot forward, his hand touched her waist.

"Don't. Stay. Please."

Once again, with the "please" she didn't move. *Couldn't* move.

His hand stroked her side lightly as he began to talk, speaking so low she had to lean in to catch his words.

"The ocean. The beach. There were no footprints in the sand but ours. We had the entire cove to ourselves. You took off your shirt . . ."

She felt his fingers skim lightly across the bare skin at her lower back. He rose slightly, shifting his hands as he moved back to the middle of the bed, drawing Erin with him.

She went willingly. In her mind, she'd watched herself take off her shirt, then his. They were on the beach and he'd grown hard, his erection tenting the front of his swim trunks. Her hands closed over his hard length, groping him through the fabric as he stripped away her bikini top.

She drew a sharp breath, feeling his hands cup her bare breasts. His fingers teased and molded her before circling in and capturing the tips between finger and thumb. Her nipples responded to his touch, tightening. She moaned when he squeezed and tugged, and she realized he mimicked the motion of her hand as she rubbed and squeezed his cock.

"I want you," she whispered. And was rewarded with a kiss. His tongue swept inside her mouth. Bold. Precise and totally irresistible.

"Say my name," he commanded.

His hands swept down her sides. *Not where she wanted them.*

"Max."

As soon as she spoke, he bolted straight up and pushed her away.

Caught off balance, Erin tumbled to the floor and was jolted back to . . . what? Reality? She shook her head, feeling dizzy.

What had just happened?

"Hades," Max snapped. "I am Hades!" Then he started making a strangled sound.

Instantly, Erin pushed away the web of confusion and scrambled back to her feet. The strangled noise meant *seizure!*

"Max!"

He didn't respond, his eyes half shut and rolled back. His jaw clenched and his body shook violently as the seizure overtook him fully.

Erin turned and grabbed the phone off the night table, but there was no dial tone.

"D-d-don't," Max hissed.

She glanced over her shoulder. "I'm calling nine-one-one. This is serious."

He lunged forward, knocking the phone from her hand before grasping her wrists and tugging her down on the bed. His strength shocked her—superhuman yet controlled.

"It's me. Max. That other—"

"Hades? Who's that?"

"He'll never hurt you." Max panted now. "Sorry. *I'll* never hurt you."

His explanation cemented what Erin had begun to suspect: multiple personality disorder. His background would surely support it.

But one aspect didn't fit. What about when she'd felt driven to seduce him? When she'd imagined them together at the beach. It was like they'd shared a dream.

"It's complicated . . ." he said.

She drew a sharp breath. "You're reading my mind!"

"Not . . . not now. Give me a minute." He was shaking now, clearly in pain.

"Shhh. Don't talk. Just relax." She grasped for his wrist, found his pulse elevated. Almost immediately it started to drop.

He released a sigh. "Don't let go. Your touch grounds me."

She tried for a softer approach. "Max, please. Let me call for an ambulance."

"I'll be fine. And—" He took a deep breath and shook his head, as if to clear it. "It worked, Erin. I made contact with Taz."

Chapter 18

The session with Erin had gone better—and worse—than Max had expected.

His skepticism that hypnosis wouldn't work on him had begun to erode while listening to her voice. Before starting, he'd seen enough of her thoughts to judge her honest, and that initial thread of trust had allowed him to relax.

It felt like he'd gone under immediately. The headache that had been present all day had even seemed to lighten, morphing into a sexual high when he subsequently projected her into the beach scenes alongside him.

Yours for the taking, mate.

The command had come out of nowhere. He heard Taz's voice and it confused him. Rejecting Taz's command, however, had plucked Max away from Erin, plunging him instead into darkness, pinning him to the ground with a crushing force.

But in the depths of that hell, Max had found

memories. Not all were good. When he tried to explore the dark caverns further, the pain spiked to an excruciating level. *Taz, where the hell are you?*

Erin had been his lifeline out of the darkness. She had touched him and he'd wanted to live, to survive. *To know more of her touch.*

Max had literally fought his way back to consciousness, fought to bring back a few precious recollections. But at what cost?

"Did he hurt you?" Max demanded.

"He?" Erin repeated.

"Hades."

Her eyes grew guarded. He had no strength left to probe her thoughts, forcing him to communicate the regular way. With words.

"I'm sorry for whatever he did."

Erin shook her head. "Nothing really happened. Nothing bad anyway."

"We were on the beach together, right?" he asked.

She nodded. "This is embarrassing . . . but do you remember kissing me?"

He'd done more than kiss her. He'd removed her shirt.

"Yeah. We did it in the sand." At her blush, Max apologized again. "I mean, I had this image of us, together. We were alone and things got . . . romantic."

"I wore a red bikini under my shirt. You had on black trunks. I think we both remember what occurred next. In our imaginations," she hastened to add. "Max, I'd say you're doing something more than mind reading. You projected images and—"

"And what?"

"You, or a part of you, may have manipulated my

reaction somewhat. I felt *compelled*. And you acted differently when you first came to."

"Different how?" Max asked.

"More calculating."

"It wasn't me. It was Hades."

"Max, I suspect Hades is a name for an aspect of yourself created as a defense mechanism to help you cope with abuse."

"Stop right there." Max finally got a few of her thoughts—enough to know she thought he was a potential nut job. "It's not a multiple personality disorder. At least not in the conventional sense. I didn't create it. *They* did. Hades was a character, a role, I played." He stopped and rubbed his head.

"You're hurting again," she said.

"But not for the reason you think. These headaches, the seizures, are booby traps. When I try to remember what I did while held overseas, it triggers an internal meltdown. Part of me wants to turn it off, but at the same time I know I'm getting closer to the truth. The hypnosis helped. I definitely want to try it again."

"Fine. But I won't be the one to do it." She shook her head, adamant. "You need to be back in the hospital, Max. These seizures could be causing damage you're unaware of. It's imperative to find their cause and get them under control."

"Your concerns are duly noted."

"Meaning you have no intention of taking them seriously."

"Not until I've found Taz."

"You mentioned making contact with him. Are you telepathic, too?"

"I don't know what you call it exactly, but Taz and I are able to communicate, at times by thought, sometimes with images. Occasionally I hear his voice. It's far from flawless and is never consistent."

"Do you know where he is now?"

"I'm not sure. He wouldn't reveal that." The connection Max had made with Taz had been brief but powerful. *Remember our plan.* "I think he's sick. He damn sure doesn't trust anyone. But he's acting on our plan. We agreed to meet at a certain cave, if we escaped and became separated. Or leave a message there."

"Was this a cave overseas?"

"No. I don't think so. In fact, I'm sure it's one from my childhood. Taz spent a summer in California as a teenager, whereas I grew up traveling all over the West. We used to talk about it. Taz probably knows my childhood stories better than I do right now."

Erin seemed to relax now as if convinced that Max wasn't loony.

"Did any of those stories involve caves?" she asked.

"Most all of them. My Uncle Stony had gold fever. His father had supposedly discovered a gold vein in an abandoned mine, but he died before disclosing specifics. Stony inherited his father's maps and journals. Every summer after the snow melted, we'd hike up into the mountains, retracing his father's expeditions, looking for the mother lode."

"Did he find it?"

"No." It angered Max that he had to wrestle to

get to that precious legacy of memories. "Stony died eight years ago. I was in the Army at the time. Stony went out alone and suffered a heart attack. Some hikers found him, but it was too late."

"I'm sorry, Max. It's hard to lose someone."

The pain in her voice was tangible, making him wonder if she, too, had been away when her father had died. Before he could ask, she changed the subject.

"Is there a particular cave that comes to mind when you think of your uncle?" she asked. "One that sticks out even if you don't recall why?"

"That would be the cave where my uncle died." Max shook his head. "The irony is I've been meaning to go back there, but never have. That's got to be the one."

"So where is it?"

"I'd rather not say." He met her gaze squarely. "It's not that I don't trust you, Erin, it's just that, I believe you'd tell someone, thinking it was in my best interests."

Her eyes narrowed. "You intend to go off alone, don't you? Max, please, I urge you not to—"

"I'm the only person Taz will trust, the only person who can convince him we're safe." *You'll never be safe. You will never be free. We will find you.* "I owe him a hell of a lot."

"I understand you feel a sense of obligation, but to risk your life helps no one."

Max felt his temper flare. "You know how many times I wanted to die over there? Just give up, eat a bullet? Taz never let me forget that if we died, they won. We knew that we had to live to put an end to what they were doing."

"What were they doing?" Erin's voice was raspy. "I saw pictures. A chamber."

"We were being brainwashed—reprogrammed. In a very ugly way. Trained to be robotic killing machines who'd stop at nothing to get the job done. No questions asked."

"Oh, God, Max."

"Near the end, I think they figured out Taz and I were each other's only hope. So if I didn't perform flawlessly, Taz paid the price. I remember him being strung up and whipped because of something I did or didn't do. I begged them to cut him down, to whip me instead. The whole time Taz sent me messages to shut up. That he could take it. That I should be stronger." Max met her gaze. "Nobody but me can go after him."

Her next words surprised him.

"Let me stay with you, Max. What if you have another seizure and fall off a cliff before you get to the cave?"

"Getting to this cave doesn't involve climbing, just hiking."

"Then think about Taz. I'm not an M.D., but I've had experience with patients suffering severe PTSDs. If he's confused, paranoid, maybe I can help. You also have to acknowledge that he, too, could be having seizures, Max."

Her points were all valid. Underlying that was the fact that Max wanted Erin to stay. He tried to read her thoughts, but sparks of pain erupted in his mind. Suddenly he felt raw. Vulnerable. His body felt on the verge of shutting down again.

"Before you agree to go with me, we need to get clear on a couple points," Max said. "First, I'm in charge. And you don't strike me as the type to take orders blindly."

"What's the next point?"

"This thing between us. I'm attracted to you, Erin. Deeply. Sexually. And while I'd never force myself on you, I'm no gentleman. You say 'yes'—and I'll be on top of you like that!" He snapped his fingers. "And before you start that doctor-patient rant again, I'll remind you we have no professional relationship."

"Um. Wow." She cleared her throat. When she spoke again, she looked him straight in the eye. "I suggest we both try to back-burner our personal feelings. Things are . . . complicated enough without that. Let's concentrate on finding Taz."

"Agreed."

"And after we explore this cave, we need to go back, Max. My boss is dead. I have responsibilities. You, too. There is a limit to how much longer we can keep on like this. Stealing cars. Sneaking around. It feels like we're Bonnie and Clyde."

"If it's any consolation, I plan to take full responsibility for all of it. Except Winchette's death, of course." He pushed up and for a moment he was tempted to kiss her. Except a kiss would only be the beginning.

He sighed. "Then let's get back on the road, Bonnie."

Chapter 19

Rufin perched nervously on the very end of the crowded bench, hiding behind a newspaper while pretending to read. He kept his left foot poised, ready to flee at the first sign of trouble.

He'd been sitting there for an hour, a total nervous wreck, watching the shop across the street. Would Bohdana show?

After days of hiding in narrow garbage-filled back alleys, avoiding most everyone, it now seemed strange to be out in such an open space. That no one even spared him a second glance made it slightly easier for him to breathe.

It was still hard to believe he'd managed to escape the Americans who'd destroyed the lab. *Destroyed his life.* The off-duty guard, who had returned early from collecting supplies, had inadvertently saved Rufin's life that day by opening fire on the Americans. Unfortunately, when the Americans fired back, the guard had sought refuge inside the lab, not realizing the building had been rigged to blow up.

And when it blew, Rufin's plight had grown even bleaker. If the Thai government knew he survived, they'd hold him responsible for everything: the loss of the lab, the loss of the data to the Americans, and the loss of the last two test subjects.

He prayed that the Thais believed him dead or captured. Dead would be better.

Rufin had ended up helping himself to the dead guard's ancient motor bike and backpack, riding it nonstop—certain the hounds of hell were after him. Before reaching Bangkok, he shaved his head in an attempt to alter his appearance. Selling the motorbike netted him some money, most of which he still had. But he'd need much more to buy papers to get passage out of the country.

It had taken tremendous courage to venture into an Internet café and set up an e-mail account. He'd been so certain that half the world was searching for him. To not be taken down by a swarm of police made him feel slightly braver.

To his surprise, Bohdana had replied quickly with the shocking news that she was also in Bangkok, having fled Jakarta in the wake of Zadovsky's death.

I have been grief stricken, she wrote, *afraid you had been apprehended.* Her cryptic e-mail went on to caution him against trusting anyone. *The authorities are seeking any and all known associates.*

Associates of Zadovsky's, no doubt.

After outlining her fears for her own safety, she agreed to meet Rufin but only if she selected the spot. She was still so naively trusting that it made him want to cry. The memories of their friendship before Zadovsky's death came back over him. They'd met only twice, but Bohdana had immediately latched on to him as if sensing a kindred soul. *"I'm glad to meet someone else who works selflessly for Dr. Zadovsky but is not appreciated,"* she'd whispered.

She had been the only person on earth he could discuss work with. The only person he ever really trusted. For the first time in days, Rufin had felt hopeful.

Now that hope blossomed to adoration as Bohdana arrived across the street. *I'll wear a red hat,* she had informed him

He almost whimpered at the sight of her. She'd lost weight. And he'd never seen her wearing such drab clothing. He watched as she milled about for a while, before paying for her groceries. Heading west, away from the market, Bohdana walked a short distance and turned down a less busy street.

Rufin stood and loped along behind her. He still hadn't decided what to tell her. Some version of the truth since he wasn't good at outright lies, but preferably something that didn't make him sound like such a fool.

Prior to the American raid, Rufin had been working diligently on his own plan to flee the lab, a painstaking plan that had included copying all critical research. Research he'd intended to use as a bargaining chip with another country. How ironic that the Americans had been at the top of his list.

Even more insane was the fact that Rufin still toyed with the idea of going to the U.S. Embassy and requesting asylum. Except without Taz, he had no proof, no bargaining chip.

In their zeal to come to the rescue, the Americans had virtually signed Taz's death warrant. Rufin had seen more than one test subject die from the violent seizures induced by faulty or interrupted programming.

Still, if the Americans had Taz's body, there was a chance.

That was one of the things he wanted to broach with Bohdana. If she would agree to accompany him to the Embassy and corroborate his story . . .

Up ahead, Bohdana turned toward a rundown high-rise. She had suggested they meet at her girlfriend's flat. And since her friend was away visiting family, Bohdana had hinted that Rufin could hide there a day or two. The woman was truly an answered prayer.

She disappeared inside the building. Rufin watched for a few minutes then went in. Following her instruction, he made his way to the fifth floor and rapped nervously on the door.

Bohdana opened it and pulled him inside with a high-pitched squeal. "I have worried about you!"

"You d-d-don't know how good it is to see you."

She wrinkled her nose, reminding him of how long it had been since he'd bathed. He took a step back and she seemed relieved.

She waved him toward the main room and moved back to the kitchen. "Go. Sit. I'll bring in food and tea."

But before he even took a step, knocking sounded at the door.

Rufin froze. Bohdana pressed a finger to her lips and eased forward.

The door burst open before she reached it. A tall, blond man stepped inside, holding a handgun. The silencer attached to the gun's barrel made it look longer. More menacing.

And it was pointed straight at Rufin.

Bohdana was talking so fast he could scarcely keep up. It was evident that she had expected this man. Her betrayal sickened Rufin. He prayed he'd pass out before the man pulled the trigger.

The man swung sideways, slamming the door behind him. Bohdana drew a sharp breath as the gun leveled at her now. She turned and ran back in the kitchen. The first shot blew off half her head.

Rufin dropped to his knees, retching as the second shot rang in his ears. He began sobbing uncontrollably. This was it. He was next.

"Come on! We've got to get out of here," the man said. "Before the others arrive."

Rufin blinked through his tears. "Others?"

"Don't you get it? She set you up. Sold you out. The Thai secret police are on their way. Let's go! I've got a car outside."

Stumbling to his feet, Rufin kept his eyes averted, away from the kitchen. He focused on the man who'd saved him.

The stranger was a Westerner. Though wearing civilian clothes and a flashy gold watch that made him look like a tourist, the man had the same build, the same chilling confidence, as the Americans who'd raided the lab. He even handled his weapon the same way.

They had come back for him! They would protect him from the Thai agents! Rufin felt fresh tears of relief blurring his vision.

Outside, the distant sounds of a siren, an everyday noise in Bangkok, took on new meaning. They were after *him*.

"We must hurry," Rufin said, panicking anew. "I swear, I'll tell you everything. Just don't let them get me."

The man flashed a cold smile. "I've got it covered. No worries."

Chapter 20

"You said you had good news." Abe Caldwell started speaking as soon as Tommy Groene came into his office.

He had just poured a cup of coffee. His first. Tara had met him at six in the private gym downstairs and run him through a grueling workout. A self-proclaimed "personal trainer with a twist," she'd finished off his session with an equally grueling round of sex. Her version of cardiofuck.

Thanks to Tara's skills, Abe's body looked more thirty-five than forty-nine. And thanks to one of his grandfather's more creative ventures with the late Victor Zadovsky, Abe's legendary sexual stamina delivered on the promise his well-sculpted body made.

How ironic that, thanks to Zadovsky's death, Abe was being forced to go public with that precious formula. All the major pharmaceutical companies had their own version of sexual enhancement drugs, cleverly marketed to aid erectile dysfunction. Caldwell Pharmaceuticals would have the twist of multiple orgasms. For *men* and women.

Without thought, Abe reached for a cigarette. He stopped.

That he chose not to smoke right now had nothing to do with his doctor's advice. It was about habitual behavior. Self-control. Willpower. Now there was a dream drug yet to be made.

Abe carried his coffee back to his desk. "Out with it."

"Allen picked up the signal again last night, in southern Arizona. This time he was able to get close enough to visually confirm it was Max Duncan. A woman was with him; her description matches that of Dr. Houston."

Abe's cup clattered against the saucer. "You haven't said they were eliminated."

"They were on the interstate. Too many witnesses and traffic cameras. Then a storm hit and Allen lost the signal. They got separated."

"Goddamnit." Abe snatched up a cigarette, but didn't light up. Yet. Lost and intermittent signals were just one of the things that kept the tracker technology off the market. For now. "Did he get a tag number? Description?"

Tommy nodded. "It came back registered to a junk dealer, who does not appear to have any connection to Duncan. It's likely stolen, though it hasn't been reported yet."

"Let's hope it stays that way. All I need is for the CIA to waltz in and spring Duncan from jail for auto theft." He lit up and inhaled deeply. "Now what?"

"Triangulation is a little harder in the area Allen lost him. But sooner or later Duncan will move back in range."

The beacon implanted in Max Duncan piggy-backed off cell phone towers. All the same problems encountered with cell service sometimes made it difficult to pick up a signal.

"If Duncan gets too far ahead, tell Allen to rent a helicopter," Abe said. "Tell him, I said no more excuses. His next call better be for body bags."

Tommy took a sip of coffee before continuing. The porcelain cup looked awkward in Tommy's large hands. "Allen was confident he'd catch up and eliminate them by nightfall."

"As much as I like the sound of that, it strikes me as optimistic."

"I agree. Which is why I think I should still go to California with the second tracker to look around for John Doe. It could speed up the process."

"I'm beginning to wonder if Doe's beacon is working," Abe said. That Allen had picked up only one signal, the one they now knew belonged to Max Duncan, seemed to confirm that the other beacon had malfunctioned. "Let's hold off on that. What have you got on the CIA's investigation?"

"They're floating the story that Duncan came to in a panic and killed Winchette accidentally. Since the CIA called Winchette in to consult on this case, they're taking responsibility, but distancing themselves. It appears the initial questions they were asking about Dr. Houston's father's ties to Dr. Winchette were simply to get information on her."

"That's a relief." It had been problematic enough erasing the trail between some old research Erin's father had worked on decades ago with Dr. Winchette. Abe didn't want that can of worms reopened. "And Winchette's files?"

"His home was sanitized last night. His personal computer and files were swapped with look-alikes so nothing appears disturbed."

Abe wondered what other secrets Winchette's records might yield about personal pet projects or even about certain competitors of Caldwell Pharmaceuticals. Of course, the latter called for even greater discretion as the fiasco with Erin's father had proven.

How unfortunate the late Dr. Marvin Houston had recognized a portion of his old research that had accidentally been used verbatim in a study. That the old research had been *classified* at least made it easier to insinuate that Houston had sold the data himself.

"Once Winchette's death is publicly announced," Tommy went on, "our PR department can issue a condolence statement, acknowledging Caldwell Pharmaceuticals' R and D relationship with Winchette's hospital. Everyone else will do likewise."

Listening to Tommy calmly outline plans deepened Abe's faith in him. For the first time in days, Abe felt cautiously optimistic. With Salvador's promise of financial backing and full access to Winchette's private records, the future didn't look as bleak.

Abe's private line rang just then. He glanced at the display then back at Tommy. "If you'll excuse me."

Tommy stood and offered the standard "call me if you need me" farewell.

Abe picked up the line. "Tell me you found him."

"Yeah," Harry said.

The news that Dr. Rufin had been apprehended had Abe springing up from his seat. "Where is he?"

"On ice. The heat here is tremendous."

"What do you need to get him out?"

"I'm handling that. The fewer people who know, the less the chance for an interception."

Abe paced, resisting the urge to bark a command. Harry wasn't as compliant as Tommy. He also wasn't an employee. And at moments like this, the man was irreplaceable. Problem was, he knew it.

"I have certain resources," Abe began.

"Resources you're going to need for something else," Harry asserted. "I don't have much time, so I suggest you let me finish. Apparently Rufin was concerned that the Thai government was going to take him out, so he fashioned his own plan to escape with the data."

The news, as sweet as it sounded, was being delivered in a tone that promised another shoe was about to drop.

Harry went on. "Rufin loaded the information on microchips that he then implanted inside the test subject known as Taz, aka John Doe. In the process, he removed Taz's tracking beacon."

Abe swore. That explained why Allen had picked up only one signal. "And how did Rufin expect to keep tabs on this man?"

"Taz was being programmed to stay with Rufin and to find him if they were parted. But the process wasn't completed. As it turns out, Max Duncan may be our ace in the hole. Rufin claims the two men had a way to communicate, even if separated. He swears Duncan can lead you to Taz. Shit! Someone's coming. I've got to go."

"Wait! I want Rufin."

"Get Taz and we'll negotiate that point. And don't get any ideas. Without Rufin to retrieve and transcribe that data, Taz is worthless."

The line went dead, leaving Abe furious. Harry just loved to play like he was an arrogant hotshot, holding all the aces.

Abe punched in Tommy's number and began snapping orders as soon as he answered. "Get ahold of Allen. Big change of plans. I need Max Duncan captured alive!"

Chapter 21

Reno, Nevada
September 23

Taz climbed down from the cab of the tractor trailer, backpack in hand. It was nearly 10 p.m., but the Double-D Truck Stop was open till midnight.

"Sorry to see you go." Larry, the truck driver who'd picked him up in Bakersfield that morning, held out a creased business card. "I'm in and out of here two, three times a week. Always looking for good help."

In addition to hitching a ride, Taz had ended up working as Larry made deliveries. It got them out of California faster, made being incognito much easier, and earned him a little extra cash.

The physical activity had helped to clear his head. And strangely, Larry's off-key singing seemed to hold Taz's headache at bay. Kill pain with pain, right?

In the middle of the afternoon he had an epiphany. He'd damn near passed out with it, but after tossing his cookies, it all became clear. He knew exactly where to find Hades.

And Hades would help him make sense of the other problems.

"Hey, you go inside the diner and find a blonde with big tits, named Linda," Larry said. "Tell her I sent you and she'll treat you right."

"Thanks, mate."

Inside the diner, a waitress called out, "Seat yourself. Be right with you."

Taz climbed into a corner booth and unfolded the map he had just purchased at the attached convenience store.

Mission incomplete.

Find Hades.

Find Rufin.

He pressed his temples, trying to ease the blurring pain that accompanied the screeching dissonance of his thoughts. Damn if he wouldn't welcome Larry's singing right now. Unable to read, he shoved the map aside and fumbled for the pocket knife tucked in the side of his backpack.

The blade was razor sharp. Like everything else in the pack, it was top quality. The guy he'd stolen it from had obviously been a pro.

After eliminating Dr. Winchette, Taz had hitch-hiked north, to Mojave. He'd had a faint memory of hiking in a nearby canyon as a teenager. He had staked out one of the trailheads and waited until a lone hiker came in.

Taz attacked the guy and shoved his unconscious body in the trunk after pulling out his gear. Stealing the car was out since the keys were in the guy's pocket and other vehicles were headed in.

The pack turned out to be well equipped. While Taz could have survived easily on his own, the clothes and food were a bonus. And the gear gave him legitimacy as a vacationing hitchhiker.

"You okay, hon?" The waitress had come up and spotted the dark stain of blood on his pants.

Fortunately, the knife was out of view. Taz tugged the map onto his lap before offering the same excuse he'd given Larry.

"I cut my thigh on a rock face while climbing. It's not as bad as it looks, Linda." He squinted at the blonde's name tag, pinned between her large breasts. "Dang thing broke open while I helped Larry unload at the last stop."

At the mention of a familiar name, she relaxed. "Larry Silvers?"

"Hi-yo Silver?" Taz's use of Larry's CB handle won him a smile.

"That rascal didn't come in to say hi? I'll remember that."

"He sent me instead."

Linda's eyes went over him. Again. "You'll do. What can I get you, hon?"

Taz ordered the special: double meatloaf. He craved protein.

As the restaurant emptied, Linda ended up spending more time at his table. Over the course of the next hour, Taz learned she was single and lonely. And judging by the pheromones she threw his way, she was also horny as hell.

"You're saving room for pie, right?" she teased when she collected Taz's empty plate.

"What kind you got?"

"Apple, peach, chocolate. Maybe blueberry, but that sells out fast."

"That'll do."

She blinked. "You mean . . . one of each?"

"With ice cream."

By the time Taz pushed away from the table, the diner was completely deserted. "Guess I better get moving if I want to hitch another ride."

"Where you headed?" Linda asked.

Taz held up his thumb. "Utah and Colorado."

"The highway will be slow till morning with all the road construction they do at night. But I'm headed up to the interstate. Meeting some friends at the Starlite. You could join us. Try your hand at slots. Maybe you'll get lucky." She winked as she spoke.

Taz nodded, recalling the one other thing that would ease pain.

Hades could wait.

So could Rufin.

Linda couldn't.

Chapter 22

It had been after midnight when Max and Erin reached the outskirts of Sedona. Shortly after leaving the Sunset Inn, they'd hit heavy rain, which had apparently triggered a catastrophic pileup that closed part of the interstate. It delayed them for hours.

Max had ended up pulling into a crowded rest stop near Sedona so they could grab a few hours' sleep. Erin wasn't eager to stop at a motel again, which was evident in the way she volunteered to climb into the backseat.

The cave Max was headed to was near the Red Rock–Secret Mountain Wilderness area. More childhood memories of exploring caves with Stony surfaced as they drew closer. But each seemed hard-won.

The more Max considered the ramifications of what had been done to him and Taz, the more infuriated he got. That none of his thoughts were complete didn't help. The feeling that he was missing *something* made him doubt and second-guess every single thought.

They awoke six hours later and cleaned up in the public bathrooms before heading off in search of food. Max found a small diner that had great food and coffee.

"Tables. Silverware," Erin joked. "If I never see another drive-through or have to use another spork, it will be too soon."

They lingered over breakfast. Erin sat across from him, reading a newspaper, while Max made notes from the phone book he'd borrowed from their waitress.

"No wanted posters," she said when she'd finished reading.

Max nodded at the newspaper. "It's unlikely you'll find news in there about Winchette's death. That'll be kept under wraps for as long as possible."

"I know."

The disappointment in her voice tugged at him. "After we check this cave, we'll try calling Dante."

"You don't sound convinced Taz will be there."

"If he's not, I'll leave a message, but—"

Max sat forward, almost like he'd been bumped. There were moments, like just now, when he swore he'd felt a connection with Taz. Something more than the perpetually echoing *remember our plan*.

And this connection felt . . . troubled.

Max closed his eyes, focusing inward as he tried to

send a mental image to Taz. Once again the attempt backfired, ratcheting up his ever-present headache.

"Max! Are you okay?"

Erin had slid into the seat beside him but it wasn't close enough. He wanted to pull her into his lap and—

"I'm fine." He blinked rapidly, trying to ease the sudden sensitivity to light.

"Liar." She reached for his wrist.

He started to pull away, but didn't. He wanted her touch. Even if it came wrapped in sympathy.

"My pulse is elevated, Erin," he said. *You do that to me.* "Already it's leveling out. It was nothing."

"You blacked out, Max. I called your name twice and you didn't respond." She reached for his chin, her voice low but firm. "Look at me. You have no business behind a wheel. It's one thing to be reckless with your own life. But what about the other innocent people on the roads? What about me?"

He wrapped his fingers around her hand. In her anger she had a death grip on his jaw.

"I'd never hurt you," he said. "And I did hear you call, but I ignored you because I was getting a memory."

Her expression softened. "What was it?"

"Nothing useful," he lied.

She tapped the phone book. "What were you looking up?"

"This particular cave is off the beaten path. If you're serous about hiking in with me, we need some gear."

"I do want to go, if for no other reason than to keep an eye on you."

He'd like more than her eyes on him. "Then let's get moving. We've got a few stops to make before we hit the trail."

They ended up finding clothes, boots, and a decent backpack at a secondhand shop, which conserved cash. They picked up a few provisions, then made a brief stop at the public library so Max could download a current topography map. He also got online to set up a free e-mail account using a false name.

"If Taz isn't at the cave, I'll leave him this e-mail address," Max explained. "We had agreed to use e-mail because it's anonymous." And if Taz *had* arrived first, he may have left a similar message for Max.

After consulting the map, Max drove out of Sedona, heading northwest. Yavapai County was awesome this time of year. He loved the red hues of the lower Rockies, the flat-topped mesas.

As if reading his mind, Erin made a sweeping gesture with her hand. "It's even more gorgeous than I'd imagined. The different rock formations are fascinating. Beautiful, yet barren."

He slowed. "I take it you haven't been here before."

"I grew up in Virginia, went to school in Maryland. A trip to the mountains meant driving to the Smokies. Did you spend a lot of time here? And if I'm asking too many questions, say so. It's not my intention to trigger a headache."

"Actually, the casual conservation, the speaking without much thought, helps. I'm kind of surprised by what flows out sometimes." He looked at her. "I probably jinxed myself saying that."

"Superstitious? Just knock on wood."

"Me? No. Stony was, though. He was obsessed with retracing his father's footsteps in the exact sequence."

"You said you moved around a lot. Where did you go to school?"

"Middle school was mostly on the Navaho reservation. As soon as school was out, we'd pack up and take off for a summer of mining. Later, Stony got a cabin in southern Colorado. We'd base out of there and divide our time between Utah, Wyoming, and Arizona. I graduated high school in Durango."

"Was your uncle ever successful?"

"Finding gold?" Max shook his head. "Not really. Just enough to keep him going. He was always so certain the next one would be the big one."

"Your voice lightens when you talk about him. You must have been very close."

"In every important way, Stony was a father to me. He was also the world's greatest uncle. We fished, we hunted, we camped, we explored. He knew stories about everything. Stony was fun." He glanced at her. "You haven't mentioned your father much. Does your voice lighten when you talk about him?"

"My father was . . . serious. Studious. A research scientist. Camping out meant sleeping on the sofa in his office while he worked late. In his own way he was fun. I miss him. Does that ever get better?"

Max sensed an underlying regret and something more, but he didn't pry. Only because he couldn't. "It never goes away, but it does get easier."

She nodded as he slowed and turned onto an unpaved road. "This is it?"

"The trailhead is not too far ahead. From there we'll hike in about four and a half miles. I'm taking a pack with food, water, and some emergency supplies, but I plan to be back out before nightfall. We don't have camping gear, though we wouldn't perish if we got stuck overnight. You good with all that?"

"I am."

Max steered around a deep rut in the road and stopped. "We'll leave the car here."

They had changed clothes in the library bathroom. Erin bent over to adjust the ties of her lightweight hiking boots. The jeans she wore hugged her ass, making Max wish she were leading their expedition.

Hoisting the backpack onto his shoulders, he adjusted the straps. The strong certainty he'd felt yesterday that this was the place to meet Taz seemed to have lessened.

Am I wrong to think this is where we're meeting? he wondered. He closed his eyes.

"It's important! Repeat after me." He had an image of him and Taz fighting—slugging each other as hard as they could. *"Repeat after me!"*

"Max? Are you getting something?"

He opened his eyes and nodded. "Taz and I were fighting, but it felt forced. Unnatural."

"Like you were being made to fight one another?"

"No. Well, maybe. Either way, it doesn't make sense."

"If you're recalling something out of context, it might not make sense now. Give it time. That you're getting more memories back is a good sign."

"You're sounding like a doctor again."

"Yeah, well, telling me to not sound like one is like telling a duck not to quack. It goes against the grain. Get over it."

He admired her spunkiness. "Then let's go. I'm eager to see if I remember the path."

The trail was easy at first, meandering along a dry creek bed. Erin found herself wanting to stop, to take it all in, but Max set a steady pace. The valley started off wide with lush spots of grass and yucca plants. As it narrowed, the canyon walls dazzled her eyes with layers of sandstone that swept up hundreds of feet.

After a couple miles, they followed another streambed into a smaller canyon. She'd been warm earlier, but in the shadowed canyon, her long sleeves felt good.

"Watch yourself here," Max said as they ascended a narrow bypass. A few minutes later they stopped.

He handed her a bottle of water. While she drank, he pointed to one of the cliff faces. "See that gray sandstone in the shape of a bird?"

Erin squinted, and then nodded.

"About a half mile beyond it is a waterfall. We'll

go off path then, for maybe a mile and a half. It'll be rockier terrain, so you'll have to watch your step."

They took off again. Erin noticed that Max grew quieter, more intense, the farther in they hiked. This was the place his uncle had died and it carried its own measure of emotion. Loss and grief were easy for her to understand; they were not only fresh memories for her; many patients had similar issues.

What Max was dealing with, however, was new ground. Personally and professionally. She'd worked with a few extreme cases, but what Max had endured and was still going through didn't happen that often.

Telepathy. Mind reading. Brainwashing. The mental and physical abuse he'd suffered while imprisoned. Combined, it made a strong case for any number of psychoses.

But she didn't believe Max was psychotic. She had experienced his powerful abilities to influence with that strange and erotic beach fantasy. And while at first she'd felt emotionally manipulated, she'd since come to realize that part of what she felt for Max was simply her own physical attraction. The man had rocked her world from the first moment she'd laid eyes on him. That undoubtedly made her more susceptible to influence.

On another level she was also troubled by the notion that her father may have been involved in mind control experiments. Not recently. But back when she was a child. Winchette hadn't exactly denied it, though he'd hinted that that type of research had been abandoned in the United States.

But what about elsewhere?

"Check it out," Max said.

They rounded on the waterfall now, but didn't stop as long as she would have liked to. The sparkling fall of water made her wish she had a camera.

As the ground took on a steeper incline, Erin had to concentrate on her footing. She found herself feeling edgy as they grew closer. If Taz was here, would he agree to return with them? What kind of physical shape was he in? Had he been troubled by headaches and seizures, too?

Just ahead Max stopped.

Erin shielded her eyes with her hands, following his gaze. She sensed they were close but where was the cave?

The canyon walls ahead were unusually bright, as if the sun hadn't baked them to a lighter color yet. Her eyes drifted lower as she tried to follow the ground, to see the way ahead. Max said no climbing was involved, but the ground here looked impassable.

"Rockslide," Max said.

His single word changed her view. The color difference she'd noticed in the wall, the brightness, the jagged edges, were all newly exposed rock. The old face of the wall lay crumbled in mounds on the ground.

"How do we get around it?" she asked.

"We don't." Max pointed. "It's gone, Erin. The entrance to the cave is a good fifty feet under that pile of rock."

She gasped. "Is Taz trapped?"

He shook his head. "It's not that recent of a land-slide."

"Should we go closer, see if he left a note or something?"

Max didn't answer. Instead he closed his eyes.

Was he recalling a memory? Or using telepathy? She knew now to simply wait. To watch for external signs of distress.

"He hasn't been here, Erin."

"We'll leave him a message, then."

"No. You don't understand. This isn't even the right cave." His voice grew sharp. "Taz is headed to Colorado."

"Do you know where in Colorado?"

"No. Damn it."

Chapter 23

By the time they returned to the car, Max's temper had evened out. He figured he owed Erin a dozen different apologies, but where to start?

Surprisingly, she'd kept up with his grueling pace without complaint. They'd come out of the canyon single-file, Max tossing the occasional "How you doing back there?" over one shoulder.

Her clipped "Fine" kept him moving.

While going downhill was easier, he'd left it up to her to call out if she needed a break. She hadn't and that allowed them to return in less time.

Outside of monosyllabic answers, Erin had remained virtually mute after Max snapped her head off.

Over her one innocent: "Now what?"

Max didn't have an answer, which royally pissed him off. Just the thought of having to say "I don't know" again set his teeth on edge.

The stuff he *didn't know* had piled up precariously,

a veritable mountain of crap that only got bigger. The questions were profound: *Where was Taz? What had Rufin done to them? What had they done for Rufin? Where were the missing pieces of Max's memory?*

How could he ever reclaim a life he couldn't recall?

He looked at Erin now. She leaned against the trunk. In spite of the fact she stared away from him, he noticed that her cheeks and nose were red; she was sunburned and breathing heavily, as if fighting tears.

The toll she'd paid was painfully apparent. God, he was an idiot. Grabbing a bottle of water, he cracked open the cap and held it out to her.

"Drink."

She glared at him and pushed his hand aside. "Leave me alone. I'm fine. Just unlock the car."

He set the water on the roof and moved to open the passenger door. That's when he realized how long they'd been gone. Jesus, it was nearly three o'clock and they hadn't eaten since breakfast.

Mr. Considerate, he'd stomped all the way back here, carrying the food on *his* back. That he'd been too angry to even think about eating was one thing. But totally forgetting her needs was unforgivable. He felt like such a shit right now. She had every right to hate his guts.

He turned to apologize. She had started to follow, to get in the car, but now stopped. He had seen her limp. It was evident that it hurt to take even a step. Now he felt worse than shit.

"I'm sorry, Erin." He swept her off her feet. Ignoring her protests, he set her lightly on the trunk.

Loosening the laces of her right boot, he gently tugged it off and peeled away the sock. Two large bloody blisters marred the back of her heel, and another on her big toe and pinky toe. He cursed himself for not thinking about checking the fit of the hiking boots they'd got for her at the secondhand store.

He removed the other boot, found more blisters there. Grabbing the bottle of water, he rinsed her feet. She drew in a sharp breath. He knew they hurt like hell.

"Why didn't you say something?"

She pulled her foot out of his grasp. "I was afraid you'd leave me."

"I'd never—"

She cut him off. "You'd have sent someone out to get me—but you'd have been long gone. I realized you were pissed. I also kept hoping you'd calm down."

Max stepped away to grab the backpack. Erin shifted as if to climb down.

"Stay put," he said.

"I'm not a damn dog, Max. Stay. Drink. Roll over."

"Please, Erin, don't move. I just want to grab the first aid kit." He shifted back to her, preventing her from sliding down. The anger had drained from him, but not from her. And rightfully so. "I owe you an apology. I was an inconsiderate ass back there. Hell, I was probably one before that. I've dragged you into something terrible and now you're paying a painful price."

He set the white plastic kit with the big red cross on the trunk beside her and flipped it open. He'd bought it in case Taz needed attention—he hadn't thought of Erin then either.

He grabbed the antibiotic salve and several bandages.

"These blisters will need to be cleaned with peroxide. This will help until we can find a drugstore. You'll need a pair of flip-flops, too. You won't be in shoes anytime soon. Are you allergic to aspirin or ibuprofen?"

"Now who sounds like a doctor?"

"Quack, quack." Finished with the last bandage, he released her foot and leaned back in close. Cupping her chin, he looked her in the eyes. "This will sound insane given how I've mistreated you coming back down the trail, but I do care about you, Erin. And I could cut off my own hand that I let you get hurt. I also apologize for snarling when you asked me about what to do next. It's no excuse, but it pissed me off to have had to say I don't know. At the same time, I did learn something valuable."

"About Taz?"

He shook his head. "About me. Being pissed at you actually felt good because I didn't get that awful backlash of pain that's been hounding me. I didn't even realize it till just now. I can worry about you, get angry at you." *Fantasize about you.* "And not get zapped." It sure as hell beat counting to thirteen thousand and beyond.

"Now there's something every girl wants to hear."

He laughed and realized it was the first time he'd done that in a long time, too.

She smiled and he knew she had accepted his apologies. That all was forgiven felt ridiculously good.

"Let's head back," he said before scooping her back up in his arms. "We'll get some food and a room. We'll get cleaned up and take care of your feet. I feel like I have no choice but to call Dante again, see if they've had better luck finding Taz." He knew she wanted to ask, "And then what?" so he added: "And then we'll figure out the rest of it."

They had just turned back onto the paved highway when the hair on the back of Max's neck prickled.

Alert, he straightened. Looked around.

Except for a tan SUV that had shot past in the opposite direction as he pulled out, the road was deserted.

He concentrated on his thoughts. The sensation had been different, yet oddly familiar. An internal radar. He'd felt it before. But when? Had Taz tried to reach him, perhaps?

So far, Max thought that he'd been doing all the work, sifting the airwaves, seeking a connection to Taz. But what if Taz was seeking him? Was this a psychic *knock-knock*?

Damn it, Taz, where the fuck are you?

Erin had her head leaned back, eyes closed. He'd gotten her to eat an energy bar and take two ibuprofen. Besides having sore feet, she had to be exhausted. They had slept in vehicles the last two nights.

As soon as they got back to town, he'd find a motel. Tonight they were sleeping in real beds.

And what about tomorrow? He didn't have a clue.

Max felt the tingling again and glanced in the rearview mirror. The tan SUV that had passed them earlier was behind him now.

And closing in.

Danger. Run.

"Hold on, Erin!" Max gunned the engine.

The SUV sped up, too.

"What's wrong, Max?" She turned around, having picked up that someone was after them.

"The SUV. Do you recognize the driver?"

She pushed her sunglasses up, squinted, tried to focus on the face. "No. It's probably an unmarked police unit." Her voice sank. "Remember, we *are* driving a stolen vehicle."

Max saw the other driver smile as if enjoying the game. "It's not the police."

Stomping on the gas pedal, Max passed a slower vehicle. The road ahead was clear. Behind him, the SUV passed the same car and kept accelerating.

Chasing them.

The stolen Taurus was no match for the SUV's more powerful engine. By rights, they should be losing ground, but the SUV had backed off. Pacing them, biding his time.

There were no cars in front of Max, but an oncoming semitruck prevented the SUV from pulling up beside them and running them off the road. Which Max had sensed was the driver's intent.

They were on a straight stretch of highway now but not too far ahead was a curvy section with sheer drop-offs. That's what the SUV was waiting for.

Max backed off the gas just a little as he eyed the oncoming semitruck, estimating its speed. Just a few more yards . . .

Counting under his breath, Max swerved into the left lane, directly into the path of the semitruck.

Erin screamed, but he ignored her. The semi's driver hit his brakes and began blasting the air horn. Speeding up, Max cut sharply to the right, darting around the jackknifing trailer.

The driver of the SUV had slowed, clearly disbelieving, but Max caught a glimpse of the handgun at the same time Erin did.

"He's got a gun, Max!"

He reached over and shoved her head toward her knees. "Get down!"

Just then the SUV disappeared from sight as the now sideways moving semitruck blocked both lanes of highway.

Max couldn't tell the extent of the damage, but the SUV didn't come after them. It had come to a stop, with part of its front end crumpled. Hell . . . the car might still be drivable.

At the next intersection Max turned and headed west.

"Who was that?" Erin asked.

"We'll figure that out after I'm sure we've lost him."

Max switched roads several more times, mostly heading north.

No one appeared to be following, but now they had a higher risk of the Taurus being targeted by police if it had been reported by the semi driver as the causative factor in a car accident.

"I'm worried about the truck driver," she said.

"The trailer stayed upright on the road," he said. "It's unlikely the driver was injured."

"But what about the guy in the SUV? He had a gun, Max! What if he shoots the truck driver?"

"The driver of the SUV isn't looking for random targets. He was after me. And he clearly wanted me dead—or incapacitated. Whatever I've forgotten must be incriminating as hell." Max cast a look at her. "I'm even beginning to wonder if Dr. Winchette was involved. I remember catching a few of his thoughts and realizing he didn't want me to awaken."

"You don't know that for sure."

"Bull. And as much as this is going to piss you off, I can tell you're wondering the same thing. What exactly do you know about Winchette's activities, especially concerning me?"

He'd been trying to read Erin's mind since the accident, but just as he had problems reaching Taz's mind, he was also having trouble probing hers.

Her expression told him a lot though. She looked angry. But when she suddenly started to cry, he panicked. Tears were Kryptonite.

He melted. "Ah, hell, sweetheart. I don't mean—"

She cut him off. "No. You may be right. I don't know what to think anymore."

"Start at the beginning. How did you and Dr. Winchette become involved in this?"

Seeming overly self-conscious of her tears, she wiped them away. "We were called in to treat Dante Johnson when he first returned last March. I'd just come back to work after taking leave following my father's death. We gained valuable experience working with Dante and I assumed that history was why we were called in to consult on your case. But when I saw pictures of that machine Taz was found in—I recognized it. I think Dr. Winchette did, too."

"Recognized it from where?" Max listened as she explained seeing a similar machine in her father's lab as a child.

"I was very young, Max. I may not be recalling it correctly."

"Did you ask Winchette about it?"

"Yes, but he was so evasive in his answer. Then, I overheard him talking to someone. He mentioned a patient going brain-dead, and I assumed it was you or Taz because he mentioned Travis Franks's name."

"What exactly did he say about Travis?"

"Not much. Something like 'Travis Franks agrees'—but I didn't catch all of it."

"And now Winchette is dead. Killed in my room, by the way, which has the word 'framed' written all over it." Max shook his head. "I'm not saying someone at the Agency's *not* behind this—but Travis Franks? I'm not buying it."

Max trusted Travis. Or used to. Had something happened in the last two years to change Travis? Something he thought Max knew? *Or Dante? Or Harry?*

"There's more, Max. I believe my father was murdered. The official cause of death was suicide. An overdose. Which I never really believed. But I was working a temporary internship at a Canadian hospital, so I was gone in the months before he died."

"What makes you think murder?"

She drew a breath. "When I went to scatter his ashes at his lake house, I found a letter he'd left me. It was left where he'd planted a tree with my mother's ashes thirty years ago. He didn't go into detail, but he clearly expected to die and wanted me to get certain papers to a colleague of his. He felt he was being watched and couldn't send them himself. But that colleague was killed in an accident. And I haven't found the papers my father mentioned."

"Did Winchette know all this?"

"No. My father warned me against telling anyone. That he didn't instruct me to take the papers to Dr. Winchette was telling. They'd been close, until just before my father resigned."

Max reached over and squeezed her hands. "I'm sorry about your dad, Erin. But I think you're right. This is all related in some manner."

He turned into a gas station and turned toward her. "Right now I need to know how they found us.

They may have found the stolen camper by now and discovered this vehicle missing. But the odds of one person spotting us randomly is slim. I suspect something we brought from the hospital is bugged, maybe the bag from Dante, maybe your purse. We'll have to ditch all of it. But first I want to call Dante. See if he knows why the Agency has its crosshairs on us."

Chapter 24

Harry needed a better place to stay. Certain he hadn't been followed, he retraced his steps back to the cheap warehouse he'd rented.

While he preferred five-star ratings, those places were too visible. And expensive. They would also be the first place Minh Tran would look for him.

Shifting the bags of food to one hand, Harry let himself in. *Lucy, I'm home.* He set the food on the table then untied Rufin.

The scientist's eyes were red. He'd been crying again. What a wimp. All brains, no guts.

But were his tears for Bohdana? Or for himself?

After learning what Rufin had done, or tried to do, to secure his own future, Harry realized everyone had underestimated Dr. Rufin. They heard his stutter, saw his slight frame, and promptly forgot the scientist's underlying genius. Maybe the little guy's balls could be seen without the aid of a microscope.

The more Harry questioned Rufin's claim of being able to re-create and complete Zadovsky's work, the more it rang true. And if Rufin had created Sugar-Cane and JumpJuice in his "spare time"—what could he do with dedicated resources?

"I brought you soup. And bread." Harry tugged Rufin to his feet and plopped him in a chair.

"How c-c-can you eat?" Rufin asked.

"After killing someone?" He knew he couldn't tell Rufin the truth. It had never bothered Harry to kill. He could soft-soap it, by saying it got easier, but that wouldn't endear him like an outright lie.

"Once I found out Bohdana had made a deal with the Thai government to trade you for her own freedom, I knew she'd stop at nothing," Harry said. "As cold as it sounds, it was her or us, buddy."

Rufin picked up a spoon and stirred his soup. "Is that how she got to Thailand? By trading secrets to the Thai agents?"

Harry nodded.

"She told me she'd come here to live with an old girlfriend." Rufin blew his nose then stirred his soup some more.

"I never met a woman that could be trusted." Harry opened the container of rice.

"What do you intend to do with me?"

Harry had quickly corrected Rufin's assumption that he worked for the United States, portraying himself instead as a high-dollar, freelance mercenary. Not necessarily Rufin's enemy, but still a threat.

Now, however, Harry wanted to cultivate Rufin's friendship.

"I was thinking about what you said," Harry went on. "And I've got a deal to propose. You and I could be partners. We'd have to figure out the whole trust thing, because neither of us trusts the other right now. And since I'm not going to make any magnanimous gestures—like free you—our relationship won't change much in the foreseeable future. But here's my proposal. I find Taz and get a lab set up. You manufacture SugarCane to help finance our operation until you can get that—what did you call it, Serum 89?—perfected. Then we sell out to the highest bidder, split the profits, and go our separate ways."

Rufin looked at him, and then back at his soup. "And what guarantee do I h-h-have that you won't k-k-kill me in the end and keep all the money?"

Harry tore off a chunk of bread. "There's a couple ways we can work that. You produce serum samples, but keep the recipe. Once it's sold, we can get half the money up front, split that, and take off in opposite directions. Then you can forward the formula to the buyer, who will then pay the balance to each of us separately. Or something like that. We can work out the details later."

When Rufin actually took a bite of food, Harry knew he'd won. He'd seen his type time and time again. Pussy.

"But for now I'm still your prisoner?" Rufin said.

Harry nodded. "Trust me. It's for your own good. I'll treat you a helluva lot better than the Thai government. Or even the U.S. They're pretty eager to get ahold of you, too. For all the wrong reasons. Just remember, I'm the only one who will offer you a collaborative deal."

Harry's phone vibrated. He read the text message, then sent a quick reply.

"I need to go meet someone. Finish eating."

"You're going to l-l-leave me here again?"

"If this deal works out, I won't be gone long."

Rufin pushed his food away. "What if you don't return?"

There was always that chance. In that case, the police would investigate when someone reported the bad smell . . .

"I'll be back. Now come on and let me tie you up."

The exclusive right to market SugarCane had made Minh Tran the number one drug dealer in Southeast Asia.

Jengho Vato, the man Harry was meeting with now was the former number one dealer. That Minh Tran had once worked for Jengho only intensified Jengho's hatred.

The deal Harry proposed was Jengho's wet dream. Getting rid of Tran and gaining the exclusive right to SugarCane, in even larger quantities than Tran had access to, was tantalizing.

Naturally Jengho was suspicious. But the majority of his skepticism died when he realized Harry— or *Doug Harold*—was the associate of the late Dr. Zadovsky that Minh Tran sought. Jengho also knew that Tran's supply of SugarCane had run drier than usual.

"What's in it for you, besides the obvious financial gain?" Jengho asked. "If you weren't happy with your deal with Tran, why not renegotiate with him?"

The unspoken question was the most important. *What would stop Harry from selling out Jengho at some point?* Just like he was doing to Tran now.

"My former colleague left me holding the bag after taking a large sum of Tran's money." Since Zadovsky was dead, Harry could blame him fully. "Quite frankly I don't feel it fair that I have to shoulder that debt alone. Once Minh Tran is dead, I can move more freely. And you can reclaim your position as top dog. We both win."

"You speak as if killing Tran is easy. Which I *know* is not fact. He's impossible to get close to," Jengho said.

"I can provide the means for you to get to him. And with the advance you pay me, I can get a lab set up and ready to produce 'Cane in the quantity you desire."

"But you're also wanting safe passage out of the country. What guarantee do I have you will return?"

"I will let you hold the scientist who will help me produce the drug. Do not think you can cut me out of the picture, though, because he doesn't have the secret recipe. I do." *Or I will*, Harry thought. As soon as Rufin was securely hidden, Harry would join the hunt for Taz.

"We will dispose of Minh Tran before you get your scientist back," Jengho said.

"Agreed."

"Then we have a deal."

Chapter 25

Sedona, Arizona
September 24

Max decided that using Erin's cell phone was less risky than being out in the open, using a pay phone. It was also faster. He needed answers now.

Besides if the Agency did have a tracking device on one of their belongings, they'd know where he and Erin were, at least until they dumped everything.

He dialed Dante's number then put the call on speakerphone so Erin could hear.

Dante answered immediately. "Erin?"

"It's Max. And I'm going to keep this brief."

"Listen, buddy, I understand your concern but we need to talk. There have been developments here."

"Like the accident involving the tan SUV?"

"What accident?" Dante's voice went from confused to concerned. "Jesus, are you, is Erin, okay?"

Max nodded at Erin, who spoke up. "I'm fine, Dante. So is Max."

"Good. Is one of you going to explain about this tan SUV?" Dante asked.

"In a minute," Max said. "First tell me if you've had any word on Taz."

"None pertaining to his whereabouts, but the developments I mentioned involve him. His fingerprints were found in your hospital room, Max. And his DNA on Dr. Winchette's body. He evaded the security cameras, but his prints were also on a lab cart outside the room. It's now believed Taz came to your room after you'd left and surprised Dr. Winchette—or vice versa."

"Damn." If Max had just stayed at the hospital, would that have been averted?

"Look, Max, come on back. Or let me meet you. I'll come alone. You call the shots."

"No offense, but I'm not sure who to trust right now. The tan SUV picked up our trail and the driver was armed. I've lost him—temporarily—but I want to know why the Agency's gunning for me. Especially if I'm no longer a suspect in Winchette's death?"

Dante swore. "It's not us, Max. And I might know how to prove it. After I escaped, I learned I had a tracking beacon implanted in my arm. Cat had one, too."

"Catalina! She was held there?"

"No, but she had her own run-in with Viktor Zadovsky."

"After the Belarus job?"

"Yes. It's a long story, Max, but Cat and I are—we're getting married. We have a son. If she hasn't already, Erin can fill in a few details, but even she doesn't know everything."

Max's head began to pound. "It'll have to keep till later. Get back to the tracking beacon."

"If you have one implanted, you can be tracked by a handheld device. Zadovsky used one to find me, but it's in pieces in a lab or I would have suggested we use it to find Taz."

"But Zadovsky's dead."

"And whoever inherited his work likely has a tracking device, too. You and Taz are both at risk," Dante said.

"How do I figure out if I've got one of these beacons?"

"Get Erin to check the underside of your upper arm."

"What would I look for?" Erin asked.

"A small round scar. Large-gauge needle. His might be somewhere else. Thigh. Buttock. The beacon will be hidden in muscle. It's a blue, rice-sized transmitter. You need to find it, pull it out so they can't track you," Dante said.

Erin was already inspecting Max's arms. "Got it. Small round puncture scar. How do I remove it?"

"You will need a scalpel and forceps. In your case a pocketknife and tweezers will probably be as much as you can get ahold of. You might have to dig for it, and it will hurt like hell, but he's had worse. Right, Max?"

"If what you're saying is true—then whoever is

tracking me might have already found Taz,"
Max said.

"It also means they might know where Harry is."

Max's head felt ready to explode, a warning to
stop or pay a higher price. "Erin and I will check for
this beacon. If I find it, I'll call you back."

"One last thing, Max. Cat told me what you did
in London. I owe you, big time. Remember that as
you weigh who you can trust. I'm here for you."

Max disconnected the call and looked at Erin.
"Feel up to performing a little exploratory surgery?"

"I shouldn't, but at this point the 'shouldn'ts'
don't matter. And I can only imagine how it must
feel to know that *thing* is inside you. If it were me,
I'd want it out fast."

"I don't want to endanger you further. Whoever
drove that SUV could be back on the road already,
closing in again. And in case you didn't notice, he's
armed. I'm not."

"His car didn't look in good enough shape to
drive. That's going to buy a little time, Max. Let's
see if what Dante said is true. If we can get that
tracker out and destroy it, they can't follow us."
Erin met his gaze squarely. "You'll also know you
can trust Dante. We can't keep running like this
forever."

Max slowed. "There's a small town about five miles
east of here. We'll find a drugstore and get what we
need to do my arm and to patch up your feet."

* * *

An hour later, Max pulled into a public boat ramp.

They were about twenty miles outside of Sedona. The place was deserted except for a few parked cars with empty boat trailers attached.

"You sure seem to know your way around here," Erin said.

"My father lived nearby." He pointed to a path in the woods. "There are restrooms just over that rise."

"Let's go. I've got what we need." Erin held up the bag of stuff he'd purchased at the drugstore.

While he'd driven here, she'd bandaged her feet and slipped on the pair of flip-flops he'd bought. They'd be hell to run in, but better than bare feet.

"No, we'll do it right here," Max said. "Once we get the tracker out, I want to plant it. See if someone comes looking for us." The SUV driver had had enough time to secure another car.

"I thought the point was to get away?"

"The point is to find Taz. If I've got a tracking beacon, so does Taz. And if they haven't found him yet, then I want to get that device they're using to hunt us."

"You plan to track Taz with it?"

"Whatever works. I'm focused on the end result—and I'm running out of options." He pulled his shirt off and braced his right arm where she could access it.

Erin opened the small pocket knife and tweezers he'd purchased and poured alcohol over them.

"This will hurt," she warned.

"As Dante said, I've endured worse." He caught her gaze. "Thank you for your concern."

He felt her swab his skin—smelled the alcohol. The memories . . .

"The scars on your chest. Is that what you meant by 'endured worse'?"

Max gritted his teeth as she sliced quickly into his arm, straight in, no hesitation. "I believe so."

When she inserted the tweezers, the headache fled on the edge of pain. A memory sprang forth.

"Taz and I discovered that physical pain, from an injury, overrode the mental anguish from the programming."

"Hold on. Sorry!" She winced as she probed inside the incision. "The good news is, the bleeding is subsiding."

"It's healing. That's another thing we discovered. We healed fast. We could hurt ourselves, or each other, in order to plan, talk."

"Got it! I think." Erin withdrew the tweezers and dropped a small bloody bead on a piece of gauze.

Max studied it while she bandaged his arm. The piece glowed like neon blue. "I know I've been gone awhile, but damn, the changes in technology are amazing." He cleaned the knife and closed it.

Erin looked at the beacon. "You think it still works?"

"We'll find out. Come on."

They climbed out of the car. Max hurried around to her side and swept her up in his arms.

"I can walk, Max."

"This is faster and I know your feet are still sore." And he liked the feel of her in his arms.

He followed the path between the trees, and then looked around, to get his bearings.

"Did you come here often?" she asked.

"My old man used to come here with one of his girlfriends. Maggie hated me and would encourage my father to leave me here to play while they went out on his boat to get drunk and screw."

"Was it good they left you behind?"

"Ultimately, yes. More than once they forgot me, which is how I ultimately came to live with Stony. My uncle went to my dad's one morning to pick me up and Maggie said, 'Oh, shit, we forgot him again.'"

"How old were you?"

"Eight or nine. And before you say how wrong it was, know that I was thrilled, not having to be around Dad and Maggie when they fought and drank. I was glad they left me behind."

There was a picnic table near the restroom. Max set Erin down long enough to plant the beacon inside the restroom. Then he scooped her back into his arms and reentered the woods on the other side.

"There's a spot up here where you can see the road. I used to throw rocks at cars coming in." At her look, he laughed. "You were obviously better supervised as a kid. We can sit here and see who pulls in."

"What if no one comes?"

"I'll hide the tracker here. I can come back for it, but I don't want it on us." He looked at the sky. "We've only got a few hours of daylight left. Park closes at sundown—so we'll need to be out by then or they'll tow the car."

That was another problem. Whoever followed them knew what they were driving. He'd need to get different wheels eventually. But for now . . .

"While we're sitting here, tell me what you know about Dante and Cat," Max said.

Trying to recall anything about Catalina was particularly painful. He also sensed a heaviness in his chest when he tried. Loss? Had he and Cat been involved?

"Dante felt certain Catalina Dion was somehow responsible for his—your—capture overseas," Erin said. "But my files indicated that she'd died while Dante was imprisoned. I don't know the specifics, but ultimately he found her, hiding from the same people pursuing him. She'd borne his son, and was protecting their child."

"They'd been lovers?" Max frowned.

"Obviously. Not ringing any bells?"

Gigantic, loud warning bells. "Nothing clear. What did Dante mean about London?"

"I have no idea, Max, but—" Erin grew quiet. "I hear a car."

Max watched as a car came into sight. It was the tan SUV. The crumpled fender had been crowbarred out away from the tire. He knew they were hidden, but still they crouched. "He doesn't look much worse for the wear."

The SUV had slowed, but went past. Then the brake lights came on. The driver did a three-point turn and headed back.

"Stay here. Please," he added.

"I can help."

"If I have to worry about you, it'll be a hindrance. I'll be back before you know it."

He slipped away, making his way through the trees, avoiding the picnic area and path.

As Max watched, the SUV circled the Taurus before pulling beyond it. The driver looked around, taking in the other cars. Then he seemed to notice the restroom sign. Parking, he climbed out.

Max got a better look at the man's face. Though he didn't recognize him, the man had obviously been military. He still had the walk.

The man carried a small device. Was that the tracker? When the man spotted the restroom he hurried up to the side and pressed against the wall. Pulling out his gun, the man inched toward the ladies' room door.

The bastard figured if Erin was inside, he'd get her first.

Without sound, Max circled and eased up to toward the building from the opposite side.

A hinge creaked as the man opened the ladies' room door.

Max rushed up behind him, shoving him inside. The man fell and tried to roll away. Max went with him. Keeping a tight grip on the man's wrist, he slammed it against the concrete floor repeatedly.

The man grunted in pain as bones shattered. The gun slipped out of his grip. Max dived and picked up the gun, fighting the urge to shoot the man.

"Stay down," Max ordered. "And keep your hands out."

The man grimaced, as he moved his broken wrist.

Max pointed the muzzle at the man's groin. "If you know anything about me, you know I start there—then move to the knee caps." The man's face lost color. "Who do you work for?" Max pressed.

The man didn't remain quiet long. "Abe Caldwell."

The name meant nothing to Max. "What does he want with me?"

"I don't know. I just follow orders."

Max raised the gun sights.

"I swear! I was sent here to help that other doctor, Winchette, find the first guy who escaped. Then you took off, too."

"Did you find the other guy?" Max reached for the blue beacon he'd put over the door frame. "I know about these."

"I haven't been able to pick up a signal on him. The implants don't always work right. I had you in southern Arizona but lost you in a rainstorm. Then you popped up a day later in Sedona."

"Hand over the tracking device," Max said.

"It's in my pocket."

"I suggest you pull it out really slow. Then slide it over here."

The man complied, shoving the unit toward Max. The tracker resembled a Palm Pilot.

"How does it work?" Max asked.

"Hit the button. It's in hibernate mode. The

beacon either shows up on the map or it doesn't. You basically zoom the map in and out."

"Now get up. And don't try anything stupid," Max said.

He directed the man back to the parking lot. It was still deserted, so Max kept the gun in view.

"Go to the Taurus."

The man looked puzzled when Max tossed him the Taurus keys. "Open the trunk."

Sweating profusely, the man tried to negotiate. "Hey, man, I'm cooperating fully."

"Yes, and for that you get to live. Empty your pockets—everything on the ground. Then climb in."

It was a tight fit, and not easy to maneuver given his broken wrist. Max slammed the lid shut after dropping the beacon down a narrow crack near the tire well.

He gathered up the man's wallet. *Allen Peterman*, the license read. He snatched the car keys but kicked the cell phone under the Taurus.

"Max!"

Erin came limping into view. She looked at the trunk. "Is he—?"

"Alive? Yes. Come on. I'll get our stuff out of the backseat. We're taking his car."

"You can't leave him like that," Erin insisted.

"I'll call Dante later and tell him where to find this guy. Right now I just want to get away from here."

Max did a quick search of the SUV and found another gun in the glove box. He turned on the tracking device and watched as the GPS-style map overlay showed the highway and a blinking red dot—the Taurus.

"Hold this while I drive." He started up the SUV and pulled out. "Make sure the dot doesn't start moving. In case I have more than one beacon implanted in me."

"Did he tell you anything about Taz?"

"He claimed he couldn't pick up a signal." Max turned back on the highway and sped off.

"Did you find out who the man works for? Why he's after you?"

Max frowned. "He claimed to work for someone named Abe Caldwell, who was supposedly working with Dr. Winchette. Sound familiar to you?"

"Abe Caldwell is one of the owners of Caldwell Pharmaceuticals, a Swiss drug conglomerate. Dr. Winchette worked with the Caldwell company in the past on drug trials, but he worked with every major drug manufacturer out there. To show favoritism—"

"Would be unethical?" Max finished. "Like conducting human experiments is unethical?"

Erin seemed at a loss for words. "I want to deny it, Max. Not so much because I know Dr. Winchette but because . . . he and my father worked together years ago. My father mentioned regretting some projects. I guess I'm afraid that if Winchette is guilty, my father was, too, even though my gut tells me he was not."

"Don't conjecture any further until we know more." He rubbed his head. Ever since Erin had removed the tracker, his headache had grown worse. "Any movement on the device?"

"No. The dot has remained steady."

"Keep watching it. Maybe by us moving around, we'll pick up a signal on Taz."

"Would it work from the air?"

"Good question. We could cover an area faster in a chopper or small plane." Max checked the setting sun. It would be dark in less than an hour. And he didn't want to be on the road at night, wondering if every set of headlights that approached was out to get them.

"For now let's put some distance between us and where we left the Taurus. Then we'll find a place to rest and regroup."

Chapter 26

Bangkok, Thailand
September 24

There was only one person Rocco would trust with his own life: himself.

And Travis Franks knew that. It was one of the ways they talked in code. If Travis had ordered Rocco straight out to go to Thailand and find Rufin, it would have destroyed Travis's fallback: plausible deniability.

Plus it gave Rocco more leeway for bending rules.

And right now a lot of people in and out of the Agency were watching Travis. Hell, if Rocco worked for the other side and were searching for Rufin, he'd look around to see who else was looking and follow them.

So while Travis stayed visible in the States, Rocco pulled another of his never-before-used aliases out of his hat, and disappeared after leaving a false trail toward the state park where Taz had been spotted two days ago.

John Doe had stolen a man's hiking and camping equipment before disappearing in a national park. This meant they wouldn't see him until he was ready to be seen—if ever. Especially if Doe was who they thought.

Travis believed he had a lead on John Doe's real identity. Three years ago, an Australian Special Air Service Regiment agent, Logan Treyhorn, was blown off course during a secret night jump into a terrorist stronghold near the Burmese border.

A ransom demand had been received with Logan's ID, but the failure to provide proof of life coupled with the lack of follow-up on the ransom demand was interpreted to mean Logan had died—if he'd even been captured alive to begin with.

Travis had two other possibilities, but the fact that John Doe had spoken with what the MRI technician described as an Aussie accent kept Logan at the top of the list. That and the nickname—Taz. Tasmanian Devil perhaps?

Because of the undercover nature of Logan's work, photos of the man were pretty much non-existent.

Travis had opted to keep his suspicions on Logan close to his vest. If the Aussies got wind their man was possibly still alive . . . ouch. Rocco had seen those SASR boys in action.

Right now, Rocco refocused on his search for Dr. Rufin. Travis's lead had turned out to be legit. They had been monitoring all of Zadovsky's last known e-mail contacts, including those of his lab personnel. Rufin had sent an e-mail to Zadovsky's former secretary, Bohdana Wulandan.

Unfortunately, someone else reached Bohdana before Rocco. He found her dead body in an apartment that had been wiped clean. He suspected someone had used her to lure Rufin in.

So far, Travis had had no luck tracing Bohdana's other e-mails, but it was clear she wasn't working alone. Someone had helped her escape Jakarta after Zadovsky's death. The Thai government perhaps? God, he hoped not.

Rocco straightened as a car pulled up to the curb just ahead of where he walked. Recognizing the driver, he climbed in the sleek BMW.

"My meter's running," Diego Marques quipped as he pulled away and began zipping through traffic.

Rocco passed an envelope of cash to the man.

Diego hefted it in his hand, then slid it in his jacket, never once taking his eyes off the rearview mirror.

Rocco watched the side mirrors as Diego turned at the next intersection then sped up an alley. He turned again and stopped.

"I think we're clean," Diego said before wheeling down another alley and racing back into traffic.

"Did you turn up anything on Bohdana?" Rocco asked.

"Nope. Whoever she worked for taught her how to cover her trail. She was lying low, paid everything in cash, even though she wasn't working anywhere."

"You think the Thai government had her on payroll?"

Diego shook his head. "They're still searching for Rufin. In fact, that search just got hotter. A group of Burmese extremists have put out feelers for Rufin, too. The extremists want him because they know the big players will pay a ransom to get him back." Diego downshifted and turned into the crowded red light district. "Minh Tran has even been seeking Rufin. I just heard that Tran's concentrating his manpower on searching for one of Jengho's camps."

"Jengho Vato?" The news surprised Rocco. The two drug lords were enemies, but rather than destroy one another with their private war, they'd supposedly worked out a boundary agreement.

"Was Jengho poaching on Minh Tran's turf again?" Rocco asked.

"The request for info I got was very soft. Tran doesn't want Jengho to know he's looking, but word is Jengho has a special guest that he's protecting."

"Rufin," Rocco said. It made sense. If someone other than the Thais had captured Rufin, they'd need to stash him somewhere until arrangements could be made to get him out of the country.

"Any idea where Jengho might have a guest house stashed?"

Diego flashed a wolfish grin. "It'll cost you."

"Why am I not surprised? Just name your price. I don't have time to dicker."

* * *

Diego's information was right on. It had also come at a lower price than Rocco had expected.

"I can't guarantee others won't beat you to this location," had been Diego's reasoning. This meant that if Rocco did indeed score, he owed Diego a favor.

Rocco had no time to get a team in place. With Diego's help, he'd hired two professional mercenaries, Joe and Dick. Not their real names, of course, but who cared? Rocco had introduced himself as "Robbie." As long as the men were skilled and trustworthy, which Diego had vouched, they could call themselves Ginger and Mary Ann.

Jengho's hiding spot turned out to be an ancient fishing vessel, no different from a thousand other ancient fishing vessels in Bangkok's harbor. It was moored near an abandoned warehouse that had recently burned and now provided cover for Rocco and company. That it was night also helped mask their presence.

He'd counted four men on the fishing boat. Two of them were acting as guards. One was the boat's captain. Rocco believed all three worked for Jengho.

The fourth man had just been dragged onto the deck and his head shoved over the rail, clearly seasick. Rocco got a glimpse of the sick man's face while he vomited over the side.

It was Rufin! His hair had been cut off, no doubt in an attempt to disguise his appearance.

Rufin being sick seemed to piss off the captain, who complained of the smell in the cabin. He wanted to move the boat, as if that would help.

The last thing Rocco wanted was for them to

move. The odds were even, three against three, and he wanted to keep it that way.

He passed the binoculars to Joe, then huddled close to discuss his plan.

"Sounds easy," Joe said.

"That's what worries me," Rocco muttered. "Let's do it."

Sneaking up to the boat was easy. The dark dock was littered with abandoned crates that provided hiding places. The only light was a dim lantern on the boat's deck. Rufin had apparently started vomiting again as soon as they'd dragged him below. The smell must have been bad because now one of the guards joined Rufin at the rail. The second guard and captain still argued over the merits of moving.

The sound of a boat engine roaring to life caught Rocco's attention. A small speed boat swung right next to the fishing vessel. Muffled shots were fired. Precise, targeted shots, not a random spray.

The guard who'd been puking fell overboard into the water. Rufin seemed frozen in place.

The speed boat zoomed away into the dark and cut its engine. Waiting.

The other guard and the boat captain had dived for cover on the deck. Rufin bolted for the cabin. The wounded guard splashed in the water below, calling out for help. After a few seconds, the captain darted forward and grabbed for a rope to toss over the rail.

Rocco knew what would happen next. The speed

boat zoomed back in, opening fire. The bright muzzle bursts made them easy to track.

"Take out the shooter," Rocco hissed to Joe.

The element of surprise worked in their favor. One shot took out the shooter, who fell forward into the murky water. Rocco heard the speed boat's engine gun full throttle as it swung back into the darkness. But this time it kept going.

"Come on!" Rocco shouted as he ran forward and jumped onto the boat. The captain was dead and the remaining guard was now hiding below in the cabin with Rufin.

"Throw out your weapons and come out with your hands up. Or we'll kill you!" Rocco shouted.

Two guns clattered across the deck. "D-d-don't sh-sh-shoot," Rufin said as he stumbled up the steps.

As soon as the guard came up, Dick hit him across the back of the head and shoved him backward.

Rocco grabbed Rufin's arm. "Stay down. Come on!"

"You!" Rufin recognized Rocco. "D-d-don't shoot me!"

"Then I suggest you move your scrawny ass off this boat before someone else does!"

He could hear the speed boat approaching again. Joe surged forward and literally picked Rufin up and carried him off the boat.

"Get him to the car," Rocco said.

Gunfire shattered the wood railing as the speed boat moved in. Rocco returned fire then jumped down onto the dock. Tires screeched as Dick pulled up now, throwing the car doors open and taking off before they closed. Rocco piled in the back with Rufin.

"Keep your head down," he ordered as Rufin slumped lower.

No one followed, but still they raced away. Surely the men on the other boat would be calling for backup now.

"Let's get back downtown," Rocco said. They had a second car ready, so they could ditch this one.

Joe leaned over the passenger seat and held up a bloody hand. "You better check your man. This ain't my blood."

Rocco looked at Rufin, noticed he hadn't moved. Shit! "Give me some light."

Tugging Rufin's shoulder, Rocco pulled him upright in the seat. Rufin's head lolled lifelessly to one side—the front of his shirt completely soaked with blood.

Chapter 27

The urge to flee Arizona kept Max driving another three hours into the night.

As they rode in silence, each seemingly lost in their own private musings, Max caught glimmers of Erin's thoughts.

Strangely, the process of contemplating *her* thoughts helped to pry loose more of his. Much the same way as their casual conversation had done earlier.

Unfortunately, Erin's silent curiosity about Dante's cryptic remark didn't bring Max any closer to answers. *Cat told me what you did in London. I owe you.*

London rang no bells. In fact, Max had noticed that whenever he tried to recall specific assignments he'd been on with Dante, he hit a familiar brick wall. As if certain memories had been all closed off with the same material. He had the feeling that if he could just loosen one key brick, the entire wall would tumble.

The knowledge that a tracking device had been implanted in his arm still infuriated him. But not nearly as much as suspecting that other things had been implanted as well. Intangibles that couldn't be cut out with a knife. He felt he had been invaded, violated, in ways he couldn't completely fathom yet.

Whether he'd been brainwashed, or mind-fucked, was no longer the question. Why and how to undo it was.

And while the CIA was no doubt very interested in knowing what classified information the mind-fuckers had accessed, Max knew the Agency couldn't care less about the personal memories he'd lost.

Catalina Dion's name struck a deep chord in Max. Had they been lovers? He had a faint glimmer of a naked woman with short blond hair, weeping in his arms. The scene, while incomplete, was stamped with heavy negative emotion.

Okay . . . naked meant lover. Weeping meant breakup. Right?

Wrong. Wrong. Wrong.

The blistering spike in his headache quickly had Max focusing back on the dark road. It was nearly 10 p.m. and they'd just crossed the state border into New Mexico.

He roused Erin, who'd drifted off to sleep. "I'm pulling into a motel," he said. "I'll get you settled in a room, then I'll go find food."

After driving to a nearby restaurant for carryout, Max parked at another motel adjacent to theirs.

As subterfuges went, it wasn't much, but at this point everything helped. The flashing red dot that represented the stolen Taurus hadn't moved, according to the tracking device. Likewise, a second red dot representing Taz hadn't popped up either.

Had Allen been discovered or had he managed to free himself? Max hadn't wanted to take the time to bind or gag the man. Getting away before someone came up had been his only concern. Since Allen had spilled his guts to Max, it was doubtful he was going to run to his boss right away.

Max had called Dante back, but got voice mail. And since Max was still keeping the cell phone battery disconnected, Dante would get Erin's voice mail.

By the time Max returned to their motel room, Erin had fallen asleep on top of one of the beds. She roused long enough to take a shower and put on clean clothes but fell back asleep before eating. He could understand why she was exhausted. Most people didn't keep this kind of pace on a day-to-day basis.

Max lifted her up and gently deposited her in the other bed, the one farthest from the door.

He would have preferred to share a bed, but realizing *that* preference was born of something more than the desire to keep her safe had him tugging the covers up over her and turning away.

Max was tired, too. It was hard to believe it had been less than a week ago that he had been rescued from the jungle and brought back to the States.

Now he was on the run with a beautiful woman. And he'd thought that only happened in the movies.

A hot shower helped revitalize him, but it didn't last. Once he ate, he felt exhaustion creep in. His headache seemed to spiral, growing worse as he tried to connect with Taz. Ultimately, the effort only increased Max's discomfort.

After checking the doors one last time, he climbed into the empty bed and turned off the light.

Erin's soft breathing in the dark soothed him. He again felt a longing to lie next to her, just to hold her—but that thought quickly morphed to thoughts of kissing her.

Of her making love to *him.*

The distinction seemed significant. He wanted to be desired freely. Not because he'd influenced her or manipulated her reactions.

Nothing wrong with that, echoed in his mind.

Oh, but there was.

There was.

At some point Max drifted off to sleep. And in his dreams, Erin welcomed him. Invited him into her arms. Her body.

"Love me, Max. Let me love you."

He heard the sounds of ocean waves, felt the warmth of the sun on his bare back. The beach. They were back on that beach again. But this time they were both naked. On a blanket, in that secluded little cove.

Erin was beneath him, moaning, writhing. It felt like he'd been dropped into the dream, midstroke, his cock already half sheathed in her tight liquid heat.

Part of him felt cheated. He'd wanted to feel her kisses go from tentative to wild. He'd wanted to undress her slowly, unwrap her like a precious gift. He'd wanted to feel her pulse slam as her body grew wet and hungry.

"More, Max."

He drew back and pushed in, going deeper. She leaned her head back, thrusting her shoulders out and offering her breasts up to him. To his mouth.

She couldn't get enough of him, her cries going from plaintive to desperate. *"More, Max. Harder."*

He felt his own release building. He held back, not wanting to let go until she'd gone hopelessly over the edge.

Run. Hide.

Taz's voice came out of nowhere.

Erin disappeared, leaving Max disoriented. The beach was gone. He was—

Hades, help! Please, Taz screamed now. *Anything. I'll do anything.*

Max recognized his new surroundings. Or the lack of them. Total darkness. The occasional flicker of light. Sound. Pain. He was back in the lab. In stasis. Waiting while Taz's memories were stripped, listening while Taz was tested by untold horrors.

Do as we say. Do not question. Do not think. There is no memory except this.

But always, he and Taz did remember. They had a pact, had sworn they would not forget. And sooner or later it all came back. Or worse, only parts of it.

Like this sensation of being buried alive. Max was in a coffin now, being sunk lower and lower into the ground, buried by an avalanche of dirt.

The horror replayed in his mind. The oxygen was running out. He was suffocating. He'd been tied down, but had broken free. But he couldn't lift the coffin's lid, the mountain of dirt was too heavy.

"Max, help me!"

He recognized Erin's voice now. The thought that she was here, buried alive in some pit beside him, threatened to snap his sanity.

Steeling his strength, Max pressed against the lid that held him trapped, felt his muscles begin to cramp, to tear.

"Erin! I'm here!"

He bolted upright in bed, dazed and confused, and realized he'd been dreaming. He was in a . . . room . . . a motel. And Erin was here—not there.

Her soft cries, however, told a different story. He heard her thrash against the sheets and caught a flash of her dreams. Jesus! He'd somehow pulled Erin into his nightmare and she was still trapped there.

Still buried in that hell.

He sprang from his bed and reached for her. "Erin. Wake up. It's me."

"Help . . . make them stop." Her hands flailed about her head as if she were trying to shove away goggles. Earphones.

Just as they'd shared the erotic beach dream earlier, she now seemed locked in Max's horrible recall of the lab.

Grabbing her shoulders, Max shook her. When she didn't awaken, he picked her up and carried her into the bathroom. Turning the shower on COLD, he held her beneath the icy spray, soaking both of them in the process.

Erin stiffened and screamed as her eyes opened and met his.

"Max! Oh, Max!" She started sobbing, her shoulders shuddering with each cry.

It didn't seem to register that she was soaking wet as she clawed her way up his chest, crawling into his embrace.

"Shhhh. I've got you, baby," he murmured. "No one's going to hurt you."

Max shut off the water and scooped her back into his arms.

She had her arms wrapped around his neck, her face buried against his throat as she continued to cry. She was shaking. Cold and scared.

Shifting her to rest against the bathroom counter, he stripped away her wet clothes. Then he wrapped her in a towel and carried her back to the bedroom.

"Don't turn out that light," she pleaded, pointing to the bathroom light he'd left on. "And don't leave me."

He set her on the bed, but she shot back to her feet as if the bed were alive.

Max knew what she was feeling, remembered it well. He also recalled how desperately he'd wanted her touch after the hypnosis session. How her touch had grounded him.

He tugged her back into his arms. She came willingly, still shaking.

Beneath the towel she kept clasped tightly around her shoulders, she was naked. But Max's wet clothes blocked the precious body heat she sought. He stepped back.

Immediately she protested. "No! Please!"

"I'm just peeling off my shirt, my jeans. I'm soaked."

"Hurry."

The moment Max kicked away his jeans; Erin pressed back into his arms. Seeking warmth. Shelter. He picked her back up and eased into the bed, slipping them both beneath the covers. The towel fell away, but she seemed not to notice.

He kept Erin on his chest with his arms crossed over her back. Her breasts flattened against him, her nipples hard little pearls.

"Don't let me go," she whispered. "Don't ever let me go, Max."

"I won't." He rocked her, making soothing noises until her trembling had subsided and her tears dried.

She wiggled and Max relaxed his grip—reluctant to let her go.

"We were sharing a dream again, weren't we?" she asked.

"Yes. It's got to be related to the link we have. I'm so sorry. I don't know how to undo it."

"What I saw . . . is that, was that what you endured?"

"Yes."

"How did you stand it? I thought I was dying."

How many times had Max prayed for death? "Taz would talk to me. We could get inside each other's head. Sharing helped some. But when the pain would get so bad I couldn't stand it, he'd remind me that one of us would escape. That we'd help the other. No matter what. And if that failed to work, he'd tell me stories of exploring with Stony. He knew the stories because I told them to him. Described every rock, every step to get there." *I'm coming, Taz.*

"But—"

"Shhh. We'll talk later. Go back to sleep."

"I can't sleep. Not after that." She pressed her nose into his chest then and drew a line of tiny kisses between his nipples.

Max's erection was instantaneous. His cock swelled and pressed against her. She shifted downward and rubbed against him.

"I dreamed about *this* first, Max. About being on that beach, kissing you. But I wanted more than a kiss."

The *more* part of him just grew harder.

"I want to make love to you, Max," she whispered. "Don't say no."

"Yes." He raised his head and kissed her.

She wrapped her arms around his neck, opening her mouth fully as she slid to his side. Max followed, never breaking the kiss. Taking the kiss deeper.

This new position, side by side, gave them each fuller access. His hand caught her breast and squeezed as her fingers closed around his swollen erection.

She moaned. "I want more."

He shifted his lips to the soft skin of her throat before moving lower. He wanted more, too. Kissing the curve of her breast, he caught a taut nipple and laved it with his tongue.

He started to suck, then lightly nipped before switching to the other breast. Her hands caressed and stroked until he had to pull away.

Pushing her onto her back, he hovered over her, running kisses down her ribs. He wanted only to bring her pleasure, wanting her to think of nothing but him. Shifting lower still, he kissed the dark triangle of curls between her legs.

She cried out. "Max. I—"

"I know." Taking his time, he kissed the insides of her thighs down to her knees. Then he slowly licked his way back up to those tempting curls. "Open for me, Erin."

She spread her legs wider and let out a soft sound as he lowered his mouth and suckled gently on her clitoris. Erin bucked, her hands encouraging, guiding.

He gave her one intense orgasm, wished he had the patience to give her another. He didn't. He slid a finger inside, teasing and massaging, giving her pleasure as he prepared her body for his.

He kissed back up from her abdomen to her breasts, settling his weight between her legs.

"I'm on the pill," she breathed. "Don't stop."

Birth control was the last thing on his mind as he

eased his throbbing cock into her, inch by inch, until he was finally in.

"You feel so good," she whispered as she lifted a leg to wrap around his hip. "Don't stop."

"I won't." Max slid deeper as she arched against him.

"Oh, God! I'm . . . I'm . . ."

"I'm coming, too," Max finished for her.

Then he was lost in the sublime and shattering sensation of hot need exploding, taking them both over the edge.

Back into a deep, soulful sleep.

Chapter 28

Singapore
September 24

There were favors; then there were big, gigantic favors.

Rocco knew he owed Diego more than money. In fact, Travis Franks now owed Diego a favor, too, which was a rare and powerful thing. In some parts of the world, you could trade a favor like that for ownership in, say, a small country.

Still Diego looked very unhappy as Rocco watched him pace outside on the porch, a cell phone pressed to his ear. They were holed up in a safe house, awaiting transport out of the country.

Bangkok was officially off Rocco's list for a while, maybe permanently. Which wasn't a bad thing. His most recent trips had all been do-or-die. That he'd survived again was sheer luck.

But Lady Luck had her limits. And Rocco knew it.

The doctor, who had been tending Rufin, now handed Rocco a small bottle of pills. "Painkillers. One every four hours. He's pretty sore from me poking around, but he should be fine after a few days of rest." The doctor, who had appeared at Travis's behest, nodded to the bed. Rufin was pale as the sheets. "He lost a lot of blood, but as bullet wounds go, his was pretty clean."

Rocco had gotten Diego to fly them under the radar, out of Bangkok, in his personal helicopter. Diego promptly went out and orchestrated a large arms deal to provide himself cover for the trip. Guns weren't typically his forte—but in economic hard times, even crooks were forced to take on odd jobs.

And in this instance, the CIA was buying the arms, through a variety of covers, naturally.

As soon as the doctor left, Rocco poured a glass of water and went over to the bed. Rufin's eyes tracked him.

"Here. This will help the pain." Rocco shook a tablet out then waited while Rufin swallowed.

"I suppose I should have gone with you in the f-f-first place," Rufin said. "Bohdana would still be alive. And this"—he glanced at his shoulder—"wouldn't have happened either."

"I wouldn't spare a lot of pity for that broad. She sold you out."

"Yes, but you didn't watch her d-d-die. Maybe it's easier for you."

"It's never easy. Anyone who tells you otherwise is lying or insane."

Earlier, Rufin had told Rocco about the man

who'd killed Bohdana. Rufin had no name and the description rang no bells. That the man had chosen to stash Rufin with Jengho Vato meant the mystery man was likely a colleague of Jengho's.

That Rufin was involved in the manufacture of SugarCane explained Jengho's and Minh Tran's interest. It also made Rufin one valuable SOB.

Rocco pulled a chair up to the bed.

"Where are you taking me?" Rufin asked.

"To the U.S. I'm sure we can arrange asylum in exchange for what you know of Dr. Zadovsky's work. We also want to know what was done to the two men we rescued. The man you called Hades is my friend, Max."

Rufin looked at him credulously. "You mean they survived? Did Taz regain consciousness?"

"Yes." Rocco wasn't going to tell Rufin that both men were on the run. "Why does that surprise you?"

"They typically need medicine to control s-s-seizures. And Taz's programming was interrupted. It should have killed him."

"What exactly were you and Zadovsky doing at that lab?" As much as Rocco held Rufin fully responsible, he was trying to keep his questions couched in sympathetic tones to get answers.

Rufin sighed and closed his eyes, but kept on talking as if tired of holding it in.

"Dr. Zadovsky had practically p-p-perfected a method of mind control. It involved drugs and cellular reprogramming; but it worked almost one hundred percent of the time."

"Cellular reprogramming?"

"Amnesia was chemically induced, then holographic sensory feedback—reprogramming—was input using all five senses. We also found that by attaching diodes to the muscles while transmitting those same programs, the input was absorbed instantly. It then became a matter of fine tuning that input. We even gave them false histories to draw from. Both subjects scored high."

"It was a game?" Rocco wished he had a tape recorder. As it was, Rufin would have to repeat this story numerous times.

"You could liken it to a form of virtual reality, but with bigger stakes."

"Could you make them do anything?"

"Almost. As long as it didn't conflict with their moral values."

"So you couldn't make them murder someone in cold blood—unless they were already cold-blooded murderers?"

Rufin looked uncomfortable. "Zadovsky was convinced that with the right programming, he could overcome even that. He was experimenting with overriding morals in other ways. Killing someone isn't inconceivable for someone l-l-like you. You have rules of engagement that are surprisingly easy to manipulate. But would you ever consider raping a woman?"

"Jesus! No!" Rocco was angry now. "Is that what you made them do?"

"Zadovsky tried with Taz. But he attempted suicide afterward. We—I erased the program from him."

"Like that makes it all better?" Rocco forced a calmer tone. "What about Max?"

"It never worked with him. No matter how much pain and abuse Max suffered, he didn't break."

Rocco held up a hand, suddenly having his own moral battle. He wanted to beat the shit out of Rufin. To make him pay. Except that wasn't how it worked. Besides, if there *was* one person in the world entitled to bend the rules and use Rufin for a punching bag, it was Max.

"There will be others with more questions, but let me ask you this. Can you really replicate Zadovsky's work?"

Rufin's eyes filled with tears. "Will they kill me if I can't?"

"No. You won't be walking the streets a free man, but you won't be abused."

"Z-Z-Zadovsky seemed unable to replicate his own work, so honestly I don't know if I can either. Perhaps with time. And provided I can recover Zadovsky's research data."

"Was that data on the computers we took from the lab?"

"Some, yes. But—" Rufin looked down at his hands. "The really critical information is on microchips that are implanted in Taz. I'll have to surgically remove them from him."

Rocco tugged his phone out, to call Travis. He didn't care what time it was in the States.

Diego came in just then. He stood in the door and motioned Rocco to follow.

Rocco knew by Diego's expression that whatever it was, it was bad.

"I'll be back," Rocco said to Rufin.

Diego didn't speak until they were in the kitchen. "The dead shooter from that speed boat has been identified. It was Minh Tran's youngest son. Apparently the kid was hoping to impress his old man by spearheading the search for Rufin. I have to find those two mercenaries before Tran does."

"I'll help," Rocco said.

"No. I can't afford any more of your help." Diego frowned, clearly worried. "I suggest you get Rufin out of here fast, too. Minh Tran's pulling out all the stops on this one. It's fixing to go supernova ugly."

Chapter 29

Max woke, realized Erin was climbing out of bed. The last time he'd looked at the clock, it was after three. O'dark-thirty. They had just made love a second time. Now it was nearly eight. The sun was up and he felt . . . incredible.

He gently grasped her wrist, stopping her.

"Did I wake you?" she whispered.

"No." His eyes caught the slight abrasions on her neck and breasts. From his beard. Call him a chauvinistic pig, but the primitive sense of seeing his mark on his woman felt righteous.

She glanced down, saw what he stared at.

"Sore?" he asked.

"Not . . . there."

He smiled and realized his headache was completely gone for the first time since he'd come to in

the hospital. Making love to Erin was deeply healing. And addictive. Already his body wanted more.

He felt his cock swell beneath the sheet. *Down
boy; the lady is sore.*

"I'm going to take a shower," she said.

"I'll make coffee."

Max rigged the small pot up to brew, and then
turned on the tracking unit. The red dot they'd left
behind no longer appeared on the screen.

Did it mean someone had found and freed
Allen? Or had the vehicle been towed out of range?
He set the machine aside. He didn't need it to find
Taz. Max knew where his friend was now—knew he
had to get to him soon.

Max could feel Taz's misery. He was confused
and scared. Something was wrong. *Help me, help me,
help me,* Taz seemed to be screaming.

Stay there, I'm on my way, Max thought. But he received no sense of a reply.

His headache returned with a vengeance. Feeling caged, Max turned on the television for a distraction.

Erin came out as he flipped through channels.
"Can we watch a little news?"

Max paused at the first cable news channel he
came to. It seemed weird to realize there was a two-
year time gap of world events that he had to catch
up on. And what about personal events? Birthdays?
Holidays? He suddenly recalled that once upon a
time he'd had an apartment in Baltimore. What the
hell had happened to it while he'd been gone?

"Coffee?"

Erin moved in and handed him a foam cup. A certain part of his anatomy was disappointed that she'd gotten dressed.

"Last night you said you know where Taz is." Erin said. "Do you intend to go after him?"

Max nodded, then stared at the television. Two photos flashed on the screen behind the announcer. ROBBERY SUSPECT, the graphic caption read. One photograph was blurred, the subject indistinct. The second photo was clearly Taz.

Max hit the volume on the remote. ". . . this is believed to be the same man wanted by Reno Police in connection with a sexual assault the night before last. The man is believed to be on foot, hitchhiking. Motorists are warned against picking up strangers. Anyone with information on this man should contact—"

Oh. Jesus. No.

Taz was wanted for sexual assault. Robbery.

Now he knew why Taz had closed him out. Shame. Guilt. *Don't be like me, mate.*

Max didn't speak until the storyline switched. "That was Taz."

Erin looked stunned. "Max, we have to call the police. That's—"

"Unforgivable. I know. And even though I know why he did it, it's no excuse."

"Why he did it?" She shook her head. "What are you saying?"

Max looked at her. "Part of Taz's programming was aimed at making him do what they called 'the morally unthinkable,' at their command. The more he resisted, the harder they pushed, and the more severe his punishments."

"Did they . . . program you this way, too?"

"No. Taz tried to hang himself. They revived him and supposedly removed the program." Max rubbed his head. "But I have to wonder if it ever really goes away."

"All the more reason he has to be stopped," she said gently.

"That's why I'm going after him."

"No, Max. Call the police. Or call Dante. Let them handle this."

"I'm the only one who can get close to him. If he senses anyone else coming, he'll flee. And if he's on the run and frightened, the robberies, the assaults, will continue." Max stood. "In spite of everything, he is my friend. He saved my life."

"What if he's gone by the time you get there?"

"I still have to try. But you don't," he said. "I'll call Dante and have him arrange to pick you up."

"No! I'm staying with you, Max. I know it sounds strange, but after the dream sharing thing, I think I understand some of what you've been through. Maybe what Taz has been through. Maybe there will be a way I can help after you bring him in."

"That's generous of you."

"Actually it's selfish, too, Max. What if I start to dream again? And you're not there?" She closed her eyes, opened them. "I don't think I could pull myself out of it. That scares me."

He tugged her close, hugged her. "I swear you have nothing to fear from me, Erin. And I swear this is the last place I'll look. If I can't find him, I'll turn it over to the police. I have to get my own life back. You, too."

The drive to Buena Vista, Colorado, their new destination, took nearly eight hours. This time Max stole a cargo van that was parked near the mall with a FOR SALE sign in the window.

Erin made a silent promise that all damage would be recompensed, even if it came out of her own pocket. It was the best she could do in the moment. She felt close to overwhelmed, trying to analyze all of it, so she stopped.

Everything about this situation, from her relationship with Max to the murder of Dr. Winchette to the strange phenomenon of shared dream memories, defied conventional explanations.

But there was one sequence of Max's dream that she couldn't let go of. A piece that seemed to tie into something Dante had mentioned yesterday.

"You saved Catalina Dion's life in London," Erin said. "Is that what Dante meant?"

Max took his eyes off the road for just a second. "Are you guessing? Or did Dante mention it before?"

"Neither. Well, maybe it is a guess. Last night I saw some images that I think were from your dream. You were holding a woman with short blond hair. She was thanking you for saving her." Erin looked away. "It seemed rather . . . intimate."

"It's not what you think." Max sighed. "There's a lot I can't tell you because it's classified, but I worked

with Catalina on a job where she posed as my girlfriend. Things went wrong and we were trapped,
held prisoner. One of the guards . . . raped her. Violently. I couldn't stop it from happening, but I did
break free and got us both out. And, yes, I did kill
the bastard who raped her."

"Oh, God, Max! How horrible."

"Cat could barely walk, but she didn't want the
others on our team to know what had happened.
She said she couldn't bear to look at them and see
the pity she thought she saw in my eyes. So I swore
to keep her secret. Then I hid with her for a week
until she could walk. I held her when she woke
screaming from nightmares, I let her pummel me
since she couldn't pummel the bastard that hurt
her. And I made her look me in the eyes every
moment I could, so she'd see there was no pity.
Only caring."

"You loved her."

"Maybe once, in the way you mean. But I was
more like a brother to her. Especially after *that*."
Max glanced over at her again. "When I talk to you
like this, the memories just unfold without effort.
Thanks."

"But I can tell you've got a headache."

"Yeah. Time to change subjects."

"Tell me about where we're headed. I've never
heard of Saint Elmo, Colorado."

"It's a small ghost town near Buena Vista. Stony
had a cabin near there. One summer, while exploring on my own, I discovered a cave that had been
totally hidden by dead trees and vines. It was filled

with quartz crystal deposits. I had been certain I'd found a diamond mine. Stony had laughed, and made a few jokes about it—called the rocks 'fool's diamonds'—as if they were the equivalent of fool's gold. But I loved that place and went back to it whenever Stony wasn't around."

"It sounds neat."

"'Neat' doesn't come close." He smiled. "You've seen a geode rock before, right?"

"Cracked open? Yes. My father had a gorgeous one on his desk. The inside was filled with crystals."

"Well, imagine sitting inside one. That's what this cave was like. Later as an adult, I realized the crystal formations were significant on their own and I always intended to go back. I had memorized the GPS coordinates—another one of Stony's superstitions was that if he wrote down the location, someone could find it."

"And Taz memorized those GPS numbers, too," she said.

He nodded. "I got an impression of him seeing the cave for the first time. I know he was there by the sense he'd expected that I'd exaggerated."

"I wish you'd let me go. Please? I'll stay in the car." Erin knew that the blisters on her feet wouldn't allow her to hike. She couldn't even wear regular shoes yet.

Max shot her a glance. "I'd feel better knowing you're at a motel. It'll be too late to hike in today, but I want to get an early start in the morning."

The meaning hit her low in the abdomen.

They'd have tonight together.

It was nearly seven by the time they reached Buena Vista. Another beautiful area that Erin longed to explore.

Max stopped for supplies again, and they ate at a small diner before checking into a motel. This time the room only had one bed. A king-size.

Embarrassment fled at the smoldering look Max gave her.

Erin had to ball her fists at her sides to keep from grabbing him, to drag him to the bed.

"I want to change the bandages on your feet," Max said. "I picked up some better ointment. It should help."

He motioned her to the bed, where he gently peeled off the bandages then moved to get a towel. He rinsed her blisters with peroxide, blowing on the stinging.

"Almost done. This has an analgesic," he said as he soothed on a new type of cream. Then he replaced the bandages. "There. What else can I do?"

Erin then looked at him. "Outside of a kiss to make it better?"

The remark had been flippant, but before she'd finished speaking, his lips brushed across hers. And when he would have pulled away, she brought her hands up, encircling his neck. Max didn't move as she explored his mouth.

"Those soft kisses drive me crazy," he said, his breath uneven. "And make me want more."

"Me, too. Please." Erin punctuated her request with an even softer kiss.

Max drew her closer then, pulling her across his lap as he caught her mouth.

She opened fully to him, her tongue dueling with his. Her fingers stroked the hair at his nape while her other hand dropped to the waistband of his jeans and moved lower, clasping at his straining erection.

"Don't make me beg," she whispered.

With a growl, he peeled her shirt off, and swept away her bra. Then, still cradling her in his arms, he lowered his head and took one of her nipples into his mouth.

Erin arched her back, offering herself more fully.

Max stood and laid her on the bed. His mouth never left her body, his lips traveling from one breast to the other, sucking, teasing. She felt him unfasten her pants, tugging them just low enough for his hand to slip in and cup her.

She rocked against his hand and met his gaze. His eyes were a dark kaleidoscope of desire.

"Got to have you." He grasped her pants and tugged them off before straightening and removing his own jeans.

Erin gasped as his cock sprang free. Her gaze shifted back to his and the raw hunger on his face made her want him even more. He knelt on the bed, hovering above her.

"You are so damn beautiful, Erin. I could come just looking at you."

She rose slightly, one hand at his shoulder, her other hand going lower, encircling his shaft. She felt his cock jump in her grip.

"The feeling is mutual," she whispered. Her lips brushed over his, then moved down his throat.

She simultaneously squeezed her hand, stroking his shaft up, then down.

Rational thought fled as desire took over. As he lowered his body, she raised her pelvis, felt the throbbing head of his penis slide against her. He positioned his cock at the slick opening between her legs. She raised one leg, welcoming him in, bathing him in heat and moisture.

Max caught her mouth, kissing her. "Lift your other leg," he whispered.

When she did, he slid fully, tightly inside her. Erin started to peak immediately. "Harder!"

He pulled back, then forward, going deeper still. "Hold on."

She felt his hands slip under her hips, cupping her buttocks, cradling her closer as he pistoned his hips in and out, pushing her over the edge and into the most satisfying climax of her life.

At her cry of release, Max pumped deeply into her, before collapsing with a shuddering explosion.

But before that even finished, he rolled over, pulling Erin on top of him, their bodies still intimately joined. "Now I just want to hold you forever," he whispered.

Chapter 30

Erin woke up to tiny kisses on her shoulder. Had she even slept? The last time they'd made love had been fast and furious. Then she'd fallen into a deep slumber.

She turned to face Max, her body responding, ready, but found him fully dressed. The bathroom light faintly illumined the room. He sat on the edge of the bed. Stoic. As if she weren't naked and wanting him.

"Don't leave." The words popped out before she could stop them. "Ignore that. I understand you have to go."

Max's hand caressed her cheek, his eyes intense, missing nothing. "I liked hearing you say that. Asking me to stay." He pressed a chaste kiss to her mouth. "You feel like the only constant in my life, Erin. I—"

She softened with expectancy, waiting for him to finish the sentence. *I— What?* She didn't expect a declaration of love. But an "I will miss you" or "I'll be thinking of you every moment" would have been nice.

"I gotta go." He whispered the words against her lips, deepening the kiss as his hand crept down to caress her breast with a possessive touch that said she was *his*. Which even she couldn't deny, not now when he was this close; not with his lips, his hands, touching her.

Abruptly he stood, releasing her. "I didn't think it would be this hard to leave."

"So stay."

He shook his head. "The room is paid for, for two days." He tugged a wad of bills from his pocket. "Here's money for food, whatever. Stay close. There's a restaurant next door. If I'm not back by nightfall—"

She cut him off. "You'll be back!"

"If I'm not, call Dante. Tell him everything I've told you. He'll know what to do. Give him the tracking device. I don't need it for finding Taz."

"Okay."

He moved to the door, opened it slightly. "And keep this locked."

"Be careful." She sat up, gathering the sheet around her, self-conscious that he was dressed and she wasn't.

"You, too." And then he was gone.

Erin curled onto her side. Feeling bereft. And dazed. How could she come to feel this way about someone she'd known such a short time?

If it weren't for all the other factors, she'd have

to wonder at the term "love at first sight." Logic didn't fit.

She heard a noise at the door, the lock clicking. She rolled over and drew a sharp breath, startled as the door opened.

Relief drenched her as Max slipped back into the room and strode straight to the bed. Not stopping, he climbed across the top of the bed, pinning her down beneath the covers.

His mouth swept close, catching hers.

This kiss was fierce. Savage and yet gentle. Domineering and giving. It spoke of caring and confusion. Love and anguish. She melted, wanting to heal him.

Wanting to be healed by him.

When he stopped, she was trembling. Pride fled. "Please, Max," she begged. "I need you. *You.*"

He leaned in close and rested his forehead on hers. "As selfish and wrong as this may sound, I needed to know that you would respond that way. I'll be back, sweetheart. And not to finish this." He pressed a gentle kiss to her cheek. "But to start again. The right way."

Then he moved off the bed and left without saying another word.

Erin lay in bed a few minutes longer but realized Max wasn't coming back. Not until he'd checked that cave.

Not until he'd found Taz.

She closed her eyes against the things she'd seen in Max's dreams. The things that had been done to these men were beyond terrible. They were also beyond her professional abilities. She'd stand by Max and support him as a friend.

And as a lover?

She didn't want to guess how they'd feel after this was over. After they dealt with all the fallout, from her father, from Dr. Winchette, from Abe Caldwell, from what was done to Max and Taz overseas.

Feeling overwhelmed, she took a shower and then started coffee.

She checked the time. Max had been gone barely fifteen minutes. How would she last all day? She looked at the phone, had a wild urge to call Dante Johnson. That Max had left her alone, free to leave, free to call anyone—spoke volumes about his trust. His faith in her.

She'd wait.

A knocking sounded at the door. She flinched. Max! She hurried to the door and opened it.

Her smile faded. It wasn't Max. But the tall man was familiar.

"Dr. Houston?" That the man knew her name relaxed her.

"Yes?"

"We need to talk. About Max Duncan."

She realized then who this man was then, had seen pictures of him in literature that Dr. Winchette had in his office.

Abe Caldwell. The man who'd hired Allen! She tried to shut the door, but he shoved his way inside, flashing a small hand gun.

"It's unfortunate that it came to this," he said.

"Now put on your shoes. Mr. Duncan needs your assistance."

Max felt certain he was doing the right thing. Leaving Erin behind while he met Taz meant he could get in and out faster.

Back to her more quickly.

Last night after she'd fallen asleep in his arms, he realized he had to turn himself in. To end this and seek answers. Only by attempting to make peace with his past could he stake a claim on the future.

A future he wanted to include Erin.

The mind reading, the bonding with her, had given him an advantage. He *understood* her on a deeper level in ways he couldn't begin to describe. There was an emotional intimacy between them that he'd only dreamed about.

When he'd been beaten and tortured and at his very lowest point overseas, he'd held on to a fantasy, a pipe dream of someone loving him like no other.

He didn't know how to explain it—but that someone was Erin.

He drove for an hour, then turned and followed a rutted trail as far as he could. No other cars were around, but he sensed that Taz had hitchhiked to a nearby point and come in by foot.

Max parked and started up the trail. That nothing had changed here was rather bittersweet. The sight of the mountains, even the sound of the birds, felt all the same as when he'd last stood here with Stony.

He missed his uncle and was grateful for the time they'd spent together. They had always been on the verge of success, always ready for a new adventure. As Max picked his way through the woods, following a faint trail through the valley, then up an incline, he remembered hoping they'd never find the gold. Because he couldn't imagine a life any richer than being with Stony in the great outdoors.

A short time later Max crested a rise and saw the cave. The opening was smaller than he remembered, a dark hole hear the ground that looked more like a shadow near the rocky edge of a cliff.

The strip of ground leading up to it was narrow, lined on one side by a steep creek bed. The other side was the sharp drop to a canyon. Erosion had washed away all but one of the massive pines that had once lined that edge, hiding the river at the bottom of the canyon.

Max tried again to sense Taz. But this time the effort only yielded a headache. He moved closer. "Taz?"

There was movement in the shadowy mouth of the cave. Then a man stepped out. Taz looked straight at him, his eyes unfocused. "Hades."

The clothes Taz wore hung in shreds, bloodied from myriad cuts. A knife was clenched in Taz's fist, the blade slicing back and forth across his thigh.

"I can't feel it anymore. He warned me nothing would help," Taz panted. "Until I found him."

"Found who?"

"Rufin." Taz lurched forward. "We gotta go back, mate. If they kill him, we'll never get free."

"We are free." Max concentrated, tried to make a connection. *Remember who you are. Max. Logan.* "We escaped, Logan. Hades, Taz, aren't real. They were holograms. Programs. That's why we could never win. It wasn't real."

"You're wrong. I am Taz." Logan lurched forward.

Max braced, prepared for Logan's attack.

A gunshot sounded. Logan stumbled backward, hit—but not by a bullet. A tranquilizer dart.

"Run!" Logan shouted before scrambling back into the cave. Max dropped to the ground and rolled backward over the edge of the creek bed, tracking the man who'd shot Logan. The man had fired the tranq gun, and then dashed behind a boulder, near the cliff.

Staying low, Max followed the creek bed back around toward the man.

A nightmare scene began to replay in Max's mind and for a moment he was back in the jungle.

They always came at the end of a mission.

Remember who you are.

"I am Max."

Remember who you are.

Logan. Dante. Rocco. Travis.

"Erin," Max whispered. Immediately the nightmare cleared.

"Come out with your hands up," the shooter shouted toward the cave, unaware that Max had slipped closer.

Max looked around for anything he could use as a weapon. Hand-to-hand combat required face-to-face distance. And the tranquilizers gave the man an unfair advantage.

That the man had come armed with tranquilizers meant he wanted them alive. But that didn't mean the man wouldn't hesitate to pull a Smith & Wesson and maim them.

"Don't shoot!" Logan called out.

Max was stunned to see Logan stagger out from the cave, into the open. Logan pitched and stumbled, but didn't fall.

Max crept closer as the shooter edged around the rocks that hid him and aimed the tranquilizer gun at Logan. Waiting for him to come closer.

Max rushed the shooter from behind.

The man turned and fired, but the shot went wide, missing Max.

Max slammed into the man before he could pull a handgun from his shoulder holster. They crashed to the ground, fighting.

Max wrenched the gun free and tossed it away. Then he slugged the man. Blood spurted from the man's nose.

Max ignored the man's yelp of pain and yanked him back to his feet. "You're not getting off that easy."

Max punched the man in the stomach, sending him back to the ground.

"Who sent you?" Max demanded.

"Go to hell!"

Before Max could snatch the man up again, a

shot fired. A bloodstain appeared on the front of the man's shirt as he let out a shrill scream.

Max whirled and found Logan standing close by with the gun still pointed at the man.

"Thanks," Max said to Logan. Then he turned back to the wounded man.

The injured man drew a breath, seeming to realize he wasn't mortally wounded.

"My buddy didn't like your answer," Max said. "I bet you work for Abe Caldwell; you probably have a tracking device like Allen did."

"Yes. And we were grateful you took Allen's device."

"You tracked me via Allen's unit," Max said.

The man sneered. "Then I followed you here. We watched you leave alone and figured you'd lead us to John Doe."

"You followed me from the motel?"

Erin!

"That's right," the man said. "Dr. Houston is with my partner. And by now Allen's probably with them, too. If you don't want to see her harmed, I suggest you cooperate. Convince your friend to drop the gun and both of you back off."

"You mean me, mate?" Logan fired again, permanently erasing the wounded man's smirk.

"No!" Max spoke too late. He closed his eyes, then turned back to Logan. "I've got to go back and find Erin."

Logan pointed the gun at Max's chest now. "We have to find Rufin."

Max recognized that Logan was no longer rational.

On top of that, he was fighting the tranquilizer. "Easy. We'll find Rufin. I swear."

"You're lying." Logan swung around and for a moment seemed to struggle with an unseen force within himself.

Max lunged forward, knocking Logan to the ground. Immediately he realized he'd underestimated Logan's strength.

They rolled across the ground, their hands locked together on the gun in Logan's grip.

"Rufin's a bastard. He was using both of us." Max squeezed the bones of Logan's wrist, but Logan retaliated with a head butt to Max's temple. He saw stars.

The men started to roll, tumbling down the incline, picking up speed, neither one willing to relinquish his hold on the weapon.

Max tried to judge how close they were to the cliff and steered them toward the lone fir tree at the edge. They slammed into it. Logan was on top and moved to straddle Max.

But Max kicked up, bowing his back and flipping Logan off. Logan hit the tree and spun sideways. Off balance, he grabbed for a tree limb. There was an awful *crack* as the limb split and Logan went over the side of the cliff.

"Logan! No!" Max rushed forward, but was unable to stop Logan's fall. He peered over the edge. Three hundred feet down, Logan's body lay unmoving, caught on a narrow rocky ledge. His legs and neck were at odd angles. He was dead.

Max pushed back to his feet and stumbled back

over to the shooter's body. Searching his pockets, he yanked out a wallet and cell phone.

Tommy Groene had a Massachusetts driver's license with a Boston address. His cell phone flashed SERVICE UNAVAILABLE.

Cursing, Max took off down the mountain. That Abe Caldwell had Erin was all Max's fault. If anything happened to her . . .

I'm coming, sweetheart!

Chapter 31

The harder Max tried to make a connection with Erin, the worse his head ached. When his vision started to tunnel, he knew he had to stop. If he went into a seizure, he'd be no help to her.

He silently vowed to go to a hospital as Erin had begged after he found her. And he would find her.

As soon as Max reached the stolen cargo van, Tommy's phone vibrated once briefly. He looked at the display. Two bars of service signal flickered. *One missed call.*

Max hit redial.

A man answered on the second ring. "Yes."

Max played his hunch. "Tommy's unavailable, Abe."

Silence.

"Duncan? Damn it! What have you done? He better be okay."

A little late for that. "Where's Erin?"

"Resting comfortably. And before you start with the

threats, let me cut to the chase. She has value as a pawn. Period. I'll release her when Tommy brings you and your pal, John Doe, to me."

"I want to talk to her."

Abe ignored the demand. "Both you and Doe will need to be drugged. Now put Tommy on the line."

"Tommy's dead."

"Shit!" The line went quiet, making Max think he had disconnected.

"Hello?" Max said.

"Shut up! Is John Doe with you?"

"No." Max knew he needed to buy time. "He spotted Tommy and took off. I'll have to go after him later."

"I suggest you find him sooner rather than later. Here's why."

Max heard muffled sounds come across the line, indistinct voices in the background. Then he heard a loud crashing noise, followed by bloodcurdling screaming. Erin!

"There's your proof of life," Abe snapped. "Any more fuckups and she screams longer. Now, you find Doe. Be prepared to bring him to me. I'll call back in two hours."

"Make it four," Max said. "It'll take me an hour and a half just to get back up the mountain."

"You got three. Better get running, Max."

This time the phone did go dead.

Max turned off Tommy's cell phone and loosened the battery to preserve power as well as to ensure it couldn't be traced. Firing up the van, he spun out of the parking lot and raced off.

Abe was likely still in the area, and could close in on Max, if Tommy had reported in his location.

And as much as Max wanted to get to Erin, he had to react with his brain, not his heart. Going in to rescue her alone would sign her death warrant. Abe would never release a witness.

After zigzagging onto another county road and assuring himself he wasn't being followed, Max pulled into a gas station and used the pay phone to call Dante.

"Hello?"

"It's Max."

"I figured it was either you or Erin when the caller ID said PAY PHONE."

"Look, I need . . . help."

Dante was instantly serious. "Anything. Where are you?"

"Colorado."

"I'm in Salt Lake City, following a lead on Taz. I can get there in a few hours."

Max kept scanning the horizon. "I don't have that much time. They've got Erin. I need help getting her back."

"They who?"

Max filled Dante in on his search for Taz and Abe Caldwell's involvement. "You were right. I had a beacon in my arm, and they found us using that damn tracking unit. I've got less than three hours before they call back. Caldwell claims he'll trade me and Taz for Erin. I don't mind walking into a trap, but I need to be sure Erin gets out."

"We're not the only ones looking for Taz," Dante

said. "Have you seen the news? He's the subject of a manhunt."

"I know. And Taz is dead. Nobody else will be hurt."

Dante swore. "I'm sorry. I know he was your friend. There's something else you should know. Rocco found Dr. Rufin. Apparently Rufin embedded microchips beneath Taz's skin. Taz is—was—a research gold mine. Rufin actually had all of the experiments done on both of you, plus Zadovsky's note, on a chip as well."

"That's why Abe Caldwell wants Taz. I need to get his body—but the place he died—I can't recover the body alone."

"Look, a private jet will get me there in an hour. We'll figure it out, buddy. Do you have a cell phone I can call you back on?"

"Not one I can keep powered up."

"Then call me back in ten minutes. Let me check on the closest airstrip and I'll give you my ETA."

"Fine. But Dante, one more thing. Nobody but you. Someone's leaking a lot of info. Abe knows more than he should."

"Not even Travis?"

"Not even Travis," Max said.

"Fair enough. I'll let you call the shots. Get back to me in ten."

Max hung up and rubbed his head. It felt ready to burst. *Hang on, Erin. I'm coming.*

Abe stubbed out a cigarette and immediately lit up another. Screw what the doctor said about cutting back, he had never felt this anxious before. If his luck would just hold a little longer.

Allen getting free before the cops came in was a godsend. At first Abe had been irate that Allen had let Max get him. Had thought it served him right to get his damn wrist snapped. Now . . . well, even with a cast, Allen could shoot a gun.

He and Allen had been driving around for the past hour, waiting until it was time to call Max Duncan.

That Tommy was dead had sealed Duncan's fate. Abe had toyed with trying to capture both men alive but John Doe was who they needed. With Allen's broken wrist, one person was as much as they could manage.

Abe glanced at the backseat. Erin Houston was bound, gagged, and blindfolded. She'd been easy enough to handle but now she, too, was a liability.

Temporarily at least. In the process of trying to bargain for Max's safety, she'd given away that she and Max had feelings for each other. This could be exploited.

Once Abe had John Doe in his custody, Max and Erin would be killed. Staging it as a murder/suicide should wrap the case. Sure the CIA would continue searching for John Doe—but Abe would have Doe out of the country, where they could safely harvest the data that had been implanted by Dr. Rufin.

Abe expected to confirm a rendezvous point with Harry Gambrel and Rufin within a day or two. And once Abe had Rufin, he technically had no use for Harry.

In fact Harry was another liability. Dealing with him would be a little trickier.

Funny to think they were in the same boat. Harry was as desperate as Abe. Each looked at the other as a weight around his neck, but necessary to get what he wanted.

"It's time," Allen said.

Abe dialed Tommy's cell phone.

Max answered on the first ring. "Let me talk to Erin."

"Tell me whether you've located John Doe."

"He's here. I had to knock him out to convince him to come."

"He better be alive! How close are you to Buena Vista?"

"We're within a couple miles."

"Head back to Saint Elmo on County Road 162. About ten miles out, watch for an electrical tower on the right. An unmarked access road is at the base of the tower. Follow it in and park at the locked gate. Then walk halfway back to the main road. I want John Doe's hands tied in front, where I can see them. And remember. The lovely Dr. Houston will pay for your screwups."

Max followed Abe Caldwell's directions, parking at the gate. Then he pulled Dante out of the back of the van. Dante's disguise, a short dark blond wig and a baseball cap, wasn't the best, but it was all they could do on such short notice.

The rope bindings at Dante's wrists were merely

glued in place, allowing him easy access to the various guns and knives he had hidden beneath the baggy plaid shirt and jeans. The bulletproof vest he wore also bulked him up to resemble Taz even more.

Max's head was pounding so badly he could hardly walk. Trying to contact Erin, or read anyone's mind, was completely out of the question at this point.

Be safe, Erin. Be safe, repeated in his head like a mantra.

To keep up the appearance that Taz was being forced to accompany him, Max carried the handgun he'd taken from Tommy and held it on Dante, who pretended to resist. Just in case anyone watched.

"Walk!" Max ordered.

"Fuck you, asshole." Dante's imitation of Taz's accent was passable.

They'd walked only a short distance down the road when headlights appeared, heading straight for them. Max stopped and pulled Dante close, shifting the gun to Dante's head where the people in the car could see it.

The car stopped about thirty feet away. The passenger and driver's doors swung open simultaneously. Since Max recognized Allen, the driver, he assumed the man with the ponytail was Abe Caldwell.

Abe moved to the back door and tugged Erin out. Her clothes were disheveled and her hands were tied, but still she fought. When Abe pressed a gun to her temple, she froze. She was blindfolded and gagged, so she didn't know Max was there.

Watching Abe manhandle her enraged Max. He willed himself to inhale deeply, to remain calm.

Allen had a cast on one wrist, a Beretta nine-millimeter in the other one. "Drop the gun," Allen ordered.

"Tommy mentioned that there was something special about my friend here," Max said. "Something that you needed him *alive* for. If you want to keep him breathing, send Erin over first."

Abe dragged Erin out in front of him, the gun still at her head. "Get rid of your gun first and she can start walking forward." Abe looked at John Doe. "Mr. Doe. Or is it . . . Taz? We're here to help you. Dr. Rufin is waiting for you."

Dante pretended to react at Rufin's name, jerking away from Max, but Max quickly stopped him.

Then Max held his gun out and threw it off to the side. "Send her forward."

Abe tugged Erin's blindfold off and shoved her forward. Max saw recognition flash across her features at seeing Dante, but she hid it. He caught her thoughts of concern, *for him*, and prayed he could send her a message that would be crucial in pulling off his next step.

Be ready to drop, sweetheart.

The moment she stepped away from Abe, Max pushed Dante forward, grabbing the gun hidden at Dante's back.

"Drop, Erin!" Max shouted.

Allen got off the first shot. Max took a bullet in the shoulder as he fired back, hitting Allen squarely in the forehead. He rounded on Abe Caldwell, but Dante already had his weapon on Abe.

"Don't shoot!" Abe dropped his gun and lifted

his hands. "Thank God! This has all been a huge misunderstanding. I was blackmailed by those men. They threatened my family."

"Save it," Dante said, shoving him up against the car hood. "Here's a phrase you're going to hear a lot of in prison: Assume the position."

Max rushed to help Erin to her feet. He tugged the gag away and freed her hands. "Are you hurt?" When he saw the bruise on her cheek, he wanted to go shoot Abe. "Damn him!"

"I'm fine." Her eyes widened as she saw blood on his shirt. "But you're not! You've been shot, Max!"

He kissed her. "I'll live."

The pain from the gunshot combined with his sense of relief over seeing Erin safe had helped to clear Max's head.

"That is Dante, right?" she asked as she split Max's shirt open to get a better look at his shoulder.

"Yes. Tell me what happened to your cheek." He touched her and she grimaced. "Sore?"

"I'll live," she said. "Allen backhanded me, mostly for your benefit. I take it you didn't find Taz."

"Actually, I did, but he's dead, Erin. I think it's probably for the better. He had lived through an unspeakable hell. And there were still people wanting to do bad things to him."

Dante came over now. "You two okay?"

"Yes," Max said.

"No!" Erin spoke at the same time. "He needs a hospital."

"Later," Max said. "What's Caldwell's story?"

"We have to call Travis," Dante said. "We're going

to need his help on this one. Caldwell's demanding we summon the police and let him call his attorney. He claims he's the victim."

"Yeah, right." Max met Dante's gaze. "Tell me straight. Do you trust Travis?"

"Completely. So does Cat."

"Then call him. I want to get Erin home immediately."

As Dante moved away, Erin tugged Max's arm. "Thank you for saving me." She reached up and stroked the side of his face lovingly before kissing him gently on the lips.

"You wouldn't have been in this mess if it weren't for me."

She shrugged. "So what happens next?"

"Fifty questions. We'll both be debriefed. I will take the blame for everything, Erin. And when they're done . . . I'd like to see you again. I want to be with you. *Please?*"

She smiled. "I want to be with you, too."

Epilogue

Langley, Virginia
Five Days Later

Erin's cab pulled up at the newly opened Marriott Resort.

Max was waiting out front. He opened her car door before offering a hand to help her out.

"You look . . . fabulous." Max's gaze swept over her slowly from head to toe and back before nodding in appreciation.

Erin had worn a blue silk dress and heels. She'd also fussed for an hour with her hair and makeup. His look told her it was worth every second.

And after this lunch meeting with Max and Travis Franks, she had another at the hospital at which she'd learn her employment fate.

"Thank you. You look rather *GQ* yourself."

Max was wearing a black suit with a white shirt, no

tie, collar open. His wraparound shades lent an air of mystery.

He followed her into the lobby. His hand at the small of her back guided her to the left, down the hall. Just past a large potted palm, he stopped and pulled her into his arms for a kiss.

"I've missed you," he said.

She rolled her eyes. "I just left six hours ago."

After returning to the East Coast, Max had spent three days in a private Virginia hospital, where he'd been debriefed nonstop. They'd also run every conceivable medical test on him. With the exception of high blood pressure and the headaches—both of which were responding to the same medication— Max appeared to be in superb physical shape.

The *non-physical* stuff was another issue and would take time to sort through. While Max had agreed to cooperate with the CIA's psychological and neurological staff, he'd refused to remain confined.

With Travis Franks's support, Max had left the hospital and gotten a room here at the Marriott. Erin had been thrilled when he'd called and invited her to dinner last night. They hadn't been able to stop talking and . . . one thing led to another. *Thank God.*

Her fears that their lovemaking had been a result of stress had quickly been put to rest. The attraction between them was hotter than ever. Her suggestion that they still take it slow was vetoed by Max.

"Life is too short to go slow," he whispered in her ear as he began to nuzzle her neck and press closer into her.

"Geez! Get a room!" Rocco Taylor's voice startled her.

"When did you get back in town?" Max shook his friend's hand and gave him a bear hug.

"Two hours ago. Dante filled me in on what happened in Colorado, but I'll be eager to hear Travis's update." Rocco hugged Erin. "Guess this means you're off the market."

"Damn straight," Max answered. He gave her hand a light squeeze and met her gaze. "At least, I hope you're off the market."

Erin smiled, enjoying the warm blush that came to her cheeks. She could get used to this. Travis had reserved a private dining room. Dante and Catalina were already seated, and after more hugs, they all took seats.

Erin had met Catalina at the Colorado clinic where Max's shoulder wound was treated. It was easy to see she loved Dante and cared deeply for Max—as a friend.

"Any word on Logan's whereabouts?" Rocco asked.

"None," Max said. "As soon as I can, I'm going back out to look around."

The morning after Erin was freed, Max and Dante had gone back to Saint Elmo with a team to recover Logan's body. But he was gone. Vanished. Max had explained to Erin that if an animal had somehow gotten to Logan's body, there would have been some signs. Tracks. Bloodstains.

The current conjecture was that Logan may not have been dead, but injured and unconscious. If he came to in the dark and went over the edge of the ledge, he could have fallen into the river even farther below.

Erin hoped the body would wash ashore to give Max closure. And of course, securing the microchips in Logan's body was paramount to the Agency.

"Dr. Rufin's been debriefed and moved to a secure location," Travis said. "Max, Dante, I'll arrange for you both to interview him soon. He's cooperating fully and agreed to work with our psychology team to assess how to treat or reverse the programming using the least invasive method. Erin, I'd like you on that team."

She nodded. "I'm eager to help."

"And I trust her judgment," Max said.

"What about the man who picked up Rufin and stashed him with Jengho in Bangkok?" Rocco asked. "Any leads?"

"Not yet. We're ninety-nine percent sure the man worked for Abe Caldwell though," Travis said. "And speaking of Caldwell, he's convinced a judge to release him on bail. Five million cash. I think the reason Caldwell quit cooperating with us is because his attorney was floating a deal."

"Money talks. Shit floats," Max said.

"Exactly," Travis agreed. "Erin, I don't have anything on your father yet, but we're working on it. We've seized Winchette's personal records and I'm confident I'll get his and your father's research, too. It's apparent Dr. Winchette and Abe Caldwell were in pretty deep."

Erin nodded her thanks. "I appreciate your help in clearing my father's name."

"One last thing before they start serving food," Travis said. "We've got Dante back. We've got Max back. But I swear to God, we will not rest until we find Harry Gambrel." He picked up his water glass for a toast. "To brothers lost. And brothers found."

His words were punctuated by the sound of three pagers beeping simultaneously. The chorus sounded urgent.

Erin watched as Travis, Dante, and Rocco all pulled out their cell phones. Their expressions grew ominous.

"What is it?" Max pressed as soon as Travis finished calling in to his office.

"One of our analysts, Madison Kohlmeyer, has been reported missing by her roommate." Travis looked toward Rocco.

But Rocco was already striding out the door.

"I'll be right back," Max said as he followed Dante and Travis out of the room.

"That name sounds familiar," Erin said to Catalina.

Cat nodded. "Rocco and Maddy have dated in the past. But recently . . . well, Maddy had just started seeing Travis Franks."

Boston, Massachusetts
Later That Same Night

Abe Caldwell poured himself a drink and lit another cigarette. While the corporate condo wasn't his first choice, he'd been glad to get out of jail! He knew they'd purposely locked him up with the worst scum to try to make him talk.

It hadn't worked.

And while the Feds weren't buying his *Mr. Innocent* act, his attorneys had obviously managed to keep Abe's arrest out of the news. They'd also been successful in peddling Abe's tell-all to Judge Anderson, who promised a plea bargain.

The big holdout seemed to be the CIA—but Abe knew exactly how to gain their favor. He felt confident that he held the winning cards.

His ace up his sleeve was Harry Gambrel.

Abe had heard through a reliable source that Travis Franks would give *anything* to find the third missing agent.

Good. Abe wanted all charges dropped. And he wanted his passport returned. The moment he got it back, he was heading to Zurich.

He'd already told his attorney to quietly orchestrate a sellout. Pagetelli Drugs would drool at the chance to take over Caldwell Pharmaceuticals. Abe could retire and leave all this crap behind for good.

Blue skies, here I come.

The rapping at the door to his study startled him out of his reverie.

"Come in, Martha," he called out to his housekeeper.

The door swung open.

Harry Gambrel strolled in like he owned the place.

"How . . . did you get in here?" Abe sputtered.

"I brought flowers for your housekeeper. A funeral spray." Harry pulled out a gun. "You've been dodging my calls."

"I was detained," Abe said, thinking fast. That the gun had a silencer was very bad. "Have a seat. No need to be hostile. I'm sure we can put a deal together."

Harry raised the gun. "I heard about your fucking deal. And I came to tell you it was a bad idea."

Abe stood, but was knocked backward by the force of two bullets.

And the last thing he heard was Harry's laugh.

More by Bestselling Author
Fern Michaels

___**About Face**	0-8217-7020-9	$7.99US/$10.99CAN
___**Picture Perfect**	0-8217-7588-X	$7.99US/$10.99CAN
___**Vegas Heat**	0-8217-7668-1	$7.99US/$10.99CAN
___**Finders Keepers**	0-8217-7669-X	$7.99US/$10.99CAN
___**Dear Emily**	0-8217-7670-3	$7.99US/$10.99CAN
___**Vegas Sunrise**	0-8217-7672-X	$7.99US/$10.99CAN
___**Payback**	0-8217-7876-5	$6.99US/$9.99CAN
___**Vendetta**	0-8217-7877-3	$6.99US/$9.99CAN
___**The Jury**	0-8217-7878-1	$6.99US/$9.99CAN
___**Sweet Revenge**	0-8217-7879-X	$6.99US/$9.99CAN
___**Lethal Justice**	0-8217-7880-3	$6.99US/$9.99CAN
___**Free Fall**	0-8217-7881-1	$6.99US/$9.99CAN
___**Fool Me Once**	0-8217-8071-9	$7.99US/$10.99CAN
___**Vegas Rich**	0-8217-8112-X	$7.99US/$10.99CAN
___**Hide and Seek**	1-4201-0184-6	$6.99US/$9.99CAN
___**Hokus Pokus**	1-4201-0185-4	$6.99US/$9.99CAN
___**Fast Track**	1-4201-0186-2	$6.99US/$9.99CAN
___**Collateral Damage**	1-4201-0187-0	$6.99US/$9.99CAN
___**Final Justice**	1-4201-0188-9	$6.99US/$9.99CAN
___**Up Close and Personal**	0-8217-7956-7	$7.99US/$9.99CAN
___**Under the Radar**	1-4201-0683-X	$6.99US/$9.99CAN
___**Razor Sharp**	1-4201-0684-8	$7.99US/$10.99CAN

Available Wherever Books Are Sold!
Check out our website at **www.kensingtonbooks.cc**

Romantic Suspense from
Lisa Jackson